DELIA

Delia o... passion, of cool irony and high resolve, is complete in itself and separate from the saga of Dray Prescot.

The Star Lords who brought Dray Prescot to Kregen appear to be changing in their attitude to him, even though he is a mere mortal man. They have favoured him with an insight into their plans for that marvelous and mysterious world four hundred light years from Earth, where men and women of many different and exotic races mingle and strive to work out their own destinies under the red and green fires of Antares.

The destiny of the island Empire of Vallia at the moment is one of faction and disarray. Mercilessly savaged by outside foes, both physical and sorcerous, and rent by internal rivalries, the country is slowly gathering itself again after the Times of Troubles. But some unscrupulous people feel that now is the moment to strike and that one more push will bring them to the summit of their ambitions.

Against this background of colour and action, intrigue and sorcery, the Star Lords have afforded Dray Prescot the privilege of vicariously sharing in the headlong adventures of Delia—Delia of Delphond, Delia of the Blue Mountains. As the narrative unfolds we know Prescot suffers. The cassettes on which the tale is told are often fuzzy and faint. But love and devotion for Delia, and pride in her courage and resourcefulness and her joyful onslaught against every challenge, stand forth clear and unashamedly. We, too, are privileged to share the story on these cassettes and go alongside Delia of Vallia as she hazards the perils of Kregen under the streaming mingled lights of the Suns of Scorpio.

Alan Burt Akers

The Adventures of Dray Prescot are narrated in DAW Books:

MANHOUNDS/ARENA OF ANTARES
FLIERS OF ANTARES
A LIFE FOR KREGEN
A FORTUNE FOR KREGEN
A VICTORY FOR KREGEN
BEASTS OF ANTARES
REBEL OF ANTARES
LEGIONS OF ANTARES
ALLIES OF ANTARES
MAZES OF SCORPIO
ETC.

DELIA OF VALLIA

by
Dray Prescot

As told to
Alan Burt Akers

DAW BOOKS, INC.
DONALD A. WOLLHEIM, PUBLISHER
1633 Broadway, New York, NY 10019

Cover art by Ken W. Kelly.

FIRST PRINTING, DECEMBER 1982

1 2 3 4 5 6 7 8 9

PRINTED IN U.S.A.

TABLE OF CONTENTS

CHAPTER ONE

From the Ochre Limits

The woman prostrate on the desert sand moved with the lax tremble of imminent death under the vulture's outspread wings. The bird inclined his stiff black wings, circling in the air, and regarded the woman with unhurried patience, awaiting the moment of her death.

She rolled sluggishly onto her side and Rippasch the vulture curved above her, his twin shadows flickering across the sand. The woman opened her eyes.

The bird lifted and the polished beak, sharp and hooked, caught the radiance of the suns and glittered. The woman's eyes half-closed. Watchfully, Rippasch dropped lower. Now she lay still, sprawled and supine, a last quiver of her limbs signal enough.

The ochre sand stretched to the horizon unbroken except for the line of footprints, faltering as they neared the point where the woman had fallen. The twin suns burned high, red and green, drenching the barren land with heat. The bird flicked his wings and curved in to land on outthrust claws. He cocked his head to one side.

The woman's arms lay loosely, her left hand across her breasts where torn russet leather revealed tanned skin, her right open at the side of her thigh. That open right hand rested limply on the hilt of a heavy sailor knife. A roll of sand partially covered the broad blade where she had fallen.

No breeze blew to muffle the scratching sound of the vulture's claws as he strutted toward the woman. His beak pointed. Her eyes remained half open.

Cracks disfigured the softness of her lips and dust stained her face into the semblance of an idol's death mask. Her breast moved in shallow rhythm, slowing, dying, stilling to quietness. Rippasch fluffed his neck feathers and strutted forward.

The woman remained motionless.

Reassured, Rippasch fluttered out his wings and hopped onto her body. His claws dug into the tanned skin; they did not break through into the flesh or draw blood.

For two heartbeats the vulture poised on the woman's breast, a black wedge against the sunslight. For two heartbeats only—then his sharp beak darted forward for the feast.

The woman's left hand struck straight up.

Her fingers closed around the thin and naked neck. Any squawking shriek of fear or astonishment Rippasch might have uttered was mercilessly choked off.

The woman's right hand closed. The knife glittered once as it swept in a flat lethal slash.

The vulture's head flew off.

Instantly, the decapitated body was turned, was twisted upside down. The spurting flood of blood cascaded out in a jutting stream. That warm wet blood splashed over the woman's face, coursed into her mouth. Greedily, she lapped the blood, swallowing, feeling the moisture wet against her parched skin—wet, wet!

She drank greedily, thirstily, gulping the red blood like a savage beast crouched over its prey.

At that moment, the woman was a savage beast, ferocious and cunning, skilled in the arts of survival, and she devoured the goodness of the kill her prowess had brought her.

Presently she licked the sailor knife clean. Moisture was so precious not a drop must be wasted. She replaced the knife in its rawhide sheath at her right side, below the main gauche that snugged sweetly against her hip. The matching rapier—plain of hilt and guard, slender and yet not too slender, not a fancy weapon—remained in the scabbard swung on plain steel lockets from her left side. Her waist was narrow and the lesten-hide belt with its silver buckle, dulled from much use, was hauled up to the penultimate slot.

Standing up, she picked the sucked-dry carcass from the sand and shook it. Her hunger was not so great, yet, that she needed to fall upon the raw flesh. But she would, if she had to.

In her present situation she was sorry that she could not husband some of the blood. But that would be the first to go. Moisture was all important. And, again, from her experience she felt regret that the vulture had not chosen to attack her corpse toward evening. She might begin to sweat again, now, and that was sheer waste.

She looked about the hostile horizon.

Her airboat had decided to crash here in the Ochre Limits after a short, sharp and nasty onslaught from beastly flutsmen, murderous slavers who thought they had sighted an easy prey. She had shot three of them with her longbow and skewered a fourth. Poor Pansi had died with a javelin through her throat and big, bluff, laughing Nath the Jokester had died with a barbed spear through his guts. Clearly, the flutsmen wished to take her alive.

After she'd taken the left eye out of the fifth—Nath had dispatched two—the remnants flew off. She'd sent a last shaft after them and taken little comfort and only minimal satisfaction from the shriek of pain from the rearmost.

So, from a wrecked airboat and two dead friends, she had begun to walk out of the desert.

Had anyone asked her if she was afraid she would have told them in her cutting way not to be such a nurdling great fool, and then ignored the question and got on with the job of survival.

If you kept on stirring blood in a bowl you could stop it from congealing; but she had no bowl and the effort would probably have taken more energy than she would lose by drinking all the blood at once and accepting the consequent loss later. She walked carefully, not hurrying, minimizing her movements, wasting nothing of her strength. Normally she walked with a grace that turned heads, not in a voluptuous hip-swinging fashion, but as though she trod moonbeams. Now she went along as though walking a tightrope across the sand.

Since the reiving flutsmen had downed her flier and slain her friends, she had maintained her direction. She knew where she was and within a few miles of just how far she had to walk to reach the river. Otherwise she would have been forced to hide up in the daytime. She cocked a brown eye up. Up there, circling high, a black dot regarded her.

She considered this new Rippasch.

No. Not yet. She still had strength and the blood had revived her. Time yet to cover more distance, get off the sand and onto the gritty dust and rocks, before she need fall down and so take off the head of that insolent creature up there.

Mind you, she said to herself, in the way her husband talked, mind you, the vulture was only being himself and acting out his nature. Rippasch was hungry and thirsty, too. And, he did help to clean up the desert. . . .

The Ochre Limits, uncomfortably thrust between the provinces of Falinur to the north and Vindelka to the south, existed mainly because the soil ran poor and sour. True desert they could hardly be called, although they would kill you from heat and thirst as finally as any of the great deserts of Kregen. The woman walked carefully as the gritty dust beneath her sandals more and more supplanted the shifting sands. She peered under her hand, looking ahead to the horizon.

She was too determined to acknowledge even to herself how much she longed for the first sight of the trees, glimmering in ghost veils through the heat whorls, to herald the river. Firmly though she might push down her feelings, they surfaced, from time to time. Then she had to fix her gaze on the shimmering horizon, and hold herself just so, and put one foot in front of the other, and march, march on.

Boulders showed here and there as she went along, and a few lizards skittered. The water table began to give sustenance to incredibly hardy growths, dusty ochre and umber like the Ochre Limits themselves. This gave her fresh heart. Those plants grew roots long enough to reach down to a Herrelldrin Hell; she'd exhaust herself trying to dig down for water. Best to keep on walking, one foot in front of the other, over and over again.

That Opaz-forsaken river had to be getting near by now, surely?

A bush of a size to reach to her knees went past as she walked on, and then another on the other side. Soon the ground, hard and dusty, could no longer be called barren. It was still useless for agriculture, fit for the wild creatures of the world. Folk said that only madmen or leem-hunters—and they were by nature mad, too—ever tried to live in the Ochre Limits. Her tanned fingers reached for the hilt of the rapier. Leems were nasty, ill-tempered, eight-legged beasts of ravening destruction and huge appetite. A rapier would be of scant use against a leem. . . .

Scurryings among the bushes caused her to keep her head turning, her eyes alert. And the twin suns sinking down the sky ahead began to dazzle, casting long double shadows from bush and rock. Her mouth was afire. The blood had made her more thirsty than ever. The pebble she picked up to roll around inside the cavern of fire that was her mouth alleviated the problem a little; a little, not much.

Small animals ran away from her now. Tiny, furry little beasts, tiny scaled beasts, tiny naked-skinned beasts, they all ran. On them the larger predators preyed, and on them the bigger, and, finally, the leem preyed on all. One of these fine days, no doubt, there would be a leem hunt on a grand scale. But other things came before that. She found herself wishing that the grand leem hunt had taken place in the past.

Reality supervened. This wild, hostile badlands could not support life enough to maintain many leems. They would be solitary, each with her or his own area, mingling only during the mating season. She was, in all sober truth, unlikely to run across a leem. Should she do so, she'd do more than many and many a leem-hunter did in a season.

The thought occurred to her that she could be walking into a vast loop of the river. If she turned to left or right, to north or south, she might meet the river in an amazingly short time. Resolutely, she thrust the thought from her. She marched on, due west.

This river, the River of Shining Spears, ran from the Blue Mountains south-southeastward into the Great River, called Mother of Waters, She of the Fecundity. It marked off the southwestern edge of the Ochre Limits. The idea of water, sparkling, splashing, *wet*, tortured her.

The Great River ran on southward in generous loopings, through the capital city, Vondium, and so on into the sea. The river, the canals, the sea—all were wet.

This wonderful island empire of Vallia had seen perilous and terrible times recently. Enemies, overseas and within the island, had sought to topple the country and seize the reins of power. Well, many of those enemies had been dealt with, and those remaining would be dealt with in due time. She could not concern herself with problems of others at this time; survival meant keeping a tenacious hold on the reality about her, the drifting dust, the sloughs of sand, the scattered bushes from which might spring deadly peril.

Seasons ago the idea that reiving flutsmen could wing freely in the skies of Vallia would have been ridiculous. The emperor maintained order in his domains. But since the Time of Troubles and the revolutions and insurrections and invasions, times had changed. The old emperor was dead and the new struggled to hold together the tattered remnants of the people loyal to Vallia, sought to bring back the old days of peace. Much of his time, perforce, was spent overseas hurling back the challenge of enemies, carrying fire and destruction into their homelands, instead of the fair island of Vallia. The emperor of Vallia, who was also King of Djanduin and Strom of Valka and lord of many broad lands, carried within himself a dream of unity. Many people followed him with fanatical loyalty, and many more opposed him for their own advantage.

The woman continued to walk on across the badlands with a determination that would not surprise those who knew her.

Her legs must have dropped off a long time ago, she felt. Weird ideas kept whirling in her head. Leems and water and flutsmen and the state of the country, all muddled up with annoyance that the trip to Delka Ob, capital of the province of Vindelka, had been interrupted. She admitted to herself that she was tired, deathly tired; but, also, she would not admit that fact. As her husband said, tiredness is a sin, particularly for people with work to do.

The first tree sprang at her, quite unexpectedly.

It appeared to be a tall, leering presence, black against the suns' glow. The sky sheeted in jade and crimson, in ochre and gold, in delicate tendrils of mauve. So there were clouds left in the world, after all. . . .

She moved aside to let the tree pass.

The next clump had to be rounded more cautiously. The fantastic notion was lodged in her head, along with the bells and the clamor and the hollow silence: the trees were sentient and walking and out to clasp her in their barky embrace.

She tried to stop, to take a breath, to force herself back to sanity.

Her legs refused to stop walking.

She went on, walking with her purposeful gait, walking on, unstoppable.

As she marched on with all the clamor bellowing away in her head and the muffled silences hollowing the edges of that uproar, she began to wonder if she had made a disastrous mistake. She knew where her airboat had been attacked, where her friends had died, the point from which she had begun her march. Perhaps she should have remained with the airboat until night, and then started. But she had had all day. . . . Perhaps that was the trouble. She fought the devils of self-doubt, and mistrust of her own judgments. She knew she was not unique in this. He who did not doubt, she who did not mistrust, must be lost.

But she had been so sure, so confident!

The distance to the river, the speed at which she walked, her own strength and determination. . . . The equation was not going to balance. Soon she would lie down. Then she would be finished.

If only those devils of flutsmen arrogant astride their saddle birds had not smashed the water jars! If only her flier had not been attacked at all . . . If only . . .

She marched on, and now her head was high, her shoulders back, chest out, and she strode on, not as though drunken but as though forcing her way forward against a whirlwind that sought to hurl her back.

She was used to marching. She'd marched through the Hostile Territories. She'd marched with armies with banners. But now the pain in her feet and ankles had ceased. She could not feel anything in her legs at all, so that *proved* they'd fallen off long ago.

The long shadows dropped down.

She had completely miscalculated. The whole thing was a miserable fiasco—a fatal fiasco.

A sound obtruded.

A tinkling, running, *splashing* sound . . .

She couldn't run.

And in those last few moments as she forced herself on toward the river she knew she had not miscalculated, and, too, she knew she was not marching on, striding out, rather she was staggering, toppling, near falling, desperately trying to reach the water before she collapsed.

Blindly in the last of the light she marched straight off the edge of the bluff and plummeted headlong into the river.

She hit with a divine splash and wetness surrounded her in bliss.

Then it became imperative to reach the little shelving beach under the bluff at once.

Jaws and claws lived in the river.

A few powerful over-arm strokes took her to the bank. She pulled herself out and lay on the mud, dripping, her wetness a cloak of benediction. The fourth Moon of Kregen, She of the Veils, rose to cast down her fuzzy pink and golden light.

The woman lay on the bank, in the mud, her brown hair spread and shining and the glory of her body abandoned to wetness. Magnificent, she looked, lying there, rounded and lissom, abandoned, sprawled, her tanned skin glowing through the rents in her leather russets.

Something hard squelched in the mud at her side.

A voice said: "By Vox! I'll fight any man who says I'm not first!"

Her eyes snapped open. She took a breath.

"Well," said another voice, thin and nasal. "She's not dead then, Hirvin."

"Out of the Ochre Limits," said another.

No one offered to fight Hirvin.

The woman turned and half sat up, leaning back on outthrust arms. The clustered men, six of them, caught their breaths. They sat their mounts at the top of the bank. Moonshine glittered on their metal. Shadows ran and concealed their faces beneath the helmet brims.

She had been concerned lest she encounter a wild and savage leem; what she had encountered was far more dangerous.

Their lances spiked up from stirrup boots, the pennons indistinct and unrecognizable in the hazy half-light. They bestrode totrixes, and the ungainly six-legged riding animals stood docilely enough, proof of harsh discipline in their management.

Hirvin cocked a leg over his saddle and dismounted.

Automatically, he took a hitch to his belt.

"Fetch her up here," he said, and the order was obeyed with betraying alacrity.

Three of the others dismounted and slid down the bank. They seized the woman, who did not resist. They brought her up to the top of the bank. The light of She of the Veils shone down. By that haloing golden light the hard hawklike faces came clearer, harsh with incessant patrols of the badlands, harsh with imposed discipline, harsh with unrealized ambitions and denied wish-fulfillments.

"A Beauty," said Hirvin, and he sucked in a breath. His face congested. An old scar shone lividly against the browned skin. He put a hand to the cheap and ornate clasp of the first of the belts girding him.

The woman put out her tongue and—as though exploring forgotten territory—licked her lips.

She swallowed and shook her head. She opened her mouth and a strangled cry changed to a wheeze. Then she could speak.

She said: "Llahal. You should know that—"

Hirvin bellowed laughter. He threw the first belt down and the axe it carried clashed against the hard packed earth of the higher bank. He roared.

"Polite, this one! Trained, I don't doubt! By Vox—Llahal to you, shishi, and play your part well, and—"

"I am not—"

"That's of no consequence." His voice sharpened. "Hold her!"

She moved her arms, in a particular way, and the two fellows grasping her were grasping thin air.

The rapier cleared scabbard sweetly. The main gauche slapped up, crosswise, in her left hand.

"You would do well to go your ways. You are swods, soldiers to be ordered. You are not brigands, murderers—"

"We are swods and we've had no fun for days on end—"

Hirvin saw something, something in the way the woman held the rapier and left-hand dagger, that made him rip his own sword free. It was a clanxer, a straight cut and thruster. He rushed, with a yell, aiming to smash past with superior weight and strength and knock the woman down with the flat.

He struck. The woman was not there.

But her rapier passed through his upper right arm.

"Do not make me kill you," she said.

"Howling Hakkachak the Hungry!" he screeched. His left hand clamped around his arm, pressing, and still a dark blot of blood stained out over his fingers. "Get behind her, you fools! Grab her! By Vox, I won't be denied my pleasure from this beauty—"

The first fellow to grab her, the one with the broken nose and the silly sly grin, fell back, staring stupidly at the dark wet line across his forearm. That was blood. He looked up, starting to yell, and Hirvin roared again.

"You miserable stupid onkers! Get around her! Trip her up! By Vox, do I have to do everything myself!"

The other two men climbed down from their totrixes hurriedly. They fanned out in the moonlight, circling the woman. She turned at once and ran toward the bank, ready to dive in and chance the jaws and claws of the river.

She was amazed at her own weakness.

A hand clamped on her arm, and a fist grabbed her brown hair. Her head was cruelly jerked back. A foot struck and knocked her legs from under her. She was aware of realizing that she did have her legs, and that was interesting, as she fell. They dragged her up to Hirvin.

A knobby fist hauled on her hair, forcing her to lift her face. She stared up at the man who looked down on her, gloating. He gloated as much from pride that he had won, as for any anticipation of what he intended. The scar moved as he spoke.

"You stuck your sword into my arm. Two can play that game."

The others—dutifully—laughed at the sally.

"Lial, do you go up to the hut and get things ready. Hot water and bandages."

The fellow with the freckles and snub nose ran off at once. The woman was dragged up by her hair. They held her, hard and harsh, and they took the rapier, main gauche and sailor knife away.

"A pretty thing like you oughtn't to play with men's weapons." Then Hirvin roared out again, his good humor restored, the sting from the rapier thrust ebbing. His men guffawed, genuinely, and they dragged the woman with them along the bank.

Their guard hut abruptly showed a light through the window as Lial struck flint and steel and caught the tump ready for the lamp. That was a cheap mineral oil lamp, and would no doubt stink all night. The place contained bunks for ten men, an audo, with a curtained alcove for the leader. The light showed his rank markings. Hirvin ranked as a ley-Deldar. The woman was pushed down on a bunk and the men stood back, staring at her.

She sat up. Sly looks passed from swod to swod. Young Nal swallowed, visibly trembling.

She said: "You are—"

"Say nothing, shishi." Hirvin held out his arm without looking as Lial bustled up with a cloth to wipe away the blood. "As soon as this little pink is bandaged, then you and I will try a fall or two, and not with Beng Drudoj, either."

Chuckles sounded in the little hut. The mud brick walls were hung with cheap and garish cloths such as could be bought for a silver sinver in any bazaar. A cooking stove built into the wall stank of grease. The bunks draped grayish bedclothes, heaped like stranded and decaying fish. The lamp, inevitably, smoked.

An arms rack, built of mud brick with some wood, held spears, stuxes, axes and short swords. The men, watching the woman, began to take off their weaponry. Outside sounded the clatter of hooves as the totrixes found their own way into their stalls.

"Watch her!" snarled Hirvin, then winced as Lial slapped a steaming cloth onto his wound. "Careful, oaf!"

The water stood ready on the stove, and it was clear the men were willing, very willing, to forgo their evening meal until afterward. Patroling the river and the edge of the Ochre Limits was a miserable existence.

When Lial finished bandaging Hirvin's arm, the Deldar took a breath, sniffed, drew in his stomach and flexed his arm experimentally. He looked at the woman.

"Will you scratch? If you do you will have to be tied down."

"I will do more than scratch—"

Hirvin shouted.

"Get the clothes off her! Tie her down! By Vox! No little shishi balks me—"

She kicked the first one so that he turned green and rolled about the floor. The second only just missed having an eye removed. The third got a grip on her hair and then keened in agony as two fingers struck up his nostrils. The other two fell on her, bearing her down by weight, and Hirvin simply leaped on top of the lot.

The door of the hut opened and the growing night breeze blew dust across the floor. Hirvin, sliding forward and hitting his wounded arm a crack on the edge of the bunk, yelled.

"Shut the door, Tandu, for the sake of Ben Dikkane! And keep that brat of yours outside if you don't want him to see man's work."

He reared up and swung about as his comrades grasped the woman, holding her. Now she struggled unavailingly, lissom, supple, her brown hair aswirl.

The four-armed man in the doorway said, curtly: "Stay outside, Dalki. See to the totrixes."

Hirvin's momentary distraction as his wounded arm cracked against the bunk edge and he shouted at the four-armed Djang gave the woman a tiny moment in which to act. The two men holding her felt her movements and could not hold her. One wrung his hands as the wrists poured molten streams of pain up his arms, the other reeled back with blood spurting from his nose. The woman leaped up onto the bunk, panting, brown hair wild, and from the last of her assailants she snatched the fighting man's dagger. Heavy, unadorned, designed to be a gut-spiller, the dagger menaced the men in the hut.

She looked a magnificent savage beast of the jungle, broken free of her chains, uncaged, no longer shackled for the delight of the passing trade.

The Djang, Tandu, used his upper left hand to sweep the dust-covered cloak up over his shoulder, out of the way. His height overtopped all. His broad, ferocious, open Dwadjang features congested with blood. He stepped forward and knocked over a three-legged stool. He did not notice. He stared at the woman, poised on the bunk. She did not brandish the dagger; she held it as a person holds a weapon they know well how to use.

Some of the swods were over the first shock of their injuries at the hands of the woman. They gathered themselves together, and stood up and wiped the blood away. They looked at their leader, at ley-Deldar Hirvin, and murderous intent disfigured their faces. They were mercenaries, hired for a mind-dulling task; they would not be balked of their prey.

"She's only a woman!" yelled Hirvin. "She will not stop us with a dagger. Get behind her, throw a blanket over her, bear her down!"

Young Nal, trembling, scampered around the end of the bunk and Lial and Long Naghan snatched up a blanket. Tandu, the Djang, stared at the woman.

His hand, his upper right, whipped out one of his swords. His lower left drew a long dagger. He advanced, he did not shut the door as he had been ordered, and his boots scratched on the blown dust. His hip collided with the edge of the nearest bunk and dislodged a marching pack there, which fell and emptied its contents onto the dusty floor. He did not notice.

He stared. His face, congested, broad, a furious ferocious frightening Djang countenance, empurpled.

He shouted. He roared in such a voice as would bring the very stars out of the sky.

"Do not touch her!" His lower right hand caught in Vogon the Amsant's hair, and jerked the bulky mercenary back. He thrust himself on, sword lifted, dagger snouting. He was visibly shaking with passion.

"What nonsense is this?" screeched Hirvin.

Tandu the Djang drew himself up. His sword swept in the ritual salute to the woman and then flickered out, a bar of lethal steel, to menace Hirvin.

"You fool! This lady is my queen! The Queen of Djanduin!" The Djang sword darted for Hirvin's throat. "This is the Stromni of Valka! The Empress of Vallia! Delia of Delphond, Delia of the Blue Mountains!"

CHAPTER TWO

The Djang Tandu and His Son Dalki Stand Watch

Deldar Hirvin staggered back, away from that reaching Djang sword. His eyes opened wide. His mouth thinned into a bitter line. He spat his words when he found his voice.

"The empress? What is that to us, *now*? If it is true, Tandu—"

The Djang swirled his sword to encompass the others. Young Nal, behind the bunk, froze, ashen.

"True? Aye, you nidges, it is true!"

"Then," said Hirvin, spittle slobbering, "then we are all dead men. What I say is so!" He twisted away from the point of the sword, gestured to his men. "It matters nothing to us, empress or queen. If she lives—we die!"

"Down on your knees!" thundered Tandu. "Down on your faces in the full incline!"

He knocked the bowl of water over from the table, and sent the table flying after it. He bloated with the enormity of his own rage, his harness straining under the immense swelling of his ribcage. He looked—he was!—frighteningly formidable.

"Thank you, Tandu," said Delia. She spoke levelly. She was in control of her breathing now, and fighting off the dreadful tiredness. She smiled.

At that smile Tandu almost exploded.

"Do we kill her first," said Sly Oswalk, "or after?"

Tandu roared his contempt.

"First, nidges, you will have to slay me!"

"That, Tandu the Onker, we will accomplish," said Hirvin, and leaped.

Delia threw the dagger.

Heavy, simple, cruel, it passed clean through Hirvin's neck.

His eyes crossed as he vainly attempted to focus on the steel transfixing his throat.

"Hai!" bellowed Tandu, and, then, remembering: "Dalki!"

Swords snapped up, and before Hirvin, tottering, fell under their feet, the men were at handstrokes.

It was a poor contest; when Dalki, a younger edition of Tandu, burst in raging, it was no contest at all.

Sly Oswalk, alone, managed to slip through the open doorway and escape into the night.

Tandu and Dalki were all for following and cutting him down without mercy.

"Majestrix! He deserves to suffer in the deepest of Herrelldrin Hells, to wander screaming among the Ice Floes of Sicce forever!"

"Aye," said Delia. "Probably. But he snatched a bow before he left. I value you, Tandu, and your son Dalki, too much—"

Tandu, stumbling over a corpse, had the sense to make no otiose reply.

Delia sat herself down on the edge of a bunk. She put a hand to her hair, smoothing the wildness back. In that brown hair, caught and embellished by the lamplight, outrageous chestnut and auburn tints glowed. Tandu, breathing hard, beamed down on his queen.

"I remember you, Tandu. Yes, I assuredly do. It is Tandu Khynlin Jondermair, is it not?"

"Yes, majestrix, may Djan Kadjiryon have you in his keeping."

"And you married one of our girls in Valka, I recall, when you came from Djanduin to train our young men to fly flutduins? Yes—Valli, I remember, beautiful Valli of the violet eyes. And Dalki is your son."

Tandu breathed so that his bronze-studded harness creaked. "Valli died, majestrix. Slain by those Djan-forsaken cramphs of aragorn. When we fought in Valka."

"I am sorry, Tandu. We have been through terrible times together."

"That is true. But there is my son, Dalki—"

As Dalki, shorter, and by a fraction less formidable than his father, bobbed his head in awed respect for this famous and indomitable woman—the Empress of Vallia! The Stromni of Valka!—it was clearly apparent that he had heard of Delia of Vallia, heard of her and shared his father's fanatical loyalty. Yet Dalki drew his harness over but two arms; he was not a true Dwadjang with four powerful fighting men's arms. He was a miscegenation; yet clear-eyed, strong-faced, proud and upright, a true son to his Djang father and Valkan mother.

"Can we stay here tonight, Tandu? I am tired."

Instantly, Dalki was at the bunks, picking up blankets, bashing straw-filled mattresses, hauling all the pillows about to find the finest.

"You are hungry, majestrix, thirsty?"

"I could drink the whole of the Sunset Sea, were it sweet water."

"A meal! Dalki, a meal for the queen!"

The mercenary frontier riders provided poor food; but the Djang and his half-Djang, half-apim son rustled up the best. They brewed strong Kregan tea and heaped a pottery dish with the golden yellow paline berries. Delia sipped the tea, and chewed a paline, as the meal was prepared. She leaned back against heaped pillows, and looked with her brown eyes level and curiously unimpassioned upon the scene. She had come through a bad ordeal. She had done so before. No doubt, in Opaz's good time, she would do so again.

The corpses were thrown outside to be cleared away in the morning. Tandu and his son would not sleep all this night. Not, by Zodjuin of the Silver Stux, when their queen slept and they stood guard.

Simple though the ingredients might be, the meal Dalki cooked up smelled delicious. It tasted very fine, also; although Delia would probably have chewed on passe biltong and sour water with her hunger. She did not consider it strange that the Djangs had not asked her why she was here, marching out of the Ochre Limits, instead of living in her great palaces—any of them—surrounded by luxury. They knew she was a woman well-used to the hard trails of life.

That lack of curiosity on their part did not make her quench her own curiosity about them. When she had finished the meal, which she had insisted they share, she said: "Tell me, Tandu. You came to Valka to train young men to fly flutduins. You were an ord-Deldar, I believe. At any rate, you would soon have passed out of the Deldar grade to become a Hikdar commanding your own pastang. Why is it that you are here, riding guard on the Ochre Limits, chasing bandits for the Kov of Vindelka?"

Tandu let his gaze linger briefly on his son. His broad,

high-colored face, suddenly took on lines Delia had not noticed before. Tandu looked, for an instant, sad.

Then he said: "Because I married my Valli."

Delia felt the shock.

"In Valka? Where I am stromni and my husband is strom? In our Valka?"

"Aye, majestrix. In the Time of Troubles, when you were away fighting our enemies. A few people only, but enough."

"My husband and I much mislike folk who do not look on all Creation as one. Djang, apim, we are all Opaz's creatures, all men and women under the hand of Djan."

Softly, Dalki said: "You suffered under many enemies then, majestrix."

His strong face, so like his father's and yet inlaid and softened by his apim ancestry, betrayed the awe and elation he felt at actually speaking to the Queen of Djanduin and the Empress of Vallia. Delia smiled.

"You were not born, then, Dalki, I know. But, you are right and have learned the lessons of history correctly. But, in one thing, there is more to learn. I have many enemies still."

"May Djondalar of the Twisted Staff strike them all low!"

"A happening devoutly to be wished," agreed the queen. She did not so much yawn as indicate that she would have yawned if she allowed yawning to figure as a part of what she tolerated in life. Instantly, the two Djangs—for Dalki thought and talked more like a Djang than a Valkan—fluffed about preparing the best bunk and smoothing the pillows and spreading extra blankets. Then, tactfully, they withdrew so the empress might complete her toilet in privacy.

Delia put her head on the pillow and went at once to sleep, confident in her Djangs and their strong right arms, all three of them. As ever, her last thought was for her husband who was—well, who the hell ever knew where he got to?

He was probably out somewhere outlandish bashing hostiles over the head with his great Krozair longsword and, as ever, thinking always of her.

What a pair they were! And then she was asleep.

Outside the guard hut the Kregen night breathed easy in the glitter of stars and the golden and roseate light of She of the Veils, soon joined by Kregan's first moon, the Maiden with the Many Smiles. The Djangs prowled watchfully. Any beast or human of evil intent would find short shrift at their hands.

Shortly after the hour of dim, which is the opposite to the hour of mid on Kregan, Delia awoke. She stretched and knew instantly where she was. She sat up. She stretched. Then she stood up and girt on her rapier, which Dalki had carefully cleaned, and went outside the hut.

Instantly, like a black shadow, Tandu stood at her side.

"Majestrix?"

"I'll stand a few burs' watch, Tandu."*

"But, majestrix—"

"Dalki needs his rest."

Tandu mulled this over. He had heard the stories concerning Delia of Vallia, so many of them true, so many far-fetched as to be fantasies; but, this!

"My queen, to stand a watch like a common swod—"

"Swods are not common, Tandu. And I have stood sentry go before."

Tandu, for one, well believed that.

"As my queen commands."

Dalki wanted to be mutinous until his father told him the queen commanded. Then he went into the hut and threw himself onto a bunk, and went to sleep dreaming of Delia of Delphond.

The high star glitter picked out the familiar constellations of Kregen. Delia sighed. Her husband had told her of other constellations and stars that he saw from his own funny little world with only a single yellow sun and a single silver moon and only apims, as he and she were, and not a diff in sight. Odd! Perhaps, one day, if the Star Lords ordained, she might herself go to that funny little world he named as The Earth. Odd.

They stood watch, queen and swod, scanning the riverbank and the trees and aware of the changing patterns in the rustle of leaves in the breeze, the smell of river and mud, the tiny scuttlings of creatures of the night. And to Tandu Khynlin Jondermair came the absolute conviction that to stand a guard duty with his Queen Delia was to confide half the safety of their mutual watch into hands as strong and capable as the toughest Djang in all Djanguraj, in all of Djanduin. He breathed easy, did Tandu the Djang.

* bur. The Kregan hour, approximately 40 terrestrial minutes.

Presently, in a soft whisper that reached only the Djang's ears, Delia spoke.

"And you never returned to our Djanduin, Tandu?"

"No, majestrix. I thought—I did not think my son Dalki would be . . . be well received there, either."

"Mayhap you were wrong in that."

"I do not know."

"I trust you were. One day, Tandu, we will put it to the test." She did not look at Tandu as she spoke; rather she kept a lookout along the river and the trees, watching for others like Hirvin or Sly Oswalk, who had escaped, to come seeking their fortune with the queen in the guardhut. "And so now you serve Vomanus, the Kov of Vindelka."

"Aye, majestrix. I had a letter from Panshi, the strom's chamberlain in Esser Rarioch. Kov Vomanus received me kindly. But that was just of him, and as he was—"

"As he was?"

"Times have changed in Vindelka, majestrix, as they have elsewhere in Vallia."

"Before those damned flutsmen brought down my flier and killed Pansi and Nath the Jokester, I was on my way to Delka Ob. I chose to fly over the Ochre Limits, for that was the shortest route. I am sorry, now, that I so chose. But I must get to Delka Ob. Vomanus is to be wed, and I must be there for the ceremony."

She did not add that when Vomanus, her half-brother, had been wed the first time she had not only not been invited, she had known nothing of it until later. Of that union had been born Valona, who was not Valona the Claw. Vomanus's wife, Saenci of the Locks, had died. Delia had felt grief at that, even though Saenci had not been of the Sisters of the Rose. Her daughter, Valona, was of the SOR. Now Vomanus was to be wed again, to a woman unknown to Delia. Natural curiosity as much as family pride impelled her to attend this wedding and, in a pathetic time-binding way, perhaps, make amends to Saenci of the Locks.

"I must get to Delka Ob, and quickly."

"We hear little out here, majestrix. We performed the ritual mourning for the kovneva. We do not know that the kov is to be married again."

"Well, he is. So, good Tandu, first thing in the morning I set off for the capital."

He turned, slowly, to regard her.

"Yes, Tandu. You and Dalki shall go with me."

He said, simply: "You do me honor, majestrix. But—what of our guard duty?"

"At your back is the River of Shining Spears, and across that the zorca grasslands of the Blue Mountains. At your front the Ochre Limits. If bandits appear, they will do little before the men we shall send arrive."

"Quidang, majestrix!"*

Not for a four-armed Dwadjang the puzzlements of command or the complexities of operations. Give a Djang his weapons, point him in the right direction, and very little if anything in the whole world of Kregen would stop him and his fellows from trampling on. But present him with a conundrum, a difficult problem in logistics or operations, strategy, and he was lost. Then he would turn to the two-armed Obdjangs with their gerbil-like faces to make the decisions and to take the command. Obdjang and Dwadjang, they lived together in fraternal friendship in Djanduin.

A long screeching cry cut through the night.

Delia cocked her head.

"A wherezik has found its prey," quoth Tandu. "Poor victim, swimming in the river at this time of night."

"No doubt," said Delia briskly, "the victim's belly was stuffed with its own victims."

"Aye. Aye, majestrix. That is the way of the world."

"Has there been any report of leems lately?"

"Not one."

"I am relieved to hear it. On the morrow we take all the totrixes and march downriver for Mellinsmot. There we should be able to find a flier, or zorcas if they have no airboats."

"Whatever the folk of Mellinsmot may have, they will gladly yield it for their empress."

"That, I hope."

"Oh," said Tandu, easily, "they will." In the star-shot darkness the lights of the moons shadowed on his hand, instinctively reaching for a sword hilt, without thought. Delia half-smiled and half-sighed.

"The Hikdar will be surprised," said Tandu, out of nowhere.

* Quidang!—Kregish for "Very good!" "Aye aye, sir!" "Your wish is my command and will be obeyed instantly."

"The Hikdar?"

"Aye. He brings a patrol along the bank, on a regular schedule. Just to see we are not all dead or run off."

"Oh!"

"Hikdar Leomer ti Vindheim will expect to see Deldar Hirvin and us—and he'll find another audo of guards." Tandu made a small breathy sound on the night air that was as near a laugh as a sentry would permit himself. It was clear that to the Djang this was a great jest. Delia felt pleasure in Tandu's enjoyment of the situation. This was a simple enough example of one of the reasons she loved her Djangs so.

They lived in Djanduin, a sizable country in the southwest of the vast continent of Havilfar, down south of the equator. Up here in the north, the large island of Vallia with the clusters of smaller islands around the shores, had seen the coming of many Djangs since the Strom of Valka became King of Djanduin. This free movement and mingling of peoples was a dream near to the heart of the Emperor of Vallia, for he foresaw the time when all of this grouping of continents and islands, known as Paz, must fight for life against enemies from overseas, the detested, despised and dreaded Shanks. So if anyone thought to question why one man should at once be strom, kov, hyrkov, king and emperor, the answer did not lie in the reply that the man was a remarkable person. He was, of course, and Delia had married him; but deeper than that, more touching the core of the future on Kregen, lay this determination to resist enemies and create a whole, free, full life for all.

A dream. Of course, a dream. But without a dream you are without everything.

The night passed. Delia said: "Before we ride for Mellinsmot there is a task I must perform. We will take all the totrixes and all the water we can carry."

A fighting man grasped the meaning without fail. A warrior maiden, a Jikai Vuvushi, probably understood even more rapidly.

Tandu cocked an eye aloft as they finished up the first breakfast of the day.

"Yes, Tandu. I know. Rippasch will be there before us. But—I must."

So, with all the saddle animals loaded with skins bulging with water, they set off into the badlands, out across the Ochre Limits.

CHAPTER THREE

A Burial Is Completed

Delia and Tandu stood, heads bowed, looking down at the wreckage of the airboat and the strewn bones. Dalki stood in a respectful way; but his eyes did not stare downward. His right hand rested comfortably on his belt beside the feathered shafts in their plain quiver, and his left hand, held down, grasped a bow. He looked up.

Presently, her private commendation to Opaz for the ibs of her friends completed, Delia said: "It is sad. But we will give them a proper burial. They will surely reach the sunny uplands beyond the Ice Floes of Sicce."

"Without doubt," said Tandu.

Scraping a grave was simple enough. It would blow streaming sand, later on, no doubt, and the graves might be stripped for the bones to lie bare and bleached under the radiance of the suns; later on the sand would blow back.

Tandu moved with caution inside the wreckage of the flier. He only knocked a few broken things over. He came out with Delia's box which he and Dalki strapped onto a totrix. That contained, besides a fine dress and other feminine essentials, wedding gifts. An earnest only. She had determined to let Vomanus see she was not pleased with him. Later on the full and lavish caravan stuffed with wedding gifts would be sent to Delka Ob. Later on.

She felt relief she had managed to persuade herself to return. Her friends had to be buried, and their ibs commended to Opaz, although such a commendation had no need of bones, corpses or graves. She controlled her shudder. She detested illness, sickness, the stink of the sick room, the fatuous smiles of people watching friends die. When her father had been ill—poisoned by secret enemies—she had managed to hold on long enough to attend to him. But if there was a flaw in Delia of Delphond, a failing, it was this, that she had to force herself into the tasks expected of people in dealing with sickness.

She had not in her life escaped those tasks.

She had been born a princess, married a prince, who had made her a queen and an empress. But she had been slave. She had emptied the golden chamberpots of those who enslaved her, and had, on and off, chopped them up into diced meat for it.

The simple ceremony over, her belongings piled on the back of a totrix, a last look at the smashed airboat, and she nodded to Tandu and they set off.

Away over the scorching wastes of the Ochre Limits lay the Dragon's Bones, a vast collection of monsters' bones of many descriptions. The place was a giant cemetery for giants. There a notable fight had taken place, where her husband—before they were married—had saved the life of her father the emperor. She thought of those long ago days as the totrixes waddled along with their six-legged gait, and she sighed. Life had been—simpler—then.

And, for all that, it had been complicated, too, Opaz knew! Just that the size of the problems these days was so much greater. Now they had half a world to ponder over.

She itched. She was used to discomfort as well as comfort; but the wash she'd managed in the river to rid herself of the mud had not been sufficient. Now dust caked over all. She longed for a wallow and a brush and a soak and a swim in the Baths of the Nine. Mellinsmot would boast such an establishment, no doubt a provincially grand place, full of gilded stout statues and flower garlands. But it would boast, also, piping hot water and steam rooms and freezing pools and an exercise salle. Yes, she closed her eyes and fought the itches, refusing to scratch, yes, she much longed for a session in the Baths of the Nine.

When the line of little dots appeared in their rear, high in the sky and winging strongly on, Delia frowned.

Tandu said, "Damned Djan-forsaken flutsmen."

The skein bore on, and Delia counted six of them.

If the flutsmen wished to attack there would be no escaping them. The Ochre Limits extended in barrenness all around. If they attacked, if they did not attack, all were as one to Tandu and Dalki.

Dalia said, and the note of crossness in her voice was not unremarked: "Why in the name of Vox do we allow these thieving murdering flutsmen so free a rein? Does not the Kov of Vindelka sweep his province clean?"

Hesitantly, Tandu said: "I know nothing of these high matters, majestrix."

"But you can see the flutsmen up there?"

"Yes, majestrix. They have grown worse just lately—"

"I thought we'd cleansed the land of them, and the aragorn and the mercenaries. I thought all our enemies were being driven back into the north. I don't know what Vomanus is playing at."

Tandu and Dalki might not worry, one way or the other, over six flutsmen—for themselves. But Tandu caught his son's eye, and for a moment they reined in to ride knee to knee as Delia trotted on ahead.

"The empress does not care for flutsmen, father."

"So I gather. I do not care, either. But we have the empress with us—so—"

"So we protect her. I know that."

"Shoot as many of the devils as you can before we come to handstrokes. After that—it is the empress, alone, who matters."

Riding up ahead, Delia wondered if the two Djangs were laying bets in the way her husband and Seg Segutorio had the habit of doing. Thoughtfully, she drew out her longbow. This was a Lohvian longbow built by Seg, who was, in his friends' opinion, the finest bowman not only in all Loh but in all Kregen. She had thought she was a good shot having been trained up by the Sisters of the Rose, until Seg had given her of his learning and experience and expertise. Seg had trained her to shoot, as he had trained her children. She had no doubt she could feather two of the flutsmen up there before they landed; but the flutsmen would shoot back.

They'd use crossbows.

Delia half-turned.

"Crossbows," she said. She spoke in that cross way, reflecting her worries, and then instantly hoped the Djangs would not think she was cross with them. Some empresses of Kregen, in this situation, would blame their retainers for any misfortune.

"We will shoot them, majestrix, before they land."

"Before they shoot us!"

"Aye, majestrix. As you say, before they shoot us."

The thought of cruel iron bolts punching into the bodies of

the Djangs upset Delia. It was bad enough to think of quarrels smashing into the totrixes. In all the marvelous diversity of life on Kregen, Delia joyed in the warmth and variety and very profuseness of life, each one precious. Except, perhaps, for inimical forms who wanted only to rip her up and eat her. Then, of course, she had to harden her heart and see they did no such thing.

Now, and with a heavy heart, she gave her orders.

"Dismount. Make the totrixes lie down. I do not like this; but it is a thing known and done."

The Djangs knew, had done it, and instantly understood.

Even then, it was nip and tuck.

The flutsmen swept on, the wings of their fluttrells beating with a pulsing rhythm that drove them through the air and sent them diving down at the little party on the sand. The totrixes didn't mind in the least that they should stop trotting along, and were no doubt highly pleased that they were actually being allowed to lie down. But, being six-legged saddle animals of contrary natures, they wanted to lie down where they wished, and not where their masters intemperately pushed and pulled them.

"Giddown!" rumbled Dalki, hauling a totrix around so that his head jutted over the rump of the one ahead.

"Stay there!" roared Tandu, as his totrix started to lumber up and move to a different place where, it was altogether probable, the sand was much softer and more comfortable.

Delia laughed.

"We must make a comical spectacle!"

"Aye, majestrix. And here come the flutsmen."

Three bows lifted and three arrowheads snouted up.

The Djangs did not have the Lohvian longbow; but their Djang bows were superb in their own fashion. Shooting at a flatter trajectory their shafts could carry almost as far as those from a longbow, and at shorter ranges they were deadly.

Delia shot in her longbow first.

The leading flutsman, his feather-streaming hair blowing wildly behind him in the wind of his passage, his accoutrements glittering, his tall aerial spear slanted up and aft, screeched. The rose-fletched shaft pierced him through his face. Delia did not stop to congratulate herself on a fortunate shot, for she had aimed at his body, but whipped out the second arrow.

Tandu loosed and then Dalki.

Neither Djang missed.

Five in ten, six in twelve, were gone.

Four crossbow bolts thudded viciously into the sand and two of the totrixes. One animal was killed instantly; the other, screaming, reared to his feet and tried to bolt, and fell over tangled legs all fouled up in his reins. Delia shut her ears to the sounds.

If these reivers of the sky were the same as those who had slain Pansi and Nath the Jokester, then her heart would harden even more. Either way, she shared most of the philosophy which attempted to stop people from killing her.

Her second shot was flailed away by a stupidly flapping wing. Tandu scored no better and Dalki's arrow skewered into the feathered underside of a fluttrell. The bird toppled forward. His rider went feet-first over the bird's awkward head vane, hit the sand, and was up, raging.

He was the first to land and whip out his sword, abandoning crossbow and bird, and come racing across the sand toward the three in the meager cover of the saddle animals.

Delia put a shaft clear through his bronze-studded leathers. He stopped running forward, yelling like a demon, waving his sword. He stopped. He stood up, the arrow through him. Then he fell down.

The remaining two flutsmen leaped from their birds in gouts of ochre sand. Their faces, hard, grimed, contorted with fury, bore a vague resemblance to human faces. Delia with those faces before her eyes was in no further doubt or wonder that these two had not flown off when their comrades had died. These flutsmen were driven to kill, they had been using kaff, and they were drugged past all reason. They spat foam and screeched, and rushed.

Delia's hand lifted to her right shoulder. Her hand, unblemished by a single ring, snapped forward.

The terchick crossed the lessening distance to the first charging man in a blurred streak of steel. The little throwing knife, sharply-pointed, cunningly balanced, left Delia's hand and sped through empty air and pierced through the right eye of the flutsman. The steel skewered on into his brain. He gyrated for a few foolish moments before he fell down.

The last one barely hesitated—if he hesitated at all—before Tandu's swords went through him and chopped him, both together.

Dalki said, "You always were greedy, Father. I was about to loose—I could have shot you."

Tandu roared, and wiped one of his swords in the sand. "My hide would have turned your shot, Dalki!"

"Well, Father, and mayhap. Next time, allow me to get a look in."

Delia refused to feel faint. After all, what were six dead men more or less in this world of suffering? She was well aware that flutsmen had kissed their families good-bye long before they took up the aerial reiving trade, and the only folk to mourn them would be the members of their own marauding band.

Still, once upon a time, under a certain moon, each one of them had had a mother. . . .

For the sake of Pansi and Nath the Jokester, Delia felt no incongruity in wishing that those mothers had never conceived, or had miscarried, or had drowned their babes in infancy. . . .

And, even that was no good. Had it not been these flutsmen, then it would have been others . . . You couldn't solve all your problems by killing. That had been tried. It worked for a time; but in the long run you simply finished up with nobody.

"Majestrix?"

She had not spoken; bluff old Tandu was wily enough to know when to jolly even an empress along.

Dalki said: "If ever it was needed to be proved, which it never was and never will be, by Djan, then the queen is a true queen of the Djangs!"

On that, Delia felt it time to gather up the totrixes, make a check, and mout up. Tandu, having come from Djanduin to teach Valkans to fly flutduins had never been a true mercenary, had never become a paktun. Similarly, Dalki was no paktun. They started to mount up.

Understanding this, Delia sighed and then laughed.

"Make a check first. See what these flutsmen have on them that is interesting to us. And, if they have gold, it is ours. Is not this so?"

"Yes, majestrix—"

"Tandu! Now hearken. You and Dalki may call me 'my lady' as well as this tiresome majestrix. You know that."

"Quidang, my lady!"

With that settled, the corpses rifled—they turned up nothing of interest and six leather bags totaling a hundred and twenty-one gold pieces, two hundred and thirty-five silver pieces and not a copper ob among them—the two Djangs and their queen set the totrixes in motion. They walked the animals, husbanding them, and so took their way out of the Ochre Limits.

As they rode Delia pondered. Portents in what had happened alarmed her. Affairs, in her half-brother's kovnate province of Vindelka, were quite clearly not running smoothly.

Flutsmen? Paid guards who attacked unfortunate women? One would think this was some wild and barbaric land instead of civilized Vallia!

Of course, much of Vallia's civilization had been stripped away during the Time of Troubles, and even now the country was not fully restored. But in Vindelka? She grew a trifle warm at the thought of some of the words she would use when she met Vomanus.

When they reached the river she was again forcefully reminded that this latter-day Empire of Vallia was not the same as the Vallia into which she had been born. She could not plunge in and go for a good long cleansing swim. Jaws and claws. . . . When she was a young girl the rivers had been made safe. Well, as in the case of the prowling leems and other savage animals, one day the rivers and the land would be made safe again.

Reaching a pleasant glade above the riverbank, they camped and cooked a meal. The men brought up as much water as they could in every container that could be pressed into service, and the queen gave herself a thoroughly good wash. Trusting in the glowing radiance of Zim and Genodras, the twin suns, she washed her hair. Some of the scents and unguents that poor Pansi would have used had been smashed in the crash of the airboat; enough remained for her to perfume her hair—subtly—and to make herself feel a little more like Delia. Despite all the titles she had had hung about her, she tended to think of herself just as Delia. Some of her titles she loved; others she was ambivalent about, and a few—a very few—she could not summon up enthusiasm for. She was too sensitive of what they meant actively to despise any one of the collection.

Tandu was fussing.

Delia eyed him.

He started to bang the fire out. "If we leave now, my lady, we will reach Mellinsmot before nightfall."

"Excellent! Then we leave now."

As the twin suns slid down the sky, and the western horizon smoked into jade and ruby flames, it was pleasant to jog along the riverbank, in the sweetness of the late afternoon and early evening, and see ahead the lights of the town waiting to welcome them.

Jogging along, Delia thought of her husband. There was no particular reason not to think of him, and the time of day made no difference, for she thought of him at any time, as, he had told her, he thought of her. Each had to go one way, for a space, until all the dangers were past. Then they would be together and not let anyone or anything part them again, ever. . . .

Riding jolting along on a saddle animal all day, biting on sand and dust, fighting off murderous flutsmen, trying to keep clean and get enough to eat, all this took a toll, drained a girl, set a dull fatigue into her bones so that the prospect of bath and bed pleased her far more than they would ordinarily. Just to wash herself clean, eat a gargantuan supper, and then stretch out and go to sleep!

Marvelous!

Of course, one vital ingredient would be missing tonight; but then he was so often away she had fashioned a life for herself that, half of a full life though it might be, had, perforce, to suffice. He felt exactly the same way.

In the last of the light as the totrixes quickened their six feet some of the pleasure of the evening waned.

They reached an avenue of tended trees; considerable cultivation had been passed in the gloaming and now they approached the northwest gate of Mellinsmot. The gates stood half-closed and a handful of travelers scurried through, dimly seen figures, to hasten away into the gathering darkness. The people were leaving Mellinsmot and heading along the beaten path by the river.

Tandu offered no comment.

Delia swiveled in the saddle. "Odd," she said. "Folk usually enter a town at night, not leave it."

"Going back to their holdings, my lady," ventured Dalki.

"Probably."

The brick archway echoed their totrix's hooves, and the guard detail would be springing out to challenge them—

There were no guards on the gate of Mellinsmot.

"Odder and odder," said Delia.

Tandu loosened one of his swords, and brought his bow forward, holding it half-drawn, arrow nocked in the practiced archer's grip. Delia brought her own bow up. Dalki, at her back, followed the example of his father and the queen.

Echoes rustled from the brick walls. The streaming radiance of the suns was almost gone. Shadows, plum-colored, bruised with darkness, fell about them.

"The Feathered Risslaca is a comfortable inn, my lady, so I have been told." Tandu did not turn to face Delia as he spoke. Beyond the next edge of twin shadows might lie danger. Tandu kept his gaze darting about, taking in everything, watching for the first suspicious movement. By now they all knew something was wrong in the town of Mellinsmot.

"Or," went on Tandu, "perhaps my lady would sooner go straight to Strom Dogan's villa, here?"

When the strom, who held this town and surrounding lands, his stromnate, at the hands of Kov Vomanus of Vindelka, understood that he was to host the empress, lavish hospitality would be immediately forthcoming. Delia, looking about at the deserted streets, the boarded-up windows, wondered.

A dog slunk away into the enveloping shadows. His tail dangled between his legs. Dalki rode with his head screwed back, alertly scanning every window, every shadowed doorway.

"D'you smell it?" demanded Delia.

"Aye, my lady." Tandu's broad face lifted. "By Djan! Like intestines left out in the suns."

Delia made a face.

"Apt, if unpleasant, Tandu."

The way lay ahead through a crossing, where the houses stood back. One side of the road lay swathed in blackness; the other was mildewed with a ghostly glow of fading red and green. A door opened and a lozenge of yellow light burst across the beaten way. A voice screamed.

A figure fell out of the door, was hurled out, for the violence of its movement sent up a swirl of dust in the half-light. The figure tottered forward, twirled about with flailing arms and as the door slammed shut fell to lie sprawled in the dust.

Delia nudged her totrix forward.

"Caution, my lady!"

Tandu was there, before her, dismounting to bend over the dark sprawled figure. He twitched away a corner of the raggedy blanket that concealed the figure's face.

He jumped back. He jumped back a clear three feet, and stood, frozen.

Delia looked down.

The face had been that of a young girl. No doubt it had been comely, with smiling eyes and smooth cheeks. Now that face was smothered in suppurating sores. The stink broke up as fresh sores burst, to run in greenish pus.

"The Affliction of the Sores of Combabbry!"

Dalki said, his voice high, "Do not touch her, my lady!"

"No." Delia's voice shook despite all she could do to hold herself steady. "This explains all. Mellinsmot is a town of contagion and death!"

CHAPTER FOUR

Affliction

Serried in rows beneath the gilded ceiling of Strom Dogan's Great Hall the suppurating sufferers lay festering in their sores. Twin white half-moons shone beside Delia's mouth; to disappear instantly as she smiled at the person for whom she ministered. Pus, vomit, blood, excrement, filth and muck—all were as one to Delia. She bathed foreheads in the approved stiffly starched yellow romantic way; she scraped the muck off the floor and scrubbed the strom's boards clean.

He, Strom Dogan nal Mellin, having cowered away in his topmost tower with his family, too frightened to risk contamination even in the short distance out of the town, had been hauled out of it by the empress.

The hauling had been done by Tandu.

"You will give orders to your people, and you will help, Dogan." Delia had spoken in such a way that Dogan's chattering teeth had almost splintered in his frenzy.

Then: "Tandu—you have my permission to pull the strom out by his ears."

"Quidang, my lady!"

So—Strom Dogan and his people had, unwillingly and fearfully, been pressed to assist the empress. The Empress of Vallia ordered, organized, controlled. She also wiped up filth and scrubbed floors.

Sickness—the very idea of sickness nauseated her.

When, as a young girl, she had been thrown by a zorca, her immediate reactions had been of fury at herself for so lamentable a display. The second thought had been one of surprise that her zorca, so brave and patient, a marvelous saddle animal, should have thrown her at all. But it was accidental.

Only then—as the third reaction—had she discovered the injury to her leg. She had been made a cripple. She dragged one leg after her like a stamped-on crab.

Getting over that, as her only way of phrasing it to herself, had involved a secret visit to the Swinging City of Aphrasöe arranged by her father the emperor, and then a surreptitious dip in the Sacred Pool of Baptism of the River Zelph arranged by the wild and savage clansman who was to become her husband. So she knew about these things.

The stink in the strom's Great Hall was prodigious.

Sweet Ibroi was burned by the bushel. Water was continually sluiced down over the floor, to be swept away in foaming sheets of brown and yellow and green. Sometimes the water swept away red—when someone's sores burst past all enduring. All the anti-pollutants available were used. How the contagion spread even the needlemen could not swear to. Better not to touch a sufferer. Better not to breathe too close to the air he or she had breathed. But, after that, what gods or demons hurled the sickness from one poor wight to the next?

Pungent ibroi, a capital disinfectant much used to wash down slaves' quarters when Vallia dealt in slaves, before the present emperor outlawed slavery, was consumed in vast quantities. At least, along with its sweet-smelling fellow it freshened the atmosphere.

Strom Dogan, a bag of lard in Delia's private opinion, quivered and shook. His wife, the stromni, was made of sterner stuff. Her fears were for her family. These, Delia excused from caring for the sick on the understanding they would roll bandages. The town was dying. Someone had to care for the sick.

If that person happened to be the empress—well, and wasn't that one reason she was empress at all?

"But, majestrix—your poor hands!"

"Do not worry about my hands, stromni. They are used to hard work."

Stromni Elspa shook her head and her soft brown Vallian hair slipped a little from the retaining pins. She could not understand the majesty and might of an empress in these conditions. By Opaz! If she, Stromni Elspa nal Mellin, was empress, she'd get the servants to handle the mess and take herself off into the country very smartly. If her husband had a little more moral fibre, they could have galloped through the infected streets and been clear away by now. They would not have been caught by this domineering woman and forced to act like common servants. The only reason Stromni Elspa tolerated the disgrace lay in the half-comforting thought that she must be storing up favors for herself with the empress.

Cartloads of little blue flowers were brought in. They trundled in through the open gates. The flowers had been culled from where they grew in weed-like profusion among the cultivations. Dalki rode out with the carts and rode back with them. No one ran away.

There were two sorts of little blue flowers. One sort possessed a tiny silver heart on each petal. These were vilmy flowers. The others were fallimy flowers.

From the vilmy flowers was made up a paste that soothed the sores and eased the pains of the sufferers.

From the fallimy flowers was made up a paste used in the normal way to scour cisterns. Now it scoured and cleansed everything that came into contact with the sickness.

Delia did not personally inspect every flower petal to make sure. If some soothing ointment paste went onto the floor, not too much harm would be done. If scouring paste was rubbed into a sore—no, that would not do. Delia gave strict—very strict—orders about that.

Stromni Elspa looked puzzled.

"But, majestrix! I mean—whoever heard of anyone putting fallimy paste on their body? It would—it would—"

"It would scour their chest most thoroughly."

"Majestrix?"

"You'd be surprised. And I laughed."

At Elspa's bewildered expression Delia bustled into caring for the next row of patients. If the sores could be kept clean, if the patient could be kept cool, there was a chance of recovery. Much of the sherbert drink, parclear, was consumed. Three days of terrible suffering, with suppurating sores breaking out all over the body, and three days of fighting to contain them and keep the patient cool, and then, if the gods smiled, the worst was over, the crisis past.

And, anyway, Delia couldn't explain about the little silver heart on the little blue flower petals. Poor Thelda! She always meant well . . .

To think about the past was as fruitless now as to think about the future. All she could do was work and work and go on working. She took this dreadful attack of pestilence in the town as a personal affront. Detesting every moment of it, fighting nausea, biting down on vomit, she forced herself to care for the sick.

Tandu made her rest. He did this with such auspicious tact and understanding for a Dwadjang as melted Delia's heart. It was clear, if she did not let herself rest and sink her abused body down into sleep, then Tandu would feel personally responsible for the consequences. Knowing her Djangs, she was aware that it was not beyond the bounds of probability that, in order to save his Queen of Djanduin, he would personally slay every last sufferer. Then, the queen could rest.

For some folk, and for Djangs, that was a normal way of thought.

The dead were burned.

Covered of faces, with gloved hands, the people dragged out the corpses and piled them up. The smell was not really tolerable; but with Delia, Empress of Vallia, standing so tall and firm, grasping a ghastly limb to help haul, gently pushing a twisted body up onto the pyre, no one could hang back. The strom and stromni, gagging, took their part. The bodies flopped, some already swollen, some with tongues jutting, some just indescribable lumps of offal.

The flames licked all clean.

The bodies melted and ran, sloughing away. Hair frizzled. The corpses crisped.

When the last were burned, there were more. In the town of Mellinsmot the doctors had been the first to die. Only one needleman remained, and he looked shriveled at the enormity of the catastrophe. As one batch of dead was burned, so another was dragged out. The process deadened the mind and calloused the spirit.

But the avenging spirits of whatever gods or demons had sent this torment upon the people would not be appeased. Townsfolk huddled in the churches and the temple, and there the Affliction of the Sores of Combabbry sought them out, and consumed them.

The needleman shook his head helplessly. His face looked like a chunk of indigestible meat after a dog had chewed and rejected it. His eyes lurked in shadowed pits beneath his eyebrows.

"We can do nothing, majestrix, nothing."

"You can, Agron the Needle! You can alleviate their pain."

Agron's leather wallet shook as he reached in to fetch out fresh acupuncture needles. In the cunning Kregen way he could insert a needle and twirl it and banish pain. He could not halt the onset or the course of the disease.

One of the churches, the structure of crumbly brick dedicated to Flamdelka the Gatherer, commandeered as an emergency hospital, was crammed with sufferers. Flamdelka the Gatherer was one of the older spirits of this part of Vallia, only half-believed in by most folk, still worshipped by many whose business took them across the Ochre Limits.

Dalki walked his totrix up slowly and dismounted. He, like everyone else, looked exhausted.

"My lady. My father bids me to remind you that you promised to rest now—"

"Yes, Dalki. Later." Delia pointed up. "Look, Dalki. A warvol flying over, looking for food."

The black wings spiraled over the church of Flamdelka. Dead bodies were being carried out and placed in carts. The smell did not offend the warvol. He was a kind of vulture, not nicknamed Rippasch, and he was hungry.

"Very good, my lady," said Dalki, and lifted his bow.

Agron the Needle nodded. He did not know how the disease was communicated. But if the warvol fed on a dead person and flew away—who knew where he might go and who knew where he might carry the disease? If he did at all.

Dalki loosed. The shaft pierced the shining black feathers. Without a cry, the warvol pitched onto the roof of Mother Hansi's Banje Store, and fell plump into the street. The corpse would be thrown onto the pyres along with the other corpses.

If she was honest with herself, Delia felt she ought to admit that some venom for Rippasch impelled her in that deed. The warvol, like Rippasch, cleaned up dead bodies, prevented the kind of disease under which they now suffered. But, in stripping an already diseased corpse, the bird might spread the contagion. Of course, it could be spread on the air, by the skin, through tears. . . . No one knew.

She was persuaded to rest only by the consideration that if she collapsed then she would only be hindering the efforts of the others. Out of pride could come blind selfishness.

"My lady?"

"Yes, Dalki. I will rest."

Walking slowly back along Fruiterer's Street and so across the dusty square of Palm Kyro, she could feel the way her legs ached. Her back ached, too; but in a different way.

Dalki, tight-lipped that the queen had chosen to walk back to the strom's grand villa instead of riding, walked a few paces in rear, leading his animal. His father had no need of dinning into his ears every few hours the sobering thought of how lucky they both were in being able to attend on the queen. As a Djang and a Vallian, Dalki needed his queen and his empress, and he was perfectly well aware of his good fortune.

There were no airboats in Mellinsmot. Most of those in private hands had been used by their owners to fly away to safety. There were very few of those. The strom's two fliers, of which he had been inordinately proud, had been commandeered by the soldiers and the mercenaries had robbed him, taken off in his airboats, and not even wished him a remberee. The black fliers used by a local Company of Friends to ship in ice had likewise all been seized. Delia was informed that in four days' time a flier might be expected bringing ice. In that time those sufferers whose temperatures rose too high would die.

Stromni Elspa wanted to fuss. Delia was brisk with the woman; not unkind. At last she could stretch out in the bed in the room they had placed at her disposal. Either Tandu or Dalki, or both, would remain just outside the door and not even an earthquake would shift them.

She thought of the poor people of Mellinsmot, of Opaz, of her friends, of her children and of her husband. Then she went to sleep. She awoke early, washed and dressed, ate a huge breakfast, and stuck straight into tending for the sick, of caring and cleaning, of soothing and swabbing. The routine established itself. Until fresh cases ceased, the routine would continue.

As for herself, she had no fears. She was concerned for her two Djangs, and kept them away from any too close contacts with diseased victims. If the damage was not already done, they might escape. Not everyone caught the Affliction of the Sores of Combabbry. The stench hung over the town. She had bathed in the Sacred Pool in far Aphrasöe. That had conferred upon her a miraculous ability to recover rapidly from wounds and to resist infections. No, she had no fears for herself, and in this knew she cheated. Naturally, this made her take on greater burdens, exposing herself recklessly. In turn, this distressed her friends. It was all a mix and extraordinarily difficult to find the correct path of conduct.

On the day when the airboat bringing the ice arrived only

ten people were so close to dying that the ice would make no difference. The three days of sores and the three days of temperature rise followed by a decline to death had already spelled destruction for too many souls. Now, the ice would make all the difference.

Even then, Tandu and Dalki with a couple of the strom's retainers only just managed to hold onto the airboat and persuade the crew to land. The smell warned them. Dalki, in particular, was most fierce.

He waved his sword under the nose of the skipper of the airboat.

"Put this voller back down, dom! Or you'll grin from a mouth under your chin!"

"It is death—" The skipper, a fat and jowly man, quivered and sweated.

"For you—yes! Down!"

The voller landed and at once the ice was unloaded.

Delia said to Tandu: "Your son cuts a fine figure, Tandu. When all this is settled, what will you two do?"

"Why, my lady, go back to guard duty, I suppose."

"We shall see. The emperor has need of good friends. I think a place will be found for you—if you so choose."

"I would choose so, my lady."

"Good. And Dalki shall be a Deldar at once."

Tandu beamed. The ice smoked as it was hurried away covered in sacking. "That pleases me, my lady. I give you thanks—"

"Of course, one cannot really have a son outranking his father. It is known. But, in this, I think you will have to be a Hikdar. I can see no other course."

"My lady!"

Delia turned away abruptly. Often and often she had discussed this thorny problem with her husband. How easy to dish out ranks and titles! How much pleasure it gave to reward good friends! And how selfish it was, giving of honor and seeing how easy it was, and taking the pleasure. Tandu was pleased and Dalki would be pleased and she was pleased so where was the error? Yet she worried over this as she knew her husband worried, also.

With the coming of the ice a crisis point was passed. From that moment no more people who could be saved died. And, significantly, there were no more outbreaks. Those men and women who had remained to fight the disease and care for the sick ceased to be stricken in their turn.

That evening by the light of a samphron oil lamp, Delia composed the necessary letter.

It was brief, said all that was appropriate, expressed regrets that she had unavoidably missed the wedding of her half-brother Vomanus. Early next morning she sent off the ice flier with the letter, charged strictly to fly at once to Delka Ob and seek audience of the kov. Her seal, stamped across the ribbons fastening the letter, would be proof enough of the importance of the errand of uncouth icemen.

She could not leave yet. There were still sufferers to be tended. Two days later a voller flew in. A girl dressed in leathers stepped down, the rapier swinging at her side, her face bright and eager, her color up, her head high.

"Majestrix!" she said, advancing with her lithe step. Then, in a softer tone, she said, "May Dee-Sheon have you in her keeping."

"Yzobel!" said Delia.

"This is a dreadful place. You are safe?"

"Perfectly. And happy to see you."

Yzobel wore white leathers. Her body complemented the beauty of her face. Yet her rapier and main gauche that hung from silver lockets were practical, hard weapons. This was a girl who could turn her hand to fighting as well as nursing. In that, she mirrored others like her.

Walking with Yzobel into the shade and already looking forward to a glass of parclear, a plate of miscils and palines, and a good chat, Delia was not surprised that Yzobel had arrived. Once the ice-flier had reached Delka Ob, the disappearance of the empress would be explained. One of the sisters, at least, would be immediately sent.

"I came on ahead," said Yzobel. "The others will be here very soon. They were gathering medicaments. But I have a message, majestrix."

"Oh?"

"The mistress wishes to see you. You are summoned to Lancival. We should leave at once."

"Of course," said Delia, Empress of Vallia, Sister of the Rose. "I am ready. Let us go now."

CHAPTER FIVE

Lancival

"Returning to Lancival is like feeling your mother's arms enfolding you." So had said a long-dead sister, and despite the sentimentality of that, Delia admitted its truth. Other sisters had said similar sentiments. One likened the feeling of going back to Lancival to resting her head on her mother's breast. This Delia regarded as sickly sentimentality—and, also, admitted of its truth. Her own mother had died when she was young, a tragedy she believed she had surmounted.

Lancival. Lancival of the red roofs and the ivy-clad walls. Lancival of the calmness and the peace, the singing and the quietness and the harsh banging of steel on steel and the panting exertions of girls in combat. Lancival of the Disciplines known only to women. Lancival of the Whip. Lancival of the Claw.

Not because she was the Empress of Vallia but because she was an initiate of the SOR of a certain exaltedness Delia possessed her own room in one of the collegiate buildings. A mere cubbyhole, it contained a narrow bed, a set of bookshelves, a dressing table with brushes and combs of plain wood and bristle unadorned and decorated with not a single stroke from a paintbrush, a single design from a chisel. A wardrobe held various robes required by the Order, a selection of undergarments of the most Spartan kind, sandals and fighting boots, a cloak and an enveloping black leather hat with a black band. The sheets were plain yellow, the pillowslip plain yellow, the towels draped over the washbasin plain yellow. The mirror set above the dressing table was not quite large enough to reflect all of her face at the same time. She was adept at tilting her proud and imperious head about, like a gawky girl, to see what was necessary to see.

This room was one of a double row along a third-story corridor, each cubbyhole like its neighbor as a pea in a pod. This particular room had once been occupied by a sister of the SOR, now long dead, renowned in the sorority's annals as Velda the Tempestuous.

The stories clustered about Velda emphasized the usual normality of her character, even her sweetness of personality. The stories told those who listened that when Velda met injustice she could not control her temper. Her temper was fierce, vicious, intemperate. A mistress of the Claw and Whip, no accurate tally had been kept of the unseemly wights she had dispatched to the Ice Floes of Sicce, she clawed and slashed them all indifferently if they offended her keen sense of justice.

This room was, therefore, always known as Velda's Room.

Just why the mistress had seen fit to assign Velda's Room to Delia of Delphond puzzled Delia. Now, she no longer concerned herself over that order of puzzlement. The room represented a haven at certain times, a sense of penitence, a place where she might strip away everything that was not Delia.

She was always glad and relieved to sink down on the narrow bed in her room at Lancival, and always ready and relieved to close the door upon that room and leave to go about her business in the wider world.

High on one wall hung a portrait of Velda the Tempestuous. It showed her in the full regalia of white leathers, long-legged, scowling of face, the Whip coiled along her arm, the Claw extended menacingly. Her rapier and left-hand dagger snugged about a narrow waist. Her hips flared in her arrogant, menacing pose. Her long white leather boots were mud-splashed. This small touch had always to Delia brought the image of Velda alive, as though the sister could not be dead but ready to answer the summons to prayer, to be met in the refectory, to be engaged in discussion at any of the formal functions of the SOR.

The Sisters of the Rose were mindful of tradition, and looked to the future, and kept themselves secret in the world in which they labored.

Beside the head of the bed stood a heavy wooden chest on legs which, in that austere room, were incongruously carved into the likenesses of rose trellises. The doors in the front of the chest were locked. The top supported a few essential items of toiletries.

Now Delia took off her raggedy russets and threw them into the wicker basket by the door. Novices would collect the laundry by rota, and wash and repair her clothes. Once, she had labored on those duties here.

She went to the end picture of the row that hung beneath the portrait of Velda. Before she opened the picture on its hinge away from the wall, she stood, brooding on the line of portraits. Each was mounted in a narrow plain frame of varnished wood. There were fifteen. As always, she gazed at the face tenth along. That frame, like the first six, was surmounted by a small nosegay, a posy, of roses carved and painted. The face looked back with its brown Vallian eyes, gentle, sweet, stunningly beautiful. Delia sighed.

Life was brutal.

You tried. You attempted to make what you could of this puzzle Opaz had given you. Yes, her grandparents, represented in the first four portraits, were dead, and it was seemly that after full lives of better than two hundred years, they should be gathered into the Benediction of Opaz the Everlasting. And her father and mother; death had claimed them. As for the seventh portrait—a little frown dented Delia's forehead. She'd left him after the Battle of the Incendiary Vosks in Hamal, unwillingly, but committed. No doubt he was off swinging his damned great Krozair longsword and adventuring in places she would rather not hear about until afterward.

As for her son Drak, in the next picture, he was being groomed to become the Emperor of Vallia and take over from his father. When he did so, Delia fully intended to speak rather intemperately to the mistress, and demand that she be allowed to join her husband in whatever nefarious goings on he was up to. They owed her that much, the SOR, surely?

She held the first picture open, still pondering.

The picture after Drak's showed Lela who was known as Jaezila. Soon there would have to be a further portrait placed below that, a picture of Prince Tyfar of Hamal. And the quicker those two decided to marry the better and so put every one of their friends out of their tantalizing frustrations at the idiocy of two young lovers.

And so to the tenth portrait.

Below it, almost a part of it, had been fixed a much smaller portrait, practically a miniature. This showed a man with black curly hair bunched on his head, with a hawklike face, bold and arrogant, with two blue bolts for eyes. His chin was like the ram of a swifter. Delia had never met this man, this

Gafard, Rog of Guamelga, the King's Striker, Prince of the Central Sea, the Reducer of Zair, Sea-Zhantil, Ghittawrer of Genod. He had married her daughter Velia and their daughter's portrait was affixed as the last in the row. This showed a babyish face, and Delia resigned herself to having a fresh portrait commissioned, for little Didi was growing up.

The small posy of red roses was echoed by a single rose fixed above the portrait of Gafard, the King's Striker, Sea-Zhantil.

Delia swung the door that was the first picture back and forth. Still looking at the face of Velia, she reached into the space beyond the picture and took out a bronze key. The handle was cast into the form of a stemmed rose.

Next to Velia her twin brother's face stared in powerful authority from the painted panel. This was Zeg, who had been called Seg in honor of Seg Segutorio. Now Zeg was King of Zandikar, and the face of his wife, Queen Miam, smiled from her own portrait. One day she and Zeg would have to visit Vallia, or Delia and her husband would have to make the long journey to the inner sea of Kregen, the Eye of the World.

As for the next portrait—and here Delia sighed in a way far removed from her patient long-suffering anguish over Velia—this was her daughter Dayra, ferocious, mischievous, led into evil ways. This was Dayra, known as Ros the Claw. She it was, surmised Delia, who was the cause of this summons to Lancival.

Dayra's twin, Jaidur, known as Vax Neemusbane, looked out from the next picture, and with him his wife, Lildra. They were now King and Queen of Hyrklana. Jaidur had served the SOR very well on secret errands, many of them not even known to his mother. Now he was settling down nicely with Lildra in the island kingdom of Hyrklana. A touch of real responsibility had worked wonders for his wildness, a wild streak he shared with his twin sister, and which she showed no signs of outgrowing.

The penultimate portrait, of Velia, a daughter born later, loved and named for the older Velia, again would soon require replacement, for Velia was growing up. Delia hoped the mistress would allow a visit with Velia here in Lancival, for Velia was being educated and trained by the SOR. It might not be possible. Discipline sometimes imposed a harshness well-nigh insupportable to a mother.

She held the bronze rose-key in her hand.

She knew—she had been told—that her dip in the Sacred Pool of Baptism in far Aphrasöe had conferred upon her a thousand years of life. She did not age. She had seen to it that her children and her friends and loved ones had also bathed. Like her husband, she had for the moment pushed aside the unanswerable questions this longevity aroused. If the time ever came for drastic measures, she, at least, would be ready.

Crossing to the chest with the rose-arbor legs, she opened the front doors.

She took out a silver-mounted balass wood box, the wood hard and black and shining. She opened the box. From it she took a thick, black, snakelike whip. This she put on the bed, quickly.

From its velvet bed she lifted her Claw.

Shining, razor-sharp steel, clawed with talons, the thing fitted up her left arm with steel splines. She turned it over. It shone with oil. With it she had been trained to rip a person's face off.

She put it back, quickly, replaced the whip, shut the lid, and pushed the box back into the chest.

Despite what the mistress might say, Delia did not intend—just yet and so soon—to wear the Claw and carry the Whip.

"Not," she said, half to herself, "not yet, by Vox!"

She shook her brown hair free about her naked shoulders. Then she picked up two fluffy yellow towels and walked along the corridor to the bathrooms. She left the door of Velda's room open.

Steam engulfed her in the suite of bath rooms. Naked women walked about, took the steam, talked, swam in the pool. Delia was quick. At this time she wished merely to wash off everything she could of her stay in Mellinsmot.

She was not sure; but it seemed more than likely, that Tandu had also written a note, sent by the icemen. He had expressed no surprise at her sudden determination on departure.

"Yes, my lady. We can do all that is necessary here until the sisters arrive."

"May Djan go with you, my lady," Dalki had said, looking up as the flier lifted.

They had called the remberees, cheerfully. Yes, Delia reflected, toweling herself briskly and bringing up the circulation, yes, it was almost certain. Her two Djangs must have said that the empress needed to be hoicked out of the plague spot at once. This was the only way she could be commanded to leave Mellinsmot.

But, all the same, she still would bet that Dayra was the cause . . .

Many of the women splashing about and gossiping and taking the steam were known to her. Many more were not. You could not expect to know every single girl personally who went through Lancival. And, of course, a goodly number of highly respected sisters of the SOR never went through Lancival at all.

She exchanged a few words with women if they talked first, giving not the Lahal form of greeting of the outside world, but the SheonFaril—the Sheonli in its usual abbreviated form. Two women near her under the hot air funnels which teased the hair into a glowing sweetness were wrapped up in each other's news.

"Taken her off, my dear, without consent."

"Did you have to castrate him?"

"No. I'd have liked to, but it was thought not necessary. The poor girl—well, she was only a Sister of Samphron, but they're not too bad."

"And her parents?"

"Everyone suffers after the Time of Troubles, although the new emperor has worked wonders. Oh, yes, they were only too happy to make a gift to the SOR. I think the mistress has dedicated that sum to some new curtains for the refectory."

"We need some of the targets to be restuffed. The girls seem to knock them to pieces wonderfully quickly these days."

"I know! It is these new bows. They are so much more powerful and accurate than our old ones."

Delia smiled and let the warm air flow over her head, turning her shoulders to feel the grateful heat spreading down. Soon she was dry and her hair, carefully prepared by one of the superior novices, gleamed with its auburn tints through the Vallian brown. Naturally, she wore no jewels.

Walking back to Velda's room she saw Yzobel waiting inside. Yzobel wore a rose-colored gown with a silver belt and dagger. She looked splendid.

"The mistress is waiting?"

"Yes, Delia. She says that she thinks you have had enough time to cleanse a regiment of Jikai Vuvushis."

"If ever you become the mistress, Yzobel—and you might, you might—I trust you will be as intolerant. It tones up the muscles."

Yzobel laughed.

Delia put on her underthings which were not of sensil, not even of silk, but of a plain smooth cotton. They happened to be scarlet. Had she been intending to wear her pale lemon-colored dress—in the color called laypom of which she was fond—she would have worn appropriately colored undergarments. As it was, when she put on the rose-colored gown, fastening it with bone buttons, what she was wearing underneath would remain a mystery.

Her sandals were flat of sole and heel, fastened by a mere three latchings of simple leather. Her belt, like Yzobel's, was fashioned from silver links. Her dagger was the long thin dagger of Vallia. She took no other weapons of steel.

From a drawer in the chest she took out her two brooches.

One was the regular circlet of roses of the SOR.

The other was small and neat, a jeweled representation of a hubless nine-spoked wheel. Delia owned more than one of these brooches. She pinned it to the rose dress firmly.

She saw Yzobel's little frown, a dint of her lip as her teeth caught.

"I know, Yzobel. But the mistress cannot deny my womanhood."

"She would be the last to do that!"

Delia nodded her head, agreeing. "Do you really need new curtains in the refectory? I heard Keshni and Lovosa talking."

"So you heard of Lovosa's latest? She was most wroth they did not let her unman him. He deserved it."

"Probably. I was not there."

Again Yzobel's lip dented under her teeth. "Yes, and we do need new curtains. A thousand orphans were discovered wandering in the Lower Mai Hills—"

"Wandering?"

"Yes. They fondly imagined they were a warband ready to fight the invaders. Some of them were barely seven years old."

"So they proved expensive."

"That is one reason we are here. As for the curtains, we do need them. I, for one, do not care if the old ones fall to pieces."

"Nor I."

Going along the corridors and down the stairs, Delia was well aware that by saying that was one reason they were here, Yzobel did not mean that Delia had been summoned here by the mistress to contribute gold. Yzobel meant that succoring orphans was one part of the reason for the existence of the SOR.

One part, an old and original, of a surety, but in these days a part that had to share resources.

She was the empress. Well, for what that was worth when set beside the work these women did to the glory of Opaz and Vallia, she had already dedicated that part of her life. The mistress would be the first to explain that a sorority that did not exert every sinew to gather in revenue from everyone, high and low, rich and poor alike, would wither. The Empress of Vallia, in great fashion, could bestow a chest of gold. Had done so. But if every sister did not make her contribution, then the feeling of responsibility died. Unpalatable facts to some, these were, and Delia knew that. As for her own financial affairs, she had never considered herself to be a rich woman. Training with the SOR had engendered in her an understanding of the satisfactions of simplicity. That was just as well, considering the troubled times through which the country had gone and was still, by Vox, going through right now. Every copper ob they could scrape up had to go to the Treasury to pay for the upkeep of the country, pay the army, buy saddle animals, both of the ground and the air, pay for education, pay for a thousand clamorous demands of empire.

She put a hand to the plain white leather pouch on the silver belt. Among the items there—a comb, a kerchief, a few pins, odds and ends—could be found not a single bottle of scent.

Scent cost money. Perfume cost more. The SOR relied on gifts together with some income from their holdings in Companies of Friends to keep them going. The lands around Lancival within its mellow valley supported them in the way of most of the food they required. They did not squander their money on resources.

All the same, perfume was a vital part of a woman's style; the SOR were not foolish enough to prohibit its use.

Natilma na Stafoing passed Delia in the shining hall leading to the lavender court. Natilma smiled. A remarkable woman, robust and yet elegant, with long hair done into coils, she wore hunting leathers and there was blood on her gloves.

"Sheonli, Delia! How nice!"

Delia smiled and spoke for a few moments. Natilma was one of the more senior sisters, and was well spoken of in the line of accession to the mistress. As they talked with the radiance of Zim and Genodras, all a lake of rubies and emeralds, flooding about them, Yzobel fidgeted. Natilma observed, and smiled again, and went on talking.

Lansi ti High Ochrun came by, and stopped to talk. She, too, with her copper hair and heavy mouth, was high in the councils of the SOR, another prospective mistress.

Yzobel shuffled her sandaled feet.

Taking pity, Delia laughed, and said: "I must really go. The mistress is waiting."

So, lightly, Delia walked out into the lavender courtyard into the radiance of the suns.

"If I were mistress," said Yzobel ominously, "I wonder what I would do about those two."

"Well, you are too young. And when you reach your hundred, they will probably not be here."

Then Delia checked herself. It was extraordinarily difficult to reconcile herself to this unexpected longevity. She was not at all sure that she wanted it. When Yzobel reached her hundred she would enter the ranks of those sisters who might look, one day, to become mistress. She would look very little different from the way she looked now. Only by the tiniest marks could one Kregan judge the age of another.

And Delia would look the young girl she truly was until she was a thousand. Was that nice? Well, time would tell.

At least four of the women who happened to be passing and stopped for a moment to chat as Delia made her way to the mistress's tower did not, she judged, happen to be passing by chance.

Yzobel clicked her dagger.

"Brazen," she said, and her nostrils pinched in.

Yzobel could get away with outrageous behavior, and Delia knew it. In the normal way of the Discipline, no sister could speak thus of another without reprimand. But, there was something planned in the way the ranking sisters just happened to be walking meekly along as Delia went toward the mistress.

Nothing overt was said. Just making their marks, as it

were. Delia fancied there would be more making of marks yet, before they ranked their Deldars and got down to the politics of the affair.

The mistress of the Sisters of the Rose could have her apartments in no other tower than the Tower of the Rose.

Thither Delia went.

The grey stone walls, ivy clad, appeared to her to shed a cooling benediction from the heat of the suns. The archway closed above her head. The rugs upon the floor were not all of Walfarg weave; there were many lesser carpets to cushion the feet. Up the blackwood stairs, a single sharp ring upon the bell, and the door opening and old Rosala smiling and beaming and stepping back to usher in the sister come to see the mistress.

"You are well, Rosala?"

"A touch of gyp in my left elbow, my dear. But I'm as chirpy as a cricket and shall be two hundred and ten next birthday."

They went along the carpeted corridor whose walls were adorned with the trophies of various past deeds. The mistress's room at the end looked just the same to Delia. Then she frowned. In one corner a curtain was half-drawn across a bed. It was a proper bed, as anyone could see with half an eye, not a day-lounger.

That bed was a new touch, an addition to the usual.

That did not, of course, mean it was abnormal.

Most of the drapes were of that pale sheer rose color that verged on the opalescence of a Zimful sky at evening, when Genodras had sunk below the horizon. When Zim sank first in the long cycles of alternations, then the evening sky held overtones of quite different natures. Against the walls and drapes the furniture stood as ever, the familiar pieces, polished, cared for, each one in its place and each one fulfilling its own duty. The desk, of balass wood, still angled across the curve of the southwestern tower window.

The mistress did not rise to greet Sister Delia.

She used one pale hand to gesture to the seat set four square before the desk. Delia sat.

Winsome to suggest this brought back vivid memories of herself as a young girl. Trite to suggest that, and trite to ignore the feeling.

The scent of flowers banked in their troughs along the wall brought back the memories! The flick-flick plant on a windowsill, set there to catch flies, would as ever have to be hand fed. A new tang hung in the air. Delia, gently, tested its meaning. Medicaments. Well, then, and perhaps now she understood a little more of the chance meetings and the markings of marks that were no chance.

"Faril Sheon, Delia," said the mistress in all formality. Her voice breathed more memories; but the tone was weaker, the full bell-note fallen away. Delia sat straight, heels together, hands in her lap, head up. She looked at the mistress.

Here in the heart of the heart of the Sisters of the Rose there was no need for the small secret sign.

"SheonFaril, mistress," said Delia.

"I am more than glad to see you. You have worried me."

The mistress had once been able to lift a full-bodied man above her head and throw him up a flight of stairs. Now she could do that, perhaps, to a fair-sized dog. Her face, unlined, bore only the marks of wisdom and experience and pain engraved upon it in the planes and the shadows. Her eyes were as bright and brown as cob nuts as ever they had been.

Like Delia, she wore the rose-colored gown. Her belt from which swung the long Vallian dagger was of plain rope, untwisted, raw. Her hair, brown as a thrush's wing, held her face in a composition at once peaceful, dominating, gentle and harsh, all in that puzzle of vaol-paol, that is a woman's face. In that eternal vaol-paol, the Great Circle of Universal Existence, was to be found more than mere philosophy.

"I grieve to have caused you concern." Delia's gaze lingered on the half-curtained bed in its alcove corner. "I apologize for my daughter Dayra. I assume that is why I am here."

At the mistress's expression, Delia added, annoyed at the tinge of alarm in her voice: "It is not little Velia?"

"No. Velia is a rose beyond price. Nor—this time—is it your Princess Dayra, who calls herself Ros the Claw."

Delia felt the breath in her. If this was bad news, she must find the strength to bear it. She said nothing. She waited as the Disciplines taught.

"You have seen my bed. I use it, in here, rather than waste my meager strength retiring to my chamber in the evening and dragging myself here in the morning."

"Mistress—"

"Wait, my daughter, wait. Once I was as you now are. But

that was long ago. It is time I sought peace with Opaz. Time I handed over to stronger—"

"Mistress!"

"Do not grieve, Delia, who was Delia Valhan, and is now Delia Prescot, Empress of Vallia."

"You know that means—"

"It means a very great deal. But I am going, no one and nothing can halt me, and you, Delia, are my chosen successor. You are to be the mistress of the Sisters of the Rose."

CHAPTER SIX

"Take this gift away from me."

"No."

"You have been selected by me, Delia, to be the mistress. Your election will follow."

"No." There was no hesitation, no doubt, in her. This was not for her. "No, mistress. I am aware of what this means. You know I am aware. But I cannot."

The mistress placed a plain square of yellow linen to her mouth. Her coughs were tiny scrabblings, as of nestlings.

"How can you refuse?"

"I do not know how. I know only that I must."

One narrow hand, doubled over, ridged and veined blue, crept onto the desk top. That hand trembled.

"Delia—"

"I cannot—I feel pain, and shame, and dishonor—all foolish feelings, I know. But take this gift away from me."

The mistress said: "Once I had a husband. He was all the world to me. But he died. Once I had children. One is still alive—somewhere. All you will need of husband and children you will find here, in Lancival."

"That I can believe, yet cannot—"

"Once I was called Elomi the Shining. I was born in Valka. Did you know that?"

"I knew."

"Valka is so beautiful it can break the heart. Yet Lancival is—"

"I cannot be the mistress, mistress. Do not ask it of me."

"And if I—?"

"You would not command. It is not in—"

"But if I did?"

"You will not."

The mistress sat back in the wide-armed overstuffed chair.

She appeared to shrink. "No," she said in that forlorn whisper. "No. I would not."

For a moment silence enfolded the two. The mistress looked across at a side table where stood a crystal parclear set, the glasses sparkling. Instantly, Delia rose, crossed to the table and poured a glass of parclear, the sherbet drink fizzing in crystal abandon. The mistress sipped, and then drank. Her neck looked fragile as she swallowed.

Delia made no move to pour parclear for herself until the mistress nodded.

A moment later, the fizz stinging her mouth, Delia was ready to battle on against an unwanted fate.

Like any general swinging his troops across a battle field to search out a fresh opening for an advance, the mistress took up a fresh subject.

"Your husband is well?"

"When I last saw him. We had just won a great battle—"

"A disgusting business of Incendiary Vosks. We heard. The SOR must do all we can against these Shanks that raid us and seek to enslave us."

"That is one of the great aims in our lives that prevents me from accepting."

"Are there not secret societies of men? They may not lay claim to our prestige. But they exist."

"That is true. My husband has never belonged to any of them in Vallia—"

"I hear differently, Delia!"

Delia smiled. This tack would not take the mistress far along the road to converting her.

"You mean the Kroveres of Iztar? Men said, when the KRVI was formed, that my husband was too proud to join one of their already existing secret orders, but must create his own. That, I need hardly say, was not true."

"No. I imagine not. And Zena Iztar would not be fooled by mere men."

"Assuredly not!"

"I have grave news concerning new Orders. There is a new Order that troubles me."

"I would have thought we women had enough already."

"In view of the new one, I agree. In some of the continents of Kregen women are not regarded in the same way they are regarded here in Vallia. In some places women have to find themselves, understand their rightful place, think of themselves as people, grow in understanding. In some places they are not treated as equals."

"Yes."

"You chose to take your husband's name when you married. You need not have done."

"I wished it. My husband is as much a Valhan as am I."

"That is true. In some places women have only a given name until they marry. They are locked into a way of thinking about themselves that—in our eyes—demeans them, and yet which they, themselves, fail to grasp. When women in those places revolt, the consequences can be ugly. Of course, in the end, it will come all right. But the learning process is painful."

Delia knew the mistress was saying this as a part of her tactical advance. She listened dutifully.

"They overreact, hate everything that is male, and carry on in ways that, while ugly, are perfectly understandable. That is the nature of revolution."

Delia found herself saying, "We have had experiences of revolutions."

"Two, at least, involved women. There was Queen Fahia of Hyrklana. And the Empress Thyllis of Hamal. The SOR played some part there."

"I know and joy in it."

"I wish first to speak to you of your friend, Jilian Sweet-Tooth."

Delia waited.

"She is a sister. She is a consummate artist with the Whip and the Claw. She is a good friend to you and your husband and those of your children she has met. Yet she sorely worries me."

"Tell me, mistress."

"I will! Do not deceive yourself on that! This new order of which I spoke. Jilian is being drawn to it. Most of the sisters composing this Order come from the SOR. There are a few from the Sisters of Samphron, the Sisters of the Sword, one or two others. Even the Little Sisters of Opaz have been sucked in. This could prove a most grave crisis."

"If they adhere to our principles—"

"That is a matter of conjecture. They are taking a new and hard line. They call themselves the Sisters of the Whip. They place the symbol of the Whip above all others."

Thinking of that thick black lash of vileness safely locked in its box, Delia felt the ominous forebodings.

"You know, mistress, I prefer the rapier and main gauche, the bow, the terchick—and this new sword my husband and his armorers have developed, the drexer."

"Yet your friend Jilian is very apt with the Whip."

"Very—apt."

"We shall not cease from teaching the disciplines of the Claw and the Whip here at Lancival. But the Sisters of the Whip. . . ." The mistress stopped speaking and put her narrow doubled-up hand to her side. Her face remained unmoved. Delia stood up at once. She could see the mistress was in great pain. Without hesitating, Delia crossed to the desk and rang the silver bell.

Rosala hurried in, cackling and clucking.

Delia called as she might call an order to her soldiers in a bloody affray.

"Yzobel!"

When Yzobel ran in, between them they carried the mistress to the bed and made her comfortable.

"Send for all the needlewomen!"

"Yes, majestrix."

From her tone of voice, Delia might have expected the swod's cracked-out answer of: "Quidang!"

After that it was a matter of arranging affairs, of seeing to protocol, of making sure the mistress was given every attention and left in peace.

She would recover, for her time was not yet. Delia did not believe this was a cunning scheme to attract sympathy and sway her to the mistress's wishes. These women were above petty schemes of that contemptible nature.

Mind you, some of the schemes of the ladies who wished to become mistress would frizzle the hair. Delia firmly intended to have her say in all that. But that time, also, was not yet. There was so much to do in Vallia and in all of Paz that at times she felt as though she was shut up in a box of feathers.

She felt an extra pang of disappointment that she could not see Velia. That sprite was out with her classmates on what was euphemistically called An Educational and Recreational Trip for Young Ladies. The description might fit a startling variety of activities. Velia might be picking wild flowers to press in her album, joying in the wonders of nature; she might be stalking another party of girls and both parties deadly determined to spot and attack the other first; she might be working in some tavern all heightened color and watching hawk-like for the people she had been sent to spy on; she might just be indulging in simple swordmastering, perhaps snapping her Whip at stuffed targets, or slashing with the practice claw at opponents armed with a variety of weapons. Delia had given strict instructions that young Velia should be taught the bow to the highest standards attainable at Lancival. After that, Uncle Seg would put on the final polish that would turn an excellent archer into a superb archer. You could not start too young learning the bow.

Sosie ti Drakanium, who was a captain of messengers, stopped Delia on the long marble sweep of staircase leading up to the Reading Rooms of the Laypom Hall. Sosie, a bright and lively girl with cropped brown hair and those deep brown Vallian eyes, hailed from Delphond.

"Majestrix. Is the mistress—?"

"She is overworked, Sosie, and needs rest. That is all."

"Thanks be to Dee Sheon! I am bid to ask you to see the Lady Almoner as soon as possible. She did not know of this dreadful news, of course, but—"

"She will certainly have more important things to do now than worry over me, I know." Delia let a small smile curve her lips, a small smile only and enough to respect the proprieties.

"As the Lady Almoner, Wilma Llandrin will be particularly busy trying to fill the shoes of the mistress until she is well again."

Sosie's bright face remained serious.

"Or until we must choose a new mistress."

"Oh, I wouldn't worry over that for a long time yet."

"But I do worry. So do others. There are some sisters who are undoubtedly most worthy and yet I would not wish to see them as the mistress. But, there is one sister I, and many others, would so wish."

Delia simply rode this as though flying a saddlebird high above the clouds.

"I am sure every sister has her own particular favorite as candidate, Sosie. You are young yet—of the junior chapel, I know—so at least you do not have the alarming thought that someone might wish to elect you!"

Sosie looked away.

"Quite, majestrix," she said. And said no more.

To rescue Sosie, Delia smiled again and said: "I will go straightaway to see Wilma. You are on your way to your Jikvar class?"

"Yes. I have to work at it. The rapier is more my weapon."

"And mine." They reached the corridor where the tall windows patterned sparkles across the carpets and marble. At the far end triple bronze-bound doors gave access to the working apartments of the sorority—working only in the sense that their work was generally regarded as work, as distinct from things like gardening and sewing and cooking and nursing which were not-work work. The distinctions were kept up, although at times they appeared nonsensical hangovers from another age.

Sosie wore black leathers instead of her usual tan tunic and she pushed the balass box straight under her arm before bidding Delia remberee in the SOR fashion of rememberer, and swinging off with her long stride after the au revoir. Delia looked after her and shook her head. Sosie had an hour or two of strenuous exercise before her. The rules of the sisterhood demanded exact obedience to a rhythm of work, play, instruction and sleep. Periods of service in the outside world came as a culmination of and an enhancement of the training. Many people could not distinguish between the Discipline of such an order and ordinary discipline. That was their misfortune; sometimes it led to petty little squabbles and misunderstandings from women outside the sorority. Despite the claims made, and the undoubted truth of many of them, it was also manifest that all women were not considered equal with men —very far from it in some places and in the eyes of some men.

As a jikmer, a captain of messengers, Sosie had particular functions to perform. Yzobel, also, was a jikmer. Delia was aware that many men believed the women had set up a rank structure of delmer and hikmer and jikmer and chukmer aping the grades within male armed forces. That this was not so did not fail to amuse her.

Yzobel favored white leathers. This was her privilege. Trouble with white leather was that in moments of activity, stretching to days of action on end, it tended to become grubby. Only the very best quality leather and finish could be employed to resist dirtying; all the same, it looked splendid, no doubt of that.

The interview with the Lady Almoner was short. Wilma Llandrin did, indeed, have much to occupy her. Sisters did not go around calling each other sister this and sister that all the time. Delia expected to be called Delia; if girls chose to address her as majestrix, that, again, was their privilege.

"Delia! This is dreadful—before I can get away to see the mistress there are a thousand and one things I must do. Yet—"

Wilma, who called herself simply Llandrin, dropping all her worldly ranks and titles within Lancival, was a small, plump, meticulous woman. She could not be called fussy. Her hair was not pure Vallian brown but contained admixtures of a darker hue. Her face, which in the normal way was a model of understanding and rectitude and calculation, now revealed the turmoil occasioned by the collapse of the mistress.

"If there is anything I can do—?"

"Oh, everything here is under control. But thank you. I wanted to give you more information on what we know of the Sisters of the Whip and of Jilian Sweet-Tooth. But that must wait a moment."

"Of course."

Here in the wide office, with many girls at their desks organizing every detail, Delia was well aware of the arcane expertise employed. Wilma could do sums in her head that lesser mortals could never do, not with all the fingers and toes Opaz gave them, not with a regiment of girls and each one with an abacus. The sisters said that Wilma could look at a set of accounts, scanning each page as fast as her fingers could turn the leaves, and tell you at the end about every misplaced copper ob. That was a gift perplexing in its subtlety and, at least in many girls' eyes, of downright torment.

For Wilma Llandrin herself, the reverse was true.

Looking at this wonderful woman before her, remembering her as little Delia Valhan, she was amazed at what the passage of time could accomplish, although this was a mere part of what the mysticism of the rose taught. Much speculation had followed Delia's accident that left her a cripple, and more when she had returned, strong and fully fit and even more beautiful than before. No—looking at the woman before her, Wilma Llandrin gave thanks to Opaz that she, Wilma, had not been called to become Empress of Vallia.

Details of protocol were easily settled, as the two sisters talked for a moment only. Then Wilma, looking down at a ledger before her, said: "Of course, Delia, the mistress is actively seeking a successor. I must tell you I do not seek that honor."

"Honor? Yes, it is an honor. But, also, it is—"

"Yes!" Wilma picked up a pen. "It can create and it can destroy. We all know that. The choice must fall upon a sister who is not only worthy, but one who can bear the burdens."

Delia started to say something that might open Wilma's confidence to her; then she changed her mind, and said: "I have so much to do, as you can imagine, and much as I love Lancival, I do not wish to remain here longer than I must."

"I am sorry to hear that."

"No more than I am to say it."

There, said Delia to herself, perhaps that will clear the air a trifle.

The pen twirled. Wilma Llandrin was not the Lady Almoner for nothing. She looked up. "You have heard about the new curtains for the refectory?"

"Yes."

"I am not going to ask you for a contribution to pay for them—or the thousand orphans."

Delia held her smile in check, inwardly bubbling with joy at dear Wilma's machinations. This method of exerting power, traditionally belonging to women down through the ages of a male-dominated world, need not be thrown away in a more modern age of equality. Some women conditioned by events and not by reason, saw only cheapness in trying to hang onto women's role as the swayers of men's actions through hidden and persuasive means. Any weapons were good weapons if they fitted the hand. Delia detested the idea of men and women having to deal in terms of weapons to oppose each other. But until all was in all, as the saying went, needs must.

Men and women were just different. That was all. It was nonsensical to claim they were the same. Provided each received fair dues from the other, and, in more enlightened areas, each received as much help and sustenance one to the other, one from the other, then Opaz would shine upon them. Men and women could get on if each had a fair crack of the whip. That reminded Delia.

"I have to attend Aimee's grakvar class in a quarter of a glass." She glanced at the clepsydra; the water was rose-colored. "I then have a jikvar class and then a hikvar—and after that I think I shall expire in the steam of the Baths of the Nine. Unless—?"

"No, no, Delia. You must conform to the rhythm. I shall call a conclave this evening."

"Very well." As Delia turned to go, she looked back. "And, Wilma, don't you overdo it. Lancival cannot spare you. You may not believe it, we all do."

Wilma Llandrin smiled and then took up the first of the incessant stream of requests for orders and instructions. Being the Lady Almoner, she had the last word. She caught Delia just as the empress's fingers trailed from the door handle.

"Oh, Delia. I am not going to ask you for a contribution for the refectory curtains. We are opening a self-denying week for that. Nor for the orphans—that has been covered. I am going to ask you for a contribution for the repairs to the hospital of the Meek Sisters of Mercy. It has been in ruins since its destruction during the Time of Troubles."

"And they cannot finance it themselves?"

"Quite out of the question. The MSM are not a wealthy Order, and we have helped them in the past. They are worthy women."

"Very well. I will see to it, sell some jewelry, something like that. At the moment I do not have any saddle animals to spare. They are still dreadfully short."

"All these wars! I know."

"When my husband returns from these wars I will have him dip into his pocket. There are other projects in mind."

"He is successful, thanks be to Opaz. Surely, Delia, he will return with caravans of loot from our defeated enemies?"

Delia, one hand on the door, shook her head. Her face remained perfectly grave.

"No, Wilma. The emperor is not in the habit of plundering cruelly. And our late enemies in Hyrklana and Hamal are now our allies. As for the Shanks—"

Wilma's face reflected her stated distaste for them . . .

"As for the Shanks, they stink of fish and have little of value that we prize. They may have, in the future."

Proving she was the Lady Almoner, Wilma said with a sniff, "Even if gold stinks of fish, it is still gold."

CHAPTER SEVEN

Unwelcome News of Jilian Sweet-Tooth

Being conscious of her own faults, Delia often became extraordinarily tired of trying to correct them all the time. She'd remained sweet and reasonable in dealing with her two Djangs, Tandu and Dalki, when all around she was almost overwhelmed by sickness and filth. Now, in the muted light of the arms salle where as a small girl she's often thought this was how the world must be below the sea, she went through the regulation exercises with her Whip.

She slashed and bashed and knocked the stuffing out of the dummies. She did not sweat. Some of the girls at practice regarded her askance, and this, too, annoyed her.

She was the empress, true. That had no bearing on the way she ought to be treated here. Here in Lancival they were all sisters.

A robust girl straining her leathers like any heavy male Deldar, flicked her whip, took out a patch of canvas on a dummy's head representing an eye, and then looked over a shoulder at Delia. Delia was about to flick at her own dummy.

"You wanted to ask me something?" Delia let her whip trail across the polished wooden floor.

The girl—Delia didn't know her—flushed up in a bright wash of blood.

"No—no, majestrix—"

"And you may call me Delia like any sister."

"Ah, yes—ah, Delia—"

"Now get on with your practice."

The girl did as she was bid. She did not cry, for that was a practice frowned on except in the most special of circumstances. But her next three blows completely missed the target.

Delia felt mean—and she also felt liberated.

By Vox! She was no angel, no spirit of perfection. Do 'em good to get the rough edge of her tongue now and again.

Anyway, her bad temper was not just because she had to slash her whip about, and then slash her claw about; she was far more worried than she liked over Jilian. Whatever was to be said about that young lady seemed, or what had not been said so far, calculated to distress her friend Delia.

Since the evening she had arrived, there had been all a hustle and a bustle, what with the mistress collapsing and the consequent preoccupation with the consequences. Now, when Delia had finished up with the Whip, the Claw and passed a pleasant period throwing other girls about the mat, really tying each other up in knots, she could go along to the pro-marshal.

Thalmi Crockhaden, the pro-marshal, stood up as Delia entered the small study room. Thalmi's hair, which remained a bright yellow despite all, marked her out as being different from the usual run of Vallians. She was of Vallia, of course; but somewhere back along the line an ancestor had strayed, given the mores in use at the time. She was not overlarge, not over-pronounced, not over anything. It was not just because of her position within the SOR that she reminded Delia of Naghan Vanki the emperor's chief spymaster. To most of the junior sisters, Thalmi spent her time arranging the most awkward timetables for training sessions. And, even then, they'd say, her assistants did all the work.

Precisely. Thalmi spent her time organizing the ramifications of the spy net operating from Lancival and elsewhere.

"You are well, Delia?"

"More or less. And you?"

"Too busy, as usual. The mistress—pray Opaz she quickly recovers—has told you, I'm sure, why you're here. It's this friend of yours, Jilian Sweet-Tooth—a remarkable product of the SOR and now about to desert us."

There seemed to be no accusations in Thalmi's straight stare, as she felt for the armrest of her chair and sat, nodding for Delia to sit. But Delia decided to get the undercurrents out of the way first.

"Before we talk of Jilian—have you any news of Dayra?"

"None. The princess has not been brought to my attention

of late. Not since she and her friends looted an abandoned temple—to a monastic local godling, to be sure."

"She has been swayed by bad companions. We know that. But I take the full blame—"

"Oh, no, Delia! Oh, no. I know better than that. Your rascal of a husband who calls himself the emperor—he is far more to blame."

"I choose not to believe that."

"Believe what you like, sister. You will not alter the truth—or, at least—" And Thalmi smiled widely, delighted at her own idiotic words. She and Delia knew that the truth was what was believed, and what was believed could be manipulated. "At least, you believe in error."

"And yet," said Delia, putting a barb of her own, "Dayra was educated and trained by the SOR."

"Yes. If she becomes embroiled with these fatuous Sisters of the Whip, we must expect even greater disasters."

"You'd better tell me about Jilian."

"She has sworn to have the manhood of that rast, Kov Colun Mogper. She will not talk of the indignities she suffered. I gather from my reports that the Sisters of the Whip can promise more than we can in the way of vengeance upon men."

"Vengeance upon men—all men?"

"Aye."

"Well, some of them deserve that, a lot of them. But all? This does not sound like Jilian to me."

"Nor me. But I am assured that she has gone sour."

That rebellious yellow hair of Thalmi's, which she was at pains to cover with a brown wig from time to time, could not spoil the effect she had of being insignificant. Her tongue might destroy the effect. Delia sat up.

"You sound bitter, Thalmi."

"I've every right to be. As Dee Sheon is my witness! When these Sisters of the Whip poach from other Orders, I feel sorrow; but it is no concern to me. When they take our girls it is my concern. And I'll tell you why they want them—it is because of the Claw. Only we can manipulate the Claw."

"Sometimes I wonder if that is so marvelous a gift—"

"Delia!"

"Clawing a man's eyes out tends to become fun to some girls—"

"Never fun. But a redressing of the balance of nature—

yes." Thalmi sat back and waited a moment before saying, "Don't worry too much about Dayra. I do not feel the apprehension for her, despite all, that I do in others. She has not gone sour in quite the same way."

"All the same," said Delia, shaking her head and feeling stubborn. "I find this very hard to believe of Jilian."

"I must confess disappointment. I was hoping you had news of her. Something timely to give me a lever to win her back. There is still a chance. But every day that chance grows more slim."

Leaning forward and helping herself to a yellow paline from the wooden dish gave Delia time to gather thought and strength. She looked up, the paline poised—she was not in the habit of popping a paline here in Lancival. "You say the Whip women need our expertise with the Claw. That I can understand. But by their title—?"

"Yes. They worship the Whip. To extremes."

"One then has to feel sorry for them."

"Oh, aye!"

The pro-marshal spent a few moments expressing her feelings on the subject. Presently, Delia said, "This means you do not know where Jilian is, either? Or where the Sisters of the Whip may be found in conclave?"

"We run across their handiwork from time to time. No, I don't know where Jilian is." Thalmi sounded personally offended, and Delia saw the spymistress *was* personally offended. She had a right to be, in nature. "We managed to trace a chapter in Vondium. But one would expect some to be found in the capital. Others exist in your own Blue Mountains—"

"It grieves me to say that does not surprise me. The Blue Mountain Girls always have been an independent crowd."

"And in various other provinces—Vomansoir, Falimur, Quken, Vindelka, Ogier—"

"Clearly, then, a locus of infection exists and is spreading." All the provinces mentioned occupied a compact area in the center of Vallia. "What other objects, do you know, are the aims apart from humiliating and killing men?"

"That, my dear Delia, is what I would dearly love to know."

The webwork of intelligence thrown over the country by the SOR was not infallible. And, in any case, the sisters were far more concerned about their rigorous pursuits of excellence in service to the generality of people to take kindly to rooting out a rival Order. Looking after a thousand orphans, rebuilding hospitals, tracking and dealing with men who thought they could kidnap girls—these were everyday pursuits, sadly enough, after the Times of Troubles.

The pro-marshal pushed the dish of palines close toward Delia. "There is one other thing that, perhaps, might give us more concern than all the rest." At Delia's delicately raised eyebrow, she went on: "Sorcery. We believe witches and wizards play a prominent part with the Sisters of the Whip."

Slowly, Delia spoke some of her mind.

"I believe I can grasp some of Jilian's thinking in this. The SOR offered me the chance of taking Witch's Vows, and as you know I declined. I am not sorry for that. We are not an Order biased heavily toward sorcery—"

"We can produce competent thaumaturgists when there is the need, Delia.

"Oh, yes, we can, of course. It could be that Jilian believes she will receive more help from the Whip Women."

"If that is all it is. . . ."

Delia took another paline, looked at the clepsydra, and said, "But it is not, you think? Well, we will see. Now it is time for us to eat and then I must attend the Fifth Sheon Service of Praise."

"I attended the Third. Very well, Delia. I will see you at Songs later."

When she'd left the pro-marshal's study, Delia realized this unwelcome news about Jilian had made her bad-tempered again. Despite her dislike of the Claw—although dislike was too strong a word: distaste, perhaps?—she was minded to fill in a private study period with a good rousing slashing session with her Claw. But she did not. Instead she read of the heroic deeds of Benga Kathyn of Tezpor, which had happened so long ago they were probably mythical.* After the Service of Praise and the study session, Delia was relaxed enough to attend Songs and join in with a will. This was one of the magics of Lancival, this capacity to soothe and calm the most unbridled passions.

And, while that was undoubtedly true, and sweet to the mind and spirit, the truth also remained that she could not spend very much longer here. No message had been received

* Benga: saint.

from her half-brother Vomanus yet. This was not surprising, in view of the circuitous route communications would have to take to reach Lancival. No man in all Vallia, in all Kregen—as far as the sisters were aware—knew of the location of Lancival. It was under their noses, of course; but that made the secret that much sweeter.

She determined to remain halfway cross with Vomanus.

Quite apart from her position as empress—a position which always amazed her—which in the most general and particular terms gave her some privileges in the knowledge of just who people intended to marry, Vomanus was, after all, her brother! He'd gone off and married before, and young Valona was the result of that. Valona had gone through Lancival like a divine wind. Well, who was this new lady her brother was marrying? Had married now, by Vox.

Many seasons ago, Delia could recall with the utmost clarity using all her influence—which even then was considerable as the Princess Majestrix of Vallia—to send out expeditions to search for the wild barbarian clansman who was to become her husband. It had fallen to the lot of Tharu of Vindelka and Vomanus to find the man so eagerly sought. Tharu had been slain in that service. Vomanus, in his open, reckless, careless way, had later on passed some casual remark about it being better had he, instead of Tharu who had willed him his kovnate province, been the one to die. His wild and reckless ways distressed Delia. She saw Vomanus as a man as well as a half-brother. Some other, deeper, hurtful, more prodigious reason impelled Vomanus in his wild ways. He had gone through a string of women, friends, acquaintances, always laughing, always reckless, never caring—he seldom bothered to clean his weapons properly after a fracas and one day his sword would snap in the midst of combat because it had rusted away undetected. Delia suffered for Vomanus because he suffered and she could not understand why.

She could not allow herself to believe the obvious answer—for in that she would sense in herself a rebellion against the mercy of the Invisible Twins made manifest in Opaz.

Her thoughts jibed with the words of the hymn that moment being carolled out to the raftered ceiling of the Lesser Hall. "In the Light of Opaz we see our beacon guide through the darkness of the world." Trite words, perhaps; but words always fervently sung and believed. Delia could not quite imagine breaking away from these beliefs, except and only in circumstances arising from her marriage.

In the course of the evening as the songs and hymns were sung, she contrived a few quiet words with people she wished to gauge. Sounding out their minds, as her old tutor, Rose Mandeling, would have said. She said with a trifle impatience to Thalmi Crockhaden, the pro-marshal, "And that is all you can tell me of this Nyleen Gillois?"

The pro-marshal did not tear that yellow hair; she looked as though she might have, had she been other than she was.

"By the Rod of Halron and the Mount of Mampe!" She took a breath. "I had a first-class agent at Delka-Ob. She provided timely, informative, detailed reports. Nothing from her until this morning—and—"

Delia turned her shoulder on the ranks of singing girls in the Lesser Hall and leaned one elbow on the balass-wood bar. Novices in pretty dresses decently covered by striped rose and yellow aprons served soft drinks like sazz and parclear, and also a wide selection of vintages. The bar area lay recessed from the main hall. The singing served as a pleasant background. Delia saw how upset the pro-marshal was, and half-guessed the cause.

Thalmi nodded savagely. "A single last message, no doubt as a gesture of defiance, perhaps, I hope as a sign of some remnants of conscience."

"She has joined the Sisters of the Whip?"

"Aye! May Dee Sheon make her run forever!"

"So we know the name of the lady Vomanus of Vindelka has wed. Nyleen Gillois na Sagaie. Sagaie is in Evir, I think?"

"Yes, right up in the far north, over the mountains, a land of furry savages. They no longer bend the knee to the emperor, they've got themselves a king up there, now, after the Time of the Troubles."

"It will probably be necessary to bring them back into the fold of Vallia, one day. There are other more pressing concerns at the moment." Delia stopped herself. She did not wish to discuss strategy of empire here. She wanted to concentrate if she could on Vomanus, on Jilian, on Dayra. Velia might, with any luck, return from her trip for ladies before her mother left. If not, Delia would not wait . . .

"Judging by the na in her name, she must be of importance."

Cattily, Delia said, "And Sagaie could be a one-shanty village."

The pro-marshal showed her teeth.

Yzobel could offer no further information. She knew only what she had been told, and had been sent to Delka-Ob to carry a message to Delia, who had been expected to be there for the wedding. As for Thalmi's spy—or, rather, ex-spy, in Delka-Ob, Yzobel knew nothing. Not only did she not know her name, she did not know of her existence.

The capital of the province of Vindelka, Delka-Ob, contained a strong group of the Sisters of the Rose. The pro-marshal was clearly worried about future defections.

"The illness of the mistress could not have come at a worse time."

Familiar words—every time was the worst time in Delia's experience—but they remained uncomfortably true in this situation. Knowledge that the mistress was stricken, rumors of strife over the election—yes, these ugly events could easily sway women who had personal grievances. And who, in this sinful world, did not have those?

"The mistress," said Delia, and she tried to speak with purposeful positiveness, struggling against the dreadful uncertainty, "she is going to be perfectly well again—"

"Of course. But for how long? I do not usually speak frankly, my dear. But I really do think that you—"

"Thalmi, as you bear me some affection—"

"Delia! Really!"

The singing reached those marvelous high notes in the Canticles of the Rose City, and for a space there was nothing any mortal with a melodious spirit could do but sink back into an inner reality and listen. Soaring and lofting, sung with all the purity of girls' voices unbridled by limping fashion, the song told of great days and great deeds. Also, it spoke to those who would hear of famous men and noble women, and, equally, of famous women and noble men. Thalmi sipped her wine and waited until the long cadences sank and died. Silence hung drab and yet pulsing with inner echoes under the rafters of the Lesser Hall.

"The Canticles of the Rose City," said the pro-marshal. "Of course, they mean something extra special to you, Delia."

"And to us all, surely? They speak of the rose, do they not?"

As though instructing a raw novice, the pro-marshal said,

"The Canticles of the Rose City are a myth-cycle at least three thousand years old. They concern, chiefly, the doings of a half-legendary, half-historical man-god." She spoke, Delia saw, with meaning. "That person's name was Drak. A name, I believe, not unfamiliar to you—"

"There is no need for this, Thalmi. I know what you imply. My family. Yes, well . . . My son Drak will be the emperor. That is arranged. And then, my dear, I shall be free to follow my own inclinations. I welcome the day."

"If I did not know you better, I would call this ingratitude and you an ingrate."

"If I am, then I am."

"Who else do you see—do you *feel*—to be right?"

"That is not for me to say."

"Everyone else will have their say—and you will, too."

"Probably." And Delia laughed.

"But, sister, you are in error." Thalmi waggled her forefinger—the forefinger of her right hand. The left hand clutched a goblet brimming with a first quality Gremivoh. "Just because you shuffle off the position of empress—no doubt your son Drak will marry Queen Lush in due time—"

"I think not." Delia spoke sharply, very stiff.

"No? Well, no matter. The point is, whether you are empress or not has no bearing on your duty with the SOR. And, you know that well!"

"That is what I have believed for a long time. Part of me still believes. But I have changed. When I was a girl the idea of being the empress escaped me, for everyone talked of the emperor my father, and of the emperor my grandfather. My mother—we used to call her Lela, out of love—was never in my eyes at least an empress. And I truly do not think she ever thought of herself as one. She married my father out of mutual love and was content to be with him. He did not really recover from her death."

Delia would not go on to say that she had felt the joy so strange to herself that her father had, at the last, found a new affection from Queen Lushfymi of Lome. It was because of Queen Lush's genuine love for the emperor that Delia did not think the ambitious queen could truly love Drak. Anyway, it was planned for Drak to marry Silda, Seg's daughter. That would take careful thought and preparation, by Vox!

Again, she did not care to mention that Vomanus, her half-brother, had been born of her mother's first marriage. There were too many worries and too many tangles. If it boiled down to being mistress of the SOR and nothing else, then she would accept nomination leading to almost certain election. Otherwise, she wanted only to be with her husband, and let the SOR manage without her for a little time.

She rubbed her right hand along her left arm, up from the wrist to the elbow, and back, in a smoothing and soothing rhythm of which she was barely conscious. Thalmi noticed, and smiled again, her teeth white.

"You do not practice enough."

"I suppose you will cite that as another dereliction of my duty!"

"I could." Thalmi sipped her wine and—lo!—the glass was empty. She reached out her hand for another goblet. "It is all one. You keep your Claw here. Have you no others at home?"

With a bitterness that shocked herself, Delia burst out: "Home? What I kept of my own possessions at my home—at my home!—is lost, gone, destroyed. I start again, and a revolution or a war or damned reiving flutsmen fly in and burn and steal! I had a Claw in its balass box in the palace at Vondium. Where it is now Opaz alone knows."

"Drink some wine." The pro-marshal proffered a glass.

"Very well." Delia understood she had overreacted. But every time she thought of the way the homes over which she had slaved had been despoiled it made her blood rise up and demand a safety valve, as the headwaters of a dammed lake used the safety-valve overspill. "At least, my home in Djanguraj is still unspoiled."

"And Strombor—"

"I have some ling furs there, soft and long and silky white, that are tatty now and need attention. I would not like to see those white ling furs stolen."

"Possessions are chained weights about our characters."

"You quote and it is true. But sometimes I know I have changed from the girl who accepted everything the SOR taught."

"I believe it, to my sorrow."

"If you remain true to me, I shall remain true to you."

"Never think otherwise."

Delia sipped her wine. "Then take from me the gift you and others are so eager to press upon me." She lifted her left hand, still tingling from that reflexive massage, and waved.

"And here comes Wilma so I suppose she will call the Conclave now."

With the inevitability of their natures there ensued a certain amount of jockeying for positions as the women entered the Conclave Chamber, a certain amount of giggling and stern rejoinders, of quick whispers, and of meaningful glances. The majority maintained a dignified mien. They had work to do and they meant to do it and have done with it.

Thinking back uneasily to those last few exchanges with the pro-marshal at the bar, Delia wished, now, that she had not made so obvious a point about the "remaining true" business. If you had to keep on proclaiming undying friendship then one might suspect that the friendship was in need of continual sustenance. She had made many friends in the outside world and her husband's blade comrades were her blade comrades. Every now and again some little vow, some small indication of the depths of feelings that existed between them might be in order.

Taking her seat in the comfortable but plainly furnished chamber, Delia rubbed her wrist and waggled the fingers up and down. No doubt about it. She was out of practice. The knack of using the Claw was taught at Lancival at an early age and the skill multiplied over the years of continual practice. This applied to most other weapons, of course—most, not all.

Some twenty women gathered in the Conclave Chamber. Those who had made their marks with Delia on her arrival, the various officers of the Order, and short-sighted Nandi ti Rondasmot who wrote down an account of what was said, they sat to their task each in her own individual fashion. Most took the duty seriously; some were conscious of their superiority; some wanted to have the thing over and done with and others wished to go on talking all night.

Rosala, with two novices there to help her unobtrusively, gave her report on the mistress. No change.

"Thank you, Rosala. We are all grateful for your devoted care of the mistress. Now you may leave."

"Thank you, my lady."

"And," added the Lady Almoner, "make sure you get a good night's rest, Rosala!"

A number of items on the agenda demanded attention. Of all the women there, Delia fancied that she alone experienced this unwelcome sense of distancing. Of course, what they did here and what was decided was of vital importance. The Sisters of the Rose wielded power. But, all the same, Delia was overwhelmingly conscious of her responsibilities in the outer world.

Natilma na Stafoing in her robust way was saying: "And so we must deal with these Sisters of the Whip. Deal with them harshly as they deserve."

Lansi ti High Ochrun pushed her copper hair back from her forehead. Softly, she said, "We refer to these Whip women freely and openly, here in Conclave and in Lancival. Might not it be wiser to treat them in the same way we treat that *other* Order, whose name we do not use openly?"

Everyone knew which Order Lansi referred to.

A number of sororities possessed names beginning with S: Samphron, the Sword, Silence, Sensibility, so that their abbreviations took notice of this fact. The Order to which Lansi referred considered themselves a cut above the rest. The old antagonism remained, ridiculous though it was, like two bitches fighting over the same bone in a dusty village street. The rivalries between male Orders were, often, of the same intensity.

This rival sorority had chosen to saddle itself with the title of The Grand Ladies Order of Gratitude. Out of disrespect and mirth, the SOR sometimes called this *other* Order the Grand Ladies. They were, of course, well aware that the GLOG meant that the Order, not the Ladies, were Grand. The GLOG habitually wore green leathers, were stronger in the north of the country—although that in normal times had no significance—and had done good work for the poor and sick, and had fought against the invaders of Vallia. They maintained what was probably a stronger force of Battle Maidens, Jikai Vuvushis, than the Sisters of the Rose. They did not use the Claw but were cunning with the Whip.

Delia's eyes closed. She opened them with a jolt of surprise. The women talked on around her. More than one sister had suggested that they referred to the GLOG euphemistically as the *other* Order because they were frightened of them and their influence. If you don't say his name the bogey can't get you.

In her clear voice, she said: "Let us treat the Sisters of the Whip as just another Order. Are they then so fearsome?"

As she listened to the various answers, reasoned, hot-tempered, cautious, her eyelids dropped down.

As a small girl learning about the Grand Ladies, she had said, "Who are they grateful to?" and had been surprised at the ladylike bellows of laughter from her tutors at the sally.

Rose Mandeling had said, beaming, "Oh, they are grateful to Opaz, of course. But it is truer to say they are grateful *for* all their worldly possessions and positions."

Delia managed to open her eyes. The chamber swam in a blue haze. She was tired—and as a hairy graint of a clansman was in the habit of saying: "Tiredness is a sin."

Well, she was sinning like mad right now, and unable to do a single thing about it.

Some items of the agenda were dealt with. Delia sat, exhausted, eyes closed most of the time, joining in when she could. Nothing was decided about the Sisters of the Whip, about the mistress, even about the new curtains for the refectory.

When, at last, the Lady Almoner brought the meeting to a close, everyone felt restless with dissatisfaction. They recognized that, just at the moment, there was precious little they could decide. Some of the women had used great skill in steering any discussion away from consideration of just who was to be considered for nomination to the position of mistress.

That suited Delia.

She smiled and said the remberers, and trailed off to Velda's Room. A thorough wash, an attention to the necessities of the toilet, an abstention from any further food or drink, and a swift and thrashing kind of onslaught on her hair, and she could fall into the narrow bed, think of all those she could not sleep without thinking of, and then drop down into nothingness.

CHAPTER EIGHT

Delia Rides the Gale

In the small cabin situated in the stern of the airboat Delia pulled down the top of her russet tunic over her breast. She tucked her chin in and squinted down. She had always had nice skin, smooth and unblemished, and now this—this monstrosity—squatted nastily on her chest like a furry grub. The patch was as big as her thumb. When she looked more closely she could see tiny yellow pimples peppering the angry red of the rash.

She did not much care for rashes and she disliked pimples.

The beastly spot did not hurt. It did not even sting. She could feel nothing even when, distastefully, she prodded it with a finger.

The hateful thing just erupted on her skin, growing larger, sitting there like an obscene grub above her breast. The flap of the door covering quivered, and a beringed hand showed, about to pull the curtain aside.

A voice bellowed: "Majestrix! I would crave a word with your puissance, your humble servant craves entrance."

Delia made a face.

She slapped the tunic up and latched it and said in a small yet firm voice: "Come in, Lathdo."

The man who entered—he was apim with brown hair—bulked in the tiny cabin with its bench seat and folding table. He wore armor. He carried swords. He bore the insignia of a Jiktar. He half-crouched under the cover and was clearly ill at ease.

"Yes?"

"A storm, majestrix. Since we quitted Delphond the weather has been kind. But Jordio swears he can smell the Riders of Notor Zan about to enfold us."

"We must descend, then, Lathdo. Is Mimi there?"

"Your orders are to be obeyed without thought, majestrix." He half turned his head, the tendons straining in his neck above the gilt rim of the corselet, and bellowed: "Mimi! *Bratch!*"

Delia did not jump. She'd called in to Vondium to see if any letters were waiting for her, and had read all the mail and no letter from him at all, and taken the opportunity to re-equip with a fresh set of clothing and necessaries. No letter from Vomanus probably meant he was as cross with her as she was with him. Most of the urgency to reach Delka-Ob had now passed, of course, since the marriage had already taken place.

She would have to go to see her half-brother and congratulate him and wish Nyleen well. She just hoped she would find her brother's new wife amenable and nice, so she would not have to lie through smiling teeth.

Drak was still prancing around in the southwest of Vallia; the country was still untidy in the view of a girl who had been brought up with the empire as a unit, the factions still plotted and the damned revolutionaries and secessionists still badgered away. The army was very thin in Vondium, what with the strong forces sent into Hamal, others into the north of the country and still others with Drak. The Lord Farris had insisted in his patient way that she must take a bodyguard and added: "Your news of flutsmen so active in Vindelka is worrying, majestrix."

"I suppose you are right. Both Yzobel and Sosie must be about their business." She could not tell a man that they were off about business of the SOR: but that was patently clear. Farris, a loyal friend for as long as she could remember, was the Crebent Justicar for the emperor, and ran things when Drak was away.

"Jiktar Lathdo the Eager has recently been promoted. He is zealous, and a good fighter. He will—"

"Yes, yes, dear Farris. You are right. Mind you send word to me the instant you hear from the emperor."

"Have I ever failed you in that?"

"I am sorry. No, never. Just that. . . ."

"And it was remiss of me to mention it." Farris was of the quality of men of whom an emperor could never have enough. His loyalty to Delia personally was beyond question. The only serious trouble with the Lord Farris was that he was approaching old age.

So she'd taken one of Farris's small but encouragingly growing force of airboats and started off. She'd gone by a swing back through Delphond to make sure a little matter at Drakanium was in order, and then set course for Vindelka. With Jiktar Lathdo the Eager, the pilot, Jordio the Hawk, and Mimi the Smile, she'd taken off with the dismal hope that she would get through this quickly and fly back to Vondium to some good—some marvelous—news.

When Mimi put her ringletted head into the tiny cabin Delia was in two minds whether or not to consult her about the rash on her chest. Probably it would go away soon. She would rub some ointment on tonight. That should do it.

Mimi looked upset.

"Very well, Mimi, my dear, I shall speak to the jiktar."

"It is so—so—degrading!"

"I agree."

The word *bratch,* which meant jump to it, although in no way as vicious as the infamous *grak,* addressed to slaves to make them hop about their work or be slashed by whips, was often heard in the ranks of the swods as the soldiers drilled. It was not, at least in Delia's hearing, addressed to her people. Mimi, young, still under training, had been overjoyed to be plucked out of her humdrum routine in the palace in Vondium to be chosen as personal handmaid to the empress. It was a tremendous boost to her ego, a real start on her career, and, more than all that, of supreme bliss to be able to be with the Empress Delia of Vallia. Mimi believed this without coaching.

"But," said Mimi, with a little return to the smile that gave her her cognomen, "I do not want to make trouble."

"I shall, if that big froth-blower Lathdo does not learn to speak to you properly."

"Thank you—"

"He is new to his position, you see. He has just been promoted ob-Jiktar from zan-Hikdar, and he is—well, he is Eager . . ."

"Oh, yes, majestrix. Very Eager."

Delia wished that her two Djangs, Tandu and Dalki, had been in Vondium. She would have welcomed their support and protection. But they had both been sent up to Vindelka with a letter from the Lord Farris, in explanation and also instruction. The Djangs would find a snug berth in Vomanus's bodyguard rather than riding patrol along the Ochre Limits.

The flier shook as wind gusts rattled past.

Mimi looked uncertain.

"This Jordio the Hawk is a good pilot, Mimi."

"Oh, yes, of course, majestrix."

"You are not afraid of fliers?"

"Oh, no, majestrix."

Delia did not smile. "You have heard the old tales of how the airboats we bought from Hamal were always breaking down. Of course you have. But now we are friends with Hamal, we can buy proper vollers, and from Hyrklana, too."

"My mother told me." Mimi moved to the topmost chest stacked along the side of the cabin and picked up a hairbrush. Delia saw that the girl wanted something to do. "Also, my mother would be amazed that the empress does not travel with a great retinue—"

"When it is necessary, I do. We shall not be away long."

Delia submitted her hair to the brush. Mimi had a nice stroke, but Delia missed the delicate touch of Rosala or Floria. But Floria—who was just as brilliant and beautiful as Rosala—was off being married, at last, and Rosala had gone, too. Since Delia's adventures in Hamal had taken her away from her handmaidens, she had not worried overmuch. And, now, poor Pansi was dead, along with Nath the Jokester, and she was going to have to train up this Mimi.

As she lay back, letting the brush stroke through her hair, she reflected that Mimi was one of the girls greatly affected by the recent Time of Troubles. The bad days had muddled up girls' education in far worse ways than boys, for a lad need only shoulder a spear and march off with the army to make a name and fortune for himself, if he did not get himself killed. For girls it was different, unless they were Jikai Vuvushis. Mimi came from the province of Forli and had not been educated by any of the sororities, at least, not to Delia's knowledge. Her mother, a shrewd woman with ambition, had applied for a place for her daughter Mimi. She had backed her application with a letter from the Kov of Forli, Lykon Crimahan. He had once been at loggerheads with the emperor, and had proved himself if not a good friend at least a man prepared to set to and work for the new emperor and let bygones be bygones. That had tilted the scales in Mimi's favor.

A slender, meek girl, Mimi's choice of career had been wisely chosen by her mother. At Mimi's age, Delia had been stomping around in black leathers slashing with her Claw and foining with rapier and main gauche. That would not have been practicable for Mimi. She was set on a career, now, and ought to be successful. In pursuance of that, Delia decided, she'd probably let the Little Sisters of Opaz have Mimi for a spell, sharpen her up, teach her the tricks of the trade. All that would help Mimi's prospects. So many girls applied and so few could be taken, Delia felt the burden upon herself. This, as with so many other aspects, was one of the abiding oppressions of being empress.

Delia was a very proud woman; but she was not so foolishly proud as to believe that being handmaiden to an empress was the summit and achievement of a girl's life.

But, by Krun, it was a damned good start.

The flier lurched again and then started a gentle descent. A consummate flier herself, Delia recognized the masterful handling. Jordio must be trying to avoid the worst of the blow by diving and attempting to find a layer of calmer air.

The brush snagged in her hair.

Delia winced.

Mimi gasped.

The brush began to stroke again, tentatively. Delia said nothing. She did not pride herself on her tolerance for not biting the girl's head off. She was sorrowfully aware that by saying nothing, she punished the poor girl far more than a swift epithet and insult ever could do.

The flier swung bodily sideways, was caught and held, and swept back onto course.

Delia said: "That is enough, Mimi. Perhaps you would like to see about that hole in the hem of the turquoise gown? You discovered the hole, which was clever. And, be careful not to stick the needle in your finger. Jordio has his hands full."

"Yes, majestrix."

As she ducked out onto the deck, Delia reflected that it was as well that not yet, not quite yet, the gentle intimacy of handmaid and empress had been established between them. Mimi would learn the empress's funny ways in time.

The wind blew her thoughts away.

Jordio, a wild shape in a flapping cloak, stood at the control levers like some phantom operator of a ghostly sky-mill. Lathdo clung to the rail at his side. Both men peered ahead, into the wildness. The sky pelted down at them, lowering, dark, massy with wind and clamor.

Delia hauled herself along the rail until she stood with the men. They were startled to see her, as though an apparition from a Herrelldrin Hell had jumped up to drag them away.

"Majestrix!" The rest was lost in the howl of the wind. Something to do with not being on deck and being in the cabin.

She said nothing. She held on. Her lips opened and the wind rushed past. This was glorious!

The flier leaped up and down like a crazed sliptinger, that beautiful salmon of Western Vallia, and Jordio met each leap and lunge and held her. Delia looked ahead and down. Were those lights below?

She banged Lathdo on a bulky armored shoulder and pointed.

He nodded.

Jordio inched his controls carefully, and the flier, responding, lunged down and kept at the angle, sweeping in through the gusts. The lights grew firmer. Wind struck into her face as a force, tearing, liberating. But however much she might exult in fronting the elements, those same elemental forces could take the flier and twist her end over end and shred her and cast her down as a mass of tumbled wreckage onto the ground below.

Her hair blew back in a whiplash of abandon. Poor Mimi! The lights brightened. A village, perhaps a small town, huddled against the fury of the storm. The place was somewhere in Vindelka, on the way to the provincial capital.

". . . get . . . down!" bellowed Lathdo. He looked furious in that dark light, his jaw muscles bulging. If aught happened to the empress!

Delia could guess his thoughts. She could feel a small sorrow for him; after all, he was new to the job and the big blow-hard was eager to do what he imagined to be the right things around an empress. He, like Mimi, could be trained.

Nothing of any of the seven Moons of Kregen could be glimpsed in that wracked sky. The darkness lashed with the wind, and the wind scourged with the darkness. No one saw it.

One moment Jordio was bringing the flier down in a steep descent, angling her to catch the wind, and the next they'd slammed slap bang into the roof of a building.

The flier simply broke up.

Upside down, whirled on the breath of the wind, Delia

caught a fantastic glimpse of Mimi flying out of the aft cabin like a kite.

Something hard struck Delia across the back. It was probably the edge of the guttering. Bits and pieces of destroyed airboat whirled about her. She saw nothing in the clamping dark of either Lathdo or Jordio. She fell off the edge of the roof, her back aching like the devil, her eyes filled with tears of pain, of fury and frustration, and her mouth wide open and yelling blue bloody murder.

She hit the dung heap.

Well, Seg and her husband knew about those kinds of adventure. She sat up, spitting straw, and glared about with such a look of savage hatred as would have fried a leem.

She could barely smell the stink, for the wind lashed it away. Her hair blew all over her face when she turned to look downwind. All she could see was the whole world leaping up and down. Then she realized this uncanny movement was merely a tree, blowing bent, and straightening, and so bowing once again to the power of the storm.

She stood up and went a dozen staggering steps to leeward. She bumped into a wall, grazed her fingers, and held on. She dragged in a few gulps of breath. That she kept on her feet meant that her legs weren't broken. That she gripped to the wall meant her arms weren't broken. That she remained upright meant her back wasn't broken—although it damnedwell felt like it. And because her head did not roll off and get blown away by the wind, her neck wasn't broken.

She gulped more air, shook her face free of hair, and crabbed along the wall. Her groping fingers felt the door long before she saw it. It fitted snugly into the jamb.

The exhilaration she'd felt at the touch of the wind faded. She felt exhausted. She was feeling far more tired lately than she should. When the rain began she knew she'd have to cave in, or, being a Sister of the Rose, think about giving in and then go marching on, stupid though the marching might be.

But the tiredness dragged at her. This was frightening, the way she could feel the fatigue deep within her bones. This was something new to her, and nauseating, unnerving.

Holding onto the edge of the jamb and getting her breath, resisting the tug of the wind, she recalled herself after she had fallen from the zorca and become a cripple. Yes, there had been something of that feeling then. Certainly, she'd never felt like this when she'd been carrying any of her children.

She put her teeth together, bit down, hunched up her shoulders, and swinging her leg vigorously, delivered a thumping great kick at the door.

She had to kick three times before she roused any answer.

The door cracked the space of a narrow nose and one eye. She put her mouth to the slot of light and bellowed.

"Let me in!"

Another thumping great thwack with her toes reinforced the demand. She was prepared to lay about her with her tongue, get 'em jumping, have a fire and a hot toddy, a meal, find a decent bed, and—first and most important—stir 'em all up into going out and scouring everywhere to find Mimi and Lathdo and Jordio.

The door slapped open. She tumbled in. An oniony sack clapped over her head. Whoever they were in here, one of them hit her over the head. The smell of onions faded with everything else, faded and went away, went with the wind.

CHAPTER NINE

A Walk in the Radiance of the Suns

She supposed, with deep rancor and considerable soul-searching, that this was what happened to girls who grew to think themselves too important. They had given her a tunic, and a breechclout. Both were of grey.

Slave grey.

Well, she'd been slave before. She had helped to outlaw slavery in Vallia. But, here she was, trudging along with a forlorn group of other slaves, all following a coach down a long and dusty road, going from where to where she had not the slightest idea.

After the onion sack she'd been kicked awake to find herself stark naked chained in a bed. And that damned spot on her chest had changed into a swelling. The swelling was ugly in her eyes, a bulging lump. A cautious swivel of her eyes revealed other lumps. When she could touch her face she felt more.

So these people, whoever they were, had led her out to the waiting coffle of slaves, and taken their chains off and affixed the slavers' chains. She trudged along with the others, and no one wanted to talk to her.

She was merchandise.

The day sparkled about her. The streaming mingled radiance of Zim and Genodras, the twin Suns of Kregen, touched everything with fire. She half-shut her eyes. The road was ochreish, dusty and dry. Her feet, naked, did not pain her, for empress or no empress, she was hardened to going barefoot. Perhaps, toward the end of the day if the march was long, her feet would pain; but, then, she was in all truth a little out of practice for this particular brand of adventure.

Her latest escapades had been more in the nature of riding a superb saddle animal at the head of armies.

The road, like most roads of Vallia, was atrocious. Relying mainly for transport on her magnificent system of canals, Vallia neglected roadworks. This specimen stretched out between fields of Strafin and Chawinseed, all glowing purple and orange above the green in the rays of the suns. If these slavers put her to work in the fields, she'd make a break and run for it.

The guards who marched beside the small column, only occasionally flicking their whips, were not apims. They were diffs, Fristles whose cat faces bristled with whiskers, and whose fur showed the patternings of various races. They did not look so much bored with their job as indifferent to what they were doing. They continually scanned the sky.

If they expected a patrol of Vallian aerial cavalry to sweep down and rescue the slaves, they would, in Delia's opinion, be expecting nothing. She trudged on. The coach up ahead swayed and jolted along. Over the heads of the intervening slaves Delia made out the ornate gildings on the coach, the real glass in the rear window, the rail at top retaining a piled mass of boxes and trunks. To trudge along as a slave at the back end of a handsome coach? There was an incongruity here.

The other people taken up into slavery smelled less than sweet. The dust stung her nostrils. The suns blazed down, pouring a conciliatory warmth upon the world for the violence of the storm. The coffle passed through a village which she did not recognize. Every door was bolted, every window shuttered; nothing moved save the gilded coach and the slavers and their merchandise.

The woman who slouched along beside Delia twisted a narrow neck to peer with filmed eyes upon the scene. Her hair straggled, dust smothered, unkempt. It was, surmised Delia with distaste, just like her own.

"All run off. Bad cess to 'em, says I. More of us there are, the lighter the work."

"Where are we going?" Delia responded with a quick eagerness to the advance. But the woman relapsed into the indifferent silence chaining them all.

They trailed on, a hopeless, miserable crew, bound for the horrors of the unknown.

Delia eyed the nearest Fristle guard who marched along with wilting whiskers, his cat face sullen, the dust staining the brass-studded leather jerkin. He carried an axe at his belt, and a spear sloped over his shoulder. Every now and again he tilted his head up, so that the leather flaps of his cap dangled free, scanning the sky.

Suppose she were such a guard, herding slaves along? And one of the slaves in her grey slave tunic and breechclout accosted her, saying something like: "I am the Empress of Vallia. Release me at once, or your head is forfeit"?

What would she think; what do?

A swift thwack with the spear, an insult? Perhaps a taste of the sharp end to keep the cramphs in order? Certainly, it would be a surprising guard who would immediately leap into a torrent of majestrixes and unshackle the chains and bow and scrape.

There was no hope there.

Not yet. When she reached their destination, and managed to gain converse with someone in authority, then would be the time. The person riding so grandly in the gold coach, Delia surmised with a chill, might believe, and, believing, dispatch her out of hand.

The aragorn and the slavemasters chased out of Vallia bore a sullen resentment against the emperor and empress for depriving them of a livelihood. Not all people welcomed the manumission imposed from above.

Only a short time after leaving the village the slaves began to falter. Soon some dropped to the ground, unable to continue. Chains clanked and dragged in the dust.

Delia was pulled down by the woman at her side.

Instinctively, she tried to help the woman up, a hand under her armpit. The woman's head lolled. Other people began to drop. The guards used their whips, and shrieks lifted, cutting in the bright air. But the coffle stopped.

A totrix came lolloping back from up front. It bore a rider in silvered armor who flourished a whip and swore most vilely. She slashed at the slaves and the guards indiscriminately, shouting at them to go on.

"Grak!" she shrieked. "Grak, you useless bunch of tapos. Grak, or you'll all have your throats cut!"

A second totrix appeared from the front of the column.

Dully, Delia wondered how many more cavalry trotted so grandly as advance guard.

The second rider reined in beside the first.

"Easy, Chica. It is clear they must have water—as I said in the village."

"Since when does anyone listen to you, Nath the Muncible? They must be whipped into marching."

"They will be whipped to death. Then who will pay you?"

"Ah—your piddling ways sicken me."

Despite this altercation, the coach up ahead rumbled to a halt and presently a few tame slaves brought pannikins of water. Delia drank. She was not at all surprised that she drank as the other slaves drank, huge greedy gulps, grasping and jostling. After a bur or so the whips snapped and the coffle slowly resumed the march.

Slavery had been outlawed in Vallia and the slavers and aragorn banished, if they failed to take up an honest living. So this nightmare could not be happening—should not be happening. But it was.

She was far stronger than most of the people in the slave coffle. She could march. She had to retain her sense of identity, bide her time. There was great danger for the empress in this situation, paradoxically, far more danger than for a citizen. Her death would be well rewarded in the circles of her enemies. By keeping on, attracting no special attention to herself, keeping herself to herself, she could survive until she met someone to whom she could talk. If the gods favored her, it would be someone she knew, someone who was a friend.

She was far more frightened of the horrible swellings disfiguring her body. Her thoughts had to be kept under control. She made her legs go up and down and carry her on as she had in the Ochre Limits. But, truly, this trudging along, even loaded with chains, was nowhere as bad as that experience. These lumps and bumps, these rashes speckled with yellow pimples that grew into obscene blemishes upon her body, growing into smooth hard lumps. . . . No. If she thought that, then she would have infected all of Lancival, those in Vondium and Drakanium . . .

No. No, that could not be the cause of the swellings.

And, if she thought rationally about this march, it was far far worse than struggling across the Ochre Limits. Then she had been a free woman, able to make her own decisions and affect, in however small a way, her own destiny. Now she was slave.

Did she have the Affliction of the Sores of Combabbry?

This pimple-speckled rash, those smooth swellings, were unlike the suppurating sores of the disease. But she had bathed in the Sacred Pool in far Aphrasöe. That would make a difference. Must make a difference to the course of the disease, surely? Perhaps she was a walking bed of infestation.

When she had spoken to the woman who dragged along at her side, her own words had sounded odd. A lump swelled beside her mouth, distorting the shape, slurring her speech. Another lump had joined those on her breast, and her face matched the general lumpiness. She must look a sight!

One leg—the left—was fully half again the size of her right leg. How odd it looked, to see one fat and one thin leg, striding forward under her!

She was growing light-headed.

Careful, girl! she said to herself, and bit down, and closed her eyes against the glare of dust, and marched on.

The course of the Affliction of the Sores of Combabbry was known. She would never have allowed herself to be taken to Lancival without complete conviction that she was free of the disease. A period of quarantine would have been necessary, and because she had not taken the disease and it was being checked in Mellinsmot, she had, along with the doctor, taken it that she was free. *Was* she free?

Just because these horrible lumps were different from the sores might not mean the disease too was different. If this woman at her side caught the infection—she would erupt in suppurating sores because she had not bathed in the Sacred Pool. All the mixed emotions experienced by Delia at thought of that magical baptism tormented her anew.

The trudging progress of the coffle degenerated to a shuffle. They made little better than two or two and a half miles an hour. When the suns at last slid down to the western horizon and the air cooled and the coach halted and tents were erected, they'd covered perhaps twenty miles or so. The slaves fell down in their tracks at the side of the road, and slept.

Those who remained awake kicked the others awake when a thin gruel, hard bread and pannikins of water came around. Then they all slept. Delia was not molested, although a few of the younger girls were removed from their chains and then, later, returned. A man slave, husky and with a mop of dark hair, was taken and likewise returned, much later than the others. He staggered in, groaning, was chained up and fell full length into an exhausted sleep.

The next day they made another twenty-five miles or so,

and picked up half a dozen new slaves from pinched-face people at a crossroads inn. Gold changed hands. The newcomers were shackled up and the dreary procession resumed.

On this day the watching of the sky, although it persisted, was far more perfunctory. From this Delia deduced the coffle must be nearing its destination.

She still could not recognize where she was. She was in Vindelka—the kovnate province of her half-brother, for Val's sake!—but that was the extent of her knowledge. When you flew so fleetly high above the ground, details below blurred. An hour or two in the air could cover all and more, far far more, than a girl could walk on her feet in a day. . . .

The cultivated fields were left behind. The coffle entered woods which thickened and deepened, cutting off the light. The track wound unevenly over bumpy ground. At the thought of bumps Delia touched herself, and winced. She was more lumpy than the ground upon which she walked.

If these damned slavers erupted all over with putrescent sores and boils, she did not think she would grieve overmuch . . . If her three companions who had crashed with her in the airboat were infected, she would not only grieve, she would have to face her own guilt.

Common sense told her that she could not be held to blame. Medical opinion held that she could not have contracted the disease. But medical opinion was unaware of the existence of that Pool in the River Zelph of far Aphrasöe. Common sense might tell her all it liked; she was Delia and she was weighed down by self-recriminations far outside common sense.

Although she had been unable to see everyone in the coffle, she was confident that Mimi, Lathdo and Jordio were not there. The two men with her in the forward part of the voller must have gone slap bang over the other side of the house. As for Mimi—she had sailed off like a kite in the cabin. Where she was now, Opaz alone knew, and Delia consigned the little handmaid's fate to that manifestation of the Invisible Twins in trust and hope.

Then she fell over a snaggly root and pitched full length.

The woman chained with her fell on top of her. Metal clanked. Guards appeared with whips, ferocious. Delia managed to wriggle around and drag the chains up so that the links took most of the blows. But some struck through, and stung, stung like liquid fire.

The thought burst into her head . . .

If I had my Whip now. . . !

The guards sorted things out with blows and lashes and the coffle moved on. Delia felt a rising terror at her own fatigue. She was just so damned tired! She stumbled along in her chains as the shouts of "Grak! Grak!" beat about them. The woman she had dragged down said nothing. She walked as though encased in ice. Blood glimmered through a rent in her grey tunic.

Delia's legs began to turn to jelly, the fat left one and the thin right one. They were still attached to her body and they continued to go up and down and forward and back; but she was sure they were jelly. She couldn't feel anything of them, and nothing from her feet. The world around her grew dark.

Just keep on marching. That was all she had to do. Keep on going forward, head up, chin in, chest out, striding on and on, and not shuffling along with her head hanging and her back bent and pains running all over her except below her thighs.

The shadows of the trees mingled with the shadows in her eyes. Nothing underfoot except clouds. The chains would soon wear away the skin. She had nice skin. Before the blotches and the lumps appeared. She couldn't see much.

The earth under her rustled with leaves. She could not remember falling down again. She was not being whipped, so she could not have fallen down. A bowl was thrust into her hands. They were resting for the night!

She drank off the gruel wolfishly and wiped her finger around the bowl, and licked it. Almost, she had been likening herself to Pakkad, who in Kregish mythology stood for the downtrodden, the pariah and outcast. If she could sleep through this night, she would gather strength for the morrow.

And on the morrow anything might happen.

CHAPTER TEN

Alyss Carries Water

Carrying water remained one of the chief occupations of slaves.

With the yoke cutting into her shoulders carrying two tubs of water, Delia walked into the stone-flagged kitchens. Greasy Nardo the Water Master shrieked at her.

"Grak, you useless lump!"

Some of the water spilled, and Nardo shouted again.

Delia took no notice. Since the end of that frightful march in the slave coffle and her selection to become a water-carrier, she had spent a sennight here and already had worked out a scheme of escape. She continued to feel fatigued. The tiredness dragged at her. Her strength was barely enough for carrying the water. And her lumps and blotches turned her reflection in the water into that of a hideous nightmare.

From all this she took hope.

No one with whom she had come into contact had contracted the Affliction of the Sores of Combabbry.

Hurrying to the trough and pouring water in, with great care so as not to spill a drop, swinging the yoke first left and tipping and then right, she emptied the tubs and started back for the kitchen door. Nardo watched her with his greasy face glistening and his switch flickering.

Outside the kitchens the wooden stockade enclosed a yard and stabling and the well, with the tops of trees showing over the palisade. Sentries prowled there. Where she was she had, of course, no idea. None of the slaves knew that.

Silly Nath at the well had already cranked up a bucket and he stood, lanky and lopsided, ready to fill the tubs.

"Smells like roast ordel today," he said, spittle glistening on his narrow chin. He was crosseyed. He wore a grey slave breechclout. The water shone silver from bucket to tub. Silly Nath did not spill much.

"Not for us," said Delia.

A totrix in the stables shook himself and stamped.

Four slaves staggered past under bundles of kindling, and more followed, dragging a lurching cart piled with logs.

"Can't you steal a little for me, Alyss?"

Delia sighed. "I'll try, Nath."

The tubs were filled. She settled the yoke so that it rested on the least sore parts of her shoulders, and started back for the kitchens.

Looking down at herself she thought—she hoped—that her left leg was not quite as fat as it had been. Was it? The skin glistened where it stretched taut. Thin white lines showed cutting in under her knee cap. Perhaps the lumps were going down at last?

Fat left leg or no fat left leg, she could ride a totrix. She marked the beast, stamping and snuffling in his stall, pampered and fed. There were six altogether, and she hungered for this particular one. When she was astride his back she'd be out through the gate, clear away if it was open, bashing it open if it was closed. After that—well, as she carried the water she descended into scarlet images of what would happen to this place when she returned leading one or two of her regiments.

No. No, that wouldn't do at all. That was quite silly.

Oh, no. She'd come back here leading one or two armies.

There would be very little left of this place by the time she and her people were finished with it.

On this mental fare she subsisted as the days passed. No one offered to molest her. The slaves slept higgledy-piggledy in dormitories above the kitchens. Facilities were primitive. From the yard looking back over the kitchen and superimposed dormitory a view could be obtained of a stone tower crowned by battlements and with a flagstaff. The pole raked up, bare.

A hint of more battlemented walls and towers beyond the first indicated that this place—wherever it was—had considerable defensive strength. Even the richest people looked twice before deciding to build castles in stone. They cost fabulous sums. This place probably consisted of a stone tower or two, and the rest of the fortifications would be of timber. Probably.

On the day that Nan the Bosom announced she was pregnant and the inevitable arguments started about who was the father, Delia really did think her left leg was just about its right size again. Nan the Bosom, outraged that the contraceptives she had paid for in kind had failed her, flailed about with her largest ladle. She was Soup Mistress, and her largest ladle was large. It cracked alongside three or four flea-bitten heads, and thwacked half a dozen grimy shins—and Nan had hardly begun.

"Not me, Nan!" and: "Musta been Nardo!"

And so on.

Delia waited outside until the water in her tubs stilled to mirrors. She had no wish to become involved. The tub-mirror showed her face as a nightmare to her, still, but not so much a nightmare as before. The lumps *were* going down. Her hair! To laugh in these circumstances could only indicate despair. It was just as well that she could view herself with some dispassionate analysis. Yes, she always tried to keep herself neat and tidy, that was true. But she did not think she was a vain woman. Just as well. The sight glaring back at her from the water mirror would have driven a vain woman past the verge.

With a savage thrust of her shoulders, she shattered the image in the water.

Putting the yoke back on, she went into the kitchens. The uproar continued. Nan, it was clear, didn't care who the father was. She just wanted to hit everybody with her ladle.

When Delia turned back from the well, Silly Nath said: "Smells like ponsho today, Alyss. Will you steal me a bit?"

"I'll try."

She turned away toward the kitchens in the never-ending drudgery. A flag flew at the flagstaff.

Instantly she stopped.

The flag flapped, infuriatingly twirling itself from side to side and pointing away from her. She could make out only the colors, not the devices. The colors were white and ochre.

Well, and what else had she expected? White and ochre were the colors of Vindelka. And that was where she was.

She remained utterly convinced that the devices on the flag were not those of her half-brother Vomanus. He would never run a degenerate hell-hole like this. A touch around her waist, a fingering pressure, brought her back with a thump from the considerations of an empress to those of a slave.

"Give us a cuddle, Alyss—"

"What, with me, Nath?"

She was so startled that was all she could think of.

"I like you. You're nice."

"But—" She moved away. Silly Nath would not leave the

well and the crank handle. He'd been flogged silly for doing that—twice. "Look at me!"

Silly Nath twisted his head on one side in his ecstasy of cleverness. "They call me Silly Nath. But I've seen you, Alyss. You're different. You're lovely."

"I'm all lumpy."

"Yes. You gimme a cuddle tonight."

Because slaves lived in squalor perhaps anything only slightly less hideous than the ugliness around would appear lovely to them. Delia was aware of the incongruity of responding to an amorous advance by denigrating her appearance. That verged on the coy. Here she was, dressed in slave grey, carrying two damn great tubs of water, her hair a mess, her lumps making her grotesque, arguing with a simpleton about cuddling. It was enough to make a girl say a rude word.

And then, amazingly, vouchsafed from Dee Sheon herself, wonderfully, she realized what that last limping thought meant. She was coming back to life. Not because poor Silly Nath felt her attractive and wanted a cuddle, but because she could see the funny side of the situation.

"Nan the Bosom is pregnant, Nath."

" 'Twaren't me."

"Now's your chance. I can't cuddle you, Nath." Then the limping humor changed, and the words whiplashed. "Stay away from me, Nath. For your own good."

All the same, on the morrow the kitchen slaves kept asking Silly Nath where he got his black eye from. He didn't say.

He looked more miserable than sullen when he filled the tubs. Delia had no need to harden her heart. Some things were done in her world and some things were not done. The question of soft or hard hearts did not enter the equation.

And the flag still flew.

When she reached the kitchen door a voice she did not know was saying: ". . . no concern. We expect some more in a few days. Until then you'll have to manage as best you can."

Greasy Nardo the Water Master wiped his forehead. He looked at once angry and chastened. The man speaking to him wore slave grey, but his tunic bore a white and ochre patch, and his switch was larger and thicker than Nardo's. His face resembled that of a half-starved water rat, with pimples.

"Is this the woman?"

"Yes, Master Uldo. This is the woman."

So, said Delia to herself, so this is the First Water Master, Uldo. He was doing a thorough job of frightening Nardo.

Uldo switched his stick at Delia.

"Alyss. Come with me." As Delia instantly obeyed, the feel of the switch on her arm, he shouted: "Onker! Do not bring the water tubs." Delia, acting as a slave would act, instantly put the tubs down and cowered away.

Surprisingly, Uldo said, "There are men in the treadmill to bring the water up. You will carry it from there."

She nodded. She did not say anything. She knew how to act like slave. She wondered if she might let this Uldo live a little longer than the others when the time came. . . .

The First Water Master strutted along importantly, slashing about with his switch, and Delia trailed along after. They went through the yard, where she gave her usual quick scrutiny of the totrix stables, and so through the open barred door beyond. Sentries looked down, mercenaries by their appearance, as the two walked into the shadows and began to climb wooden stairs into the interior of the building.

They went by flang-infested stairways and dusty corridors until they reached a panel, jutting from the wall. These back stairs and runnels were to be found in most of the palaces and castles of Kregen. Uldo pushed the door open and they went through.

The room was low-ceilinged and the walls were stone-faced. Very little could be seen, for the room was filled with steam. The sounds of rushing water mingled with the hoarse thump of a bellows. A blurred halo of reddish-yellow light and a wash of heat told of a furnace being stoked to greater output. A faint cloying taint of heavy scents hung on the steam-laden air.

Uldo pointed with his switch.

"When you are told, Alyss, you will take the hot water into the bathroom. You will make sure it is very hot."

"Yes, master."

Then, again surprisingly, Uldo said, "Ninki fell and scalded herself. You will do her work until she is well."

"Yes, master."

"And there is time for you to comb your hair. Velia!"

At this Delia started, and turned pale.

A gross form waddled on stumpy legs from the steam.

The woman was vast. Her arms were dripping wet. She

wore only a grey slave breechclout. She would have made a middling-sized vosk look small. She ran with moisture. She shook. But her face with its multiple chins and piglike nose and small bright eyes smiled.

"Come on, dearie. I'll make you look presentable."

Uldo brushed moisture from his eyebrows. His expression remained that of a worried man run off his legs.

"We're short-handed, Velia, and Ninki scalds herself. I wonder if she did it on purpose. Remember, Velia, you'll have to see to it. You're responsible."

"Oh, that's all right. My lady knows me." Velia's enormous body quivered with amusement. "She trusts me."

"More than me—"

"That's because I'm a woman."

"So," said Uldo, turning to leave the steam room, "I see."

When he had gone Velia drew Delia off to the side where curtains concealed an alcove where the steam coiled less thickly. A few shelves with unguents and scents, a truckle-bed, a chest, toilet articles, indicated the place where the Steam Mistress spent her entire life. Scraps of food drying on a plate would have fed a couple of the slaves down below. Delia repressed the growl from her stomach.

"Now, let's have a look at you, dearie."

The Steam Mistress produced a cheap but ornate comb and started to tear away at Delia's scalp. Any protest would have been futile. Delia, perforce, allowed her hair to be dragged into some semblance of order. With that out of the way— "A start only, dearie, a start only, for it's in a terrible mess!"—she was washed thoroughly. There was, in any event, a copious supply of hot water. The grey slave tunic and breechclout could only be brushed and the worst of the spots either got off or rubbed over with a grey chalk. The chalk slicked in the heated atmosphere. Delia touched her face.

She had been speaking normally. The lump at the side of her mouth had disappeared. She looked down. Her legs looked the same size—almost. She fancied the left was still a teeny weeny fraction fatter than the right. The lumps noticeable on her two days ago were now quite gone. She felt and looked all over. She could find not a single blotch.

"All right, dearie, all right. You're fine. There'll be plenty of that, later on, I don't doubt."

Delia chose not to inquire what the Steam Mistress meant.

She could still feel the shock that had flashed through her when Uldo had called out the Steam Mistress's name.

Suppose her little Velia should be slave here!

"Now, Alyss. You must be quick. My lady will have her bath hot. You must run. And don't spill a drop."

"Yes, Velia, no, Velia."

"H'm," said Velia the Steam Mistress, "you'll do."

After that they waited. The water boiled in the pans. Velia gave a series of thunderous strokes upon the bellows and the furnace roared and the steam spouted. Everything was drenched in moisture. Delia adjusted the yoke, a smaller and more refined version than the one used in the kitchens. She balanced the copper pans. If they splashed and the water hit her, she'd be scalded red. They waited until the very last moment, until a bell jangled, before the boiling water fumed into the copper pans. Then Delia ran.

The bathroom next door was hot. It smelled of exotic perfumes from the far corners of Kregen. Ceramic pots of Pandahem ware bulged with flowers. Drapes hung artistically.

The bath itself lay sunk into the marble flooring. Velia had given Delia a pair of wooden-soled slippers, for the floor heated by ducts was far too hot even for a slave to walk upon barefoot. A woman wearing a long white gown and carrying a silver rod beckoned imperiously. Delia poured the water into the bath and then raced off for more.

By the time she had completed four trips she was beginning to glow a trifle.

The water in the copper pans now bubbled all the way to the bath.

"Hurry, you ninny!" commanded the woman with the silver nod. She looked harrassed. She darted to a curtained doorway and peered out, the door just cracked ajar. She turned back.

"One more, and hurry, girl!"

Delia flew.

When she returned, the water bubbling and steaming, the woman looked surprised. "Very well. One more. *Grak!*"

Delia grakked.

She was just pouring the last of the water into the bath when the flunkey woman opened the door, bowing, and a woman walked in who, immediately, took Delia's attention. She stood back, holding her copper pans still, partially concealed by the fronds of a fern, and watched. As usual with many great ones of the world, they took no notice of a slave, the grey slave clothing blending with the background.

This woman walked with studied poise. She was attended by a handmaid clad in pearls and little else, a fashion Delia considered either offensive and decadent or just plain tasteless. Some people liked the fashion, though.

Clad in a draped white gown, the woman reminded Delia of a lazy cat, curled before the fire. The latent sensuality concealed by satisfaction in her face was perfectly complemented by the perfection of her form as she threw off the gown. Her hair was not chalk-white, not silver, but of that platinum luster that so often occurred in Vallian women. The blondeness sheened platinum in the overheated atmosphere.

Her face was not remarkable for beauty, and perhaps its own icy perfection marred any warmth that lack of external beauty might have lent it. She was, judged by almost any standards, a remarkable woman.

Poised, posed, she stood on the lip of the bath. She extended one foot, the toenails painted and polished a deep purple. Her foot arched. Clearly, this moment of the bath was for her a moment of sensual pleasure.

In the next instant, she would have plunged her foot into the water.

Quite without thought, perfectly instinctively, Delia darted forward.

"Careful, my lady! The water is boiling hot—you will scald yourself!"

The woman hesitated, and in the same moment, tottered. She began to overbalance. If she went full length into that water she'd be parboiled. Delia ran. She got an arm around the woman's waist, locked into the swell of the hips, and pulled back.

In an undignified tumble of naked arms and legs, the pair sprawled on the matting surrounding the bath.

The flunkey woman shrieked.

She rushed forward and yanked Delia up. She thwacked out with her silver rod, striking Delia about the shoulders.

"Imbecile! Onker! Look what you have done!" The silver rod slashed. "Now you will be flogged jikaider until you are shredded to death!"

CHAPTER ELEVEN

Nyleen Gillois

The silver rod struck again.

Tangled up with a naked woman as she was, Delia had to make up her mind.

Her instinct was simply to get up and take the silver rod away and give the flunkey woman a taste or two. That was also the act of a slave who wished to commit suicide. The flunkey woman, dragging at her to pull her off, hit again.

With a twisting heave as though struggling to get free, Delia half-hunched around and so took the silver rod into her left hand. Naked flesh, pink and glowing, bulged up before her eyes. Concealing her movements, she gave the rod a hefty pull and then instantly rolled the other way. She started to yell, adding to the shrieks from the other two.

"Your pardon, my lady! I was trying to help!"

That vicious pull on the rod yanked the flunkey woman forward, caught unexpectedly and off balance. She staggered. In the next instant she would go head first into the bath.

Delia considered enough was enough.

She got her body in the way, rear-ended the woman off, and then bent to the other who screamed in her nakedness upon the matting. Delia hauled her up.

"There, there, my lady. It's all right. You are unhurt, praise be!"

She did not care to give the praise to any particular deity or spirit until she knew a little more of this platinum-haired woman's predilection in religious matters.

"You touched me, slave!"

"Yes, my lady. You would have been boiled—"

"Silence!" screamed flunkey-woman.

"Oh, do hold still. Ilka, do!"

"Yes, my lady."

"Now you, slave. What is your name?"

"Alyss, my lady."

"Alyss. I see. And you saved me from the boiling water?"

"I could do nothing else, my lady."

Let her chew on that one. Delia had the idea that too great a pressure on a sense of gratitude would be wasted on this woman.

"Let me look at you—" The great lady stood up, gave herself a genteel shake and, oblivious of her nudity, sized up the slave before her.

At that moment the opposite doors burst open and three hulking great warriors burst in, swords drawn, shields up, glaring and spitting, ready for blood. They skidded to a halt on the marble, and then began to hop up and down.

"My lady!" the Hikdar shouted.

"I'm perfectly all right, thank you, Nadia. You'd better leave. Otherwise you'll burn your feet off clear up to the ankles."

"Yes, my lady!" And: "Quidang!" The three Jikai Vuvushis bashed their swords against their shields, turned smartly, and trotted off. Smartly.

As though the antics of her guards cleared the atmosphere, the great lady unbent graciously. A dent at each corner of her mouth might have been mistaken for amusement. Delia stood, unmoving, silent, waiting for events. Great ladies were unpredictable—by Krun! who better than her to know that?—and it might be very necessary in the next moment or two to be cunning, groveling, tearful or grateful.

The woman flunkey, this Ilka, came forward with the white robe, which she wrapped about her mistress. All the time the pearl-clad handmaid had remained in a stasis of terror, her hands clasped together on her breast.

The great lady settled the robe about her shoulders. She drew her head up so that the platinum hair sheened.

"I have taken a liking to you, Alyss. I think it will be amusing for you to serve me. If you continue to do as well, you will do well." And she laughed, delighted at her own quip.

"Yes, my lady."

"Do you think the water of the correct temperature now?"

Delia did not hesitate. If this was how the fish felt when the hook whipped out of his mouth, she did not know. But it was a chance, and she grabbed it.

Going to the edge of the bath, she knelt down and tested the water with a tentative finger. It stung only a little.

"It stings only a little, my lady."

"Then I will chew a palmful of palines. Sissy!"

The pearly maiden jumped and blushed and ran to fetch the yellow berries so that her mistress might savor their flavor while she waited for her bath to cool.

Ilka, the flunkey woman, glowered at Delia.

When the water reached the right temperature, and Delia reported the fact, the great lady once more removed her gown and stepped forward. She dipped that purple-painted toenailed toe into the water, and smiled, and sank down into the depths. The water sluiced away from under her. Perfumes were poured in, and soft scents filled the room. The place stank rather too high for Delia's tastes, but she had been told by other ladies that her tastes were far too refined in some directions, and far too coarse in others.

Gently laving the water about her breast, the great lady looked up.

"Ilka. See to it that Alyss is taken away and bathed, cleaned up, her hair combed, given decent clothes. I think Sissy cannot teach her very much, but let her try. Then bring her to me."

"Yes, my lady."

This was done.

As they went through the performance in an adjoining and less splendid bath chamber, Delia said: "Who is the lady, mistress?"

Ilka, superintending the operations upon her new charge, sniffed.

"Why, you fambly. She is Nyleen Gillois na Sagaie, who is now Kovneva of Vindelka."

In an even voice, Delia said: "She is newly married to the kov, is she not?"

"Oh, him," said Ilka, and slapped her silver rod at the slave braiding up Delia's hair.

"Is he here?"

"No. And speak properly, girl!"

"Yes, mistress."

Presently, when they were clothing her in silver tissue and dangling strings of pearls about her in strategic positions, she said: "Mistress. Is there something I might eat?"

"Eat? You cannot be hungry?"

"I am hungry, mistress."

Ilka sniffed, as though the clepsydra had sprung a leak. "Oh, very well. You, slave, fetch food. And Grak!"

The slave girl prodded by the silver rod ran off, to return shortly with a copper bowl of bread and bird's wings, roasted in brown gravy and smothered in Tarnton dressing. Delia made herself eat it all, although she was not overfond of Tarnton dressing with its rich mixture of fruits and honeys. She liked fruit and she liked honey; but she liked them as they came and not adulterated by would-be culinary artists.

As she ate she reflected that it was sheer bad luck that her half-brother was absent. Any appeal to this Nyleen would, in her judgment, prove fatal. Quite clearly, Nyleen ran this household of slavery and Vomanus could know nothing of it all. He couldn't, surely? No—Delia would not believe that of Vomanus, despite all his feckless ways.

She consoled herself with the hope that this removal to a higher sphere within the castle would afford her better opportunities for escape.

In the old evil days when slavery was the norm in Vallia, if slaves ran off they were usually recaptured very quickly, simply because they had nowhere to hide. Once Delia ran off she'd have a very different future. Oh, yes, very different, by Vox! As she rearranged the strings of pearls and pulled the silver tissue straight she dwelled for a time on what might happen here when, say Nath Karidge, the commander of her personal bodyguard, turned up with his cavalry. . . .

"Grak, girl!" Ilka, frowning, harassed, shooed the slaves away. These slaves appeared to be a poor lot, pinched and hollow-eyed, and reserved for the most menial work. That they were employed this close to the great lady reinforced the impression of emergency everywhere apparent. At the same time Delia winced within herself at her own categorization of these poor creatures, and then she chastised herself again for that demeaning thought. People were people in the light of Opaz.

The emergency, to put it in overstatement, was easily understood. This Nyleen was from Evir, and that northernmost province of the empire had broken away, revolted, got itself a king and carried on the practice of slavery. Nyleen expected to be served by slaves. Just how Vomanus had happened on her was beyond Delia's grasp at the moment. But he had and he had married her. So here she was, kovneva of the kovnate, and damned-well determined to go on being a slavemistress. The countryside was being raided for human merchandise. Until the stock of slaves could be built up, they'd be short.

Delia fumed, hurrying along with Ilka through corridors showing every sign of new and uncompleted furnishings. This place had probably been just three or four stone towers joined by short curtain walls, an ancient sax, a frontier fort. Now they'd built new timber halls and walls and kitchens and were furnishing the whole up like a palace. Well, Delia felt even more convinced as they hurried through the antechamber that Vomanus could know nothing of all this.

Two bulky female slaves wearing just grey breechclouts and carrying a sofa with gilded legs and upholstery of a bright green and yellow shrank aside to let Ilka pass. The flunkey woman—she was called with respect Silver Rod—pushed past without noticing. Delia followed.

Through the antechamber the great lady's retiring room beyond was not quite what Delia had expected.

Yes, there were quantities of furniture in dubious taste, and feathers and fans and drapes, and side tables bearing wine and munchables. The carpets floated one ankle deep. The air stank of perfume. All this was tiresomely normal for women suddenly catapulted into affluence. But, also, there were more tasteful refinements. Three or four good pictures adorned the walls. The mirror was a marvel, tall and cunningly swiveled. In an alcove stood a harp. The instrument had not been tampered with in the sense that many women ordered grotesque carved representations of gods and goddesses to be applied all over the frame. This specimen stood upright and was there to do what it had been built to do.

Delia recognized the handiwork, of course. This one had been built by Master Nalgre the Strings, for there was no mistaking his supreme craftsmanship. He was dead now for over three hundred seasons. If she cared to look down low at the side of the soundboard she would find a name scratched into the varnished wood. Her mother had been cross. Harps, young Delia, she had said, are for playing on and not for writing your name on, as though you can claim the instrument as yours. And, in her strict old-fashioned and loving way, her mother had sent the harp to Vomanus and brought in a new one. Well, that was all a long time ago.

"Stop gawping, girl! Arrange your clothes. And recline on the lowest step of the divan!"

Stopping gawping was not too difficult, for the harp brought back a gush of memories. And reclining on the lowest carpeted step of the divan was easy. The divan itself, smothered in silks and furs, waited under its freight of feathered fans. But arranging her clothes—well, now, how did you arrange a scrap of silver tissue and few strings of beads?

She finally decided to get a string each side and the rest down the middle when Nyleen walked in. She came with her retinue. This was small. Sissy hovered, still unsure of herself. A big strapping wench waved a feathered fan, for the overheated atmosphere needed to be siphoned off and fresh air imported to make any real difference. Nadia, the guard Hikdar, led her pair of fighting women. They wore silvered breastplates, deeply curved. Delia had always thought girls comical when they adopted brass breastplates, but these girls in their breastplates corselets, breast and backs, looked likely in a fight.

"Parclear, Alyss!"

In a weird reprise of her actions with the mistress, Delia rose and poured and fetched the sparkling drink. Nyleen slouched in her divan and the others took up their ritual positions. A large dark girl wearing the black and white skin of a wersting led a couple of werstings in on leashes. These black and white striped hunting dogs had been thoroughly tamed. They hunched together for comfort, and rolled their eyes. No doubt their fangs had been blunted.

Wondering what was to happen next, Delia resumed her reclining position on the lowest step. She had seen queens and empresses in their thrones, with slaves and chail sheom, chained slave handmaids, and savage beasts chained, with handlers to control them, and enormous slaves waving faerling fans. This Nyleen aped her betters and aimed high. It was, Delia decided, comical and also farcical. Also, it was dangerous.

A bell rang. A woman wearing a deep green gown and girded by a belt from which hung many keys entered and began a long conversation with Nyleen. The kovneva listened, pettishly, every now and then sipping her parclear or taking a biscuit crumb from Sissy and throwing it to the werstings. Delia lay and schemed plans of escape.

Then she discovered what her main duties for the kovneva were to be.

She was not at all surprised.

After all, hadn't she been along this road before?

Fat Queen Fahia of Hyrklana had used golden bowls. As for that poor unfortunate wretch, rumor had it she'd been chewed up by her own vicious black neemus. In any event, as Delia's son Jaidur was now King of Hyrklana, with Lildra as queen, Fahia would never again be queen and snap her fingers for her golden pot.

Nyleen, Kovneva of Vindelka, favored silver pots with a furry rim. Much, my dear, more comfortable.

At least she retired behind a screen to wash. Delia did all that was necessary. In truth, compared with the muck and mess she'd scrubbed up in Mellinsmot, this was a mere tiresome chore. Throwing the soiled linen into the basket and washing her hands before fetching fresh, she debated if she should break this Nyleen's neck now. No. Perhaps it would be better to unriddle the puzzle first. Nyleen, aloof, her platinum hair in the almost capable hands of Sissy, returned more than once. Delia soldiered on, nursed on, sistered on.

There were no men in close attendance on Nyleen.

She managed to snatch a bite to eat now and again, for any idea of the Kregan's regular six or eight meals a day was quite out of the question. Only when Nyleen slept was Delia free to sleep. Common sense made her decide not to escape that night. Sleep was the first priority. After all, she wouldn't run far when she could barely drag herself to her new cot and fall, flat out.

The next few days witnessed a gradual improvement in her bodily strength. Soon, she bubbled with confidence, soon she'd be back to her full natural vigor.

Kovneva Nyleen's routine varied but little. When she went out riding she left her handmaids in the fortress and rode with Nadia and an escort. No banquets were held. Dancing was arranged for the next evening. On the appointed hour people began to appear in the wide hall which, now cleared of its benches, normally served as the refectory. Not a single man was present.

Being cut off from news of the outside world always gave Delia a claustrophobic feeling. What was going on, right now, in Vondium, in Valkanium, in Delphond? Had there been any news of her husband? Were her children still well?

Had the Shanks attacked again from around the curve of the world? There were a million and one items the answers to which she desperately required. Yet during this time she remained calm. She planned her escape. She stole food and clothes and found a loose flagstone and scooped a hole and hid her loot there. She was ready on the night of the dance.

The slaves with whom she had worked in the kitchens could only stare enviously. Only Silly Nath yelled out, some nonsense about cuddling that night. Nan the Bosom thwacked him over the head with her second largest ladle.

These slaves had been trundled in to stoke up the fires and provide hot food from a railed area at one side. They kept looking at the piles of food and racked amphorae, and licking their lips. Depending on what manner of slavemistress Nyleen was, they might this evening get a wet or get a thrashing.

Nan the Bosom started a racket among the slaves, fiercely accusing some scoundrel of stealing her best onion-slicing knife. "How can I make soup if I can't slice onions, and how can I slice onions if I don't have my best onion slicer?"

The knife—it had a black handle and was thin and exceedingly sharp—was not found. Naturally. By that time it lay snugged under a flagstone.

If any wight was foolish enough to try to stop Delia, then she or he or it would serve in lieu of an onion.

Nyleen showed no great discrimination among her women as to rank. All those who were free danced. The slaves slaved. Forming an opinion about the inclinations of Nyleen, Delia grasped at another thread. Nyleen detested men, clearly, and surrounded herself with women. That was her privilege up to a point. But Silly Nath was here, and other male slaves. They were not seen as men. They were seen as slaves.

The orchestra proved abominable.

Five women scraped and blew and banged away, and Sissy jangled on the great harp made by Nalgre the Strings over three hundred seasons ago. The superb instrument had been carted down to the converted refectory. Delia chose not to listen to the so-called music. But it served to provide a background and a tempo for the various dances. The lines formed and broke apart and reformed, hands joined and parted. Couples gyrated in the waltz brought to Kregen by the emperor. Eyes sparkled and teeth glistened and the glowing aromas rose.

They were circling in the dance called the Broken Vaol Paol when Delia slipped away unnoticed. In this dance the circle is broken at a certain point and a general excuse me follows as partners change in order to reform the Vaol Paol, the great circle of life of the philosophers. Delia hurried away.

Down through ways she now knew well she pattered on bare feet. Her flagstone would yield a pair of stout sandals one of the Jikai Vuvushis had spent one hell of a time yelling over and searching for. Torches cast their streaming orange hair in the night breeze. Stars prickled above. In the yard the well looked lonely without Silly Nath as its constant companion.

The kitchens still operated, pre-preparing the food for its final cooking aloft in the refectory. Delia avoided the light, skulked over to her flagstone. She put on the drab brown clothes, girded up the belt, fingered Nan the Bosom's black-handled onion knife. She put on the sandals and made for the totrix stalls.

The far doors opened on the yard and many torchlights glittered through, blowing in the breeze. The sounds of zorca hooves, the noise of totrixes and the groaning protestations of wheels reached her. A procession entered the yard. She shrank back into the shadows, cursing this inopportune interruption. Now she would have to wait until these idiots had taken themselves off.

The ornate coach which had led her coffle of slaves ground to a halt a scant dozen paces from her. Totrix riders reined in and zorcamen jangled to a halt. Lances slanted, their pennons whipping. The sound of armed men and women surrounded her. She lay as quiet as a woflo from a chavnik.

"They have begun the dance already, blast your eyes, Nath! We are late!"

The coachman turned his head. "Yes, master."

"You will be given ten strokes, Nath. Ten."

"Yes, master."

The coach disgorged a man wrapped in a cloak, a helmet upon his head, an air of force and bluster about him. He stamped booted feet. A totrix rider dismounted, flung the reins to a waiting Jikai Vuvushi, and approached this blustery blowhard of a man.

"Chica! Go and tell my sister I am here. Bid her send her tame slaves to attend me before I dance!"

"At once, jen," said that same Chica who had been so severe to the slaves in Delia's coffle on the way here. She strode off, long-legged, virile and potent, a fighting maid from sole to crown. A nasty customer, that one, judged Delia.

Looking from the shadows, listening, cursing these fools for interfering with her meticulously planned escape, Delia waited as the man Nath the Muncible approached this stamping blowhard who was Kovneva Nyleen's brother. A right pair, then. She eyed the zorcas. One of those, now, under her, and they'd never catch her. . . . Few animals on Kregen were as fleet as a zorca over ground.

"Your orders, jen?" Nath the Muncible spoke in his even voice.

"See to the men. Keep them well away. You know how my sister detests all men."

"Aye, jen. All save you, thanks be."

"She cannot do without me." The words came out big and puffed. Delia felt it time to begin to creep away in the shadows and see about a zorca. The big man went on talking, spitting his words out with venom. "She married that fool Vomanus and so we are one step nearer the throne. The moment the empress arrives and can be killed the quicker we can take the second step."

CHAPTER TWELVE

Just Delia, Playing the Harp

The empress stopped moving.

Breathing evenly, alert, motionless, still as a reptile waiting to strike, the empress crouched in the shadows and the words she had just heard reverberated in her brain.

"The moment the empress arrives and can be killed. . . ."

Escape this night, then, was out of the question.

Delia fancied she wanted to know a little more of the plot to kill her. If she ran off now . . . ? Well, she could always return with the armies, as she had planned. That way something might be decided. But she was Delia. She was Delia of Delphond, Delia of the Blue Mountains. She was Delia of Valka, and Empress of Vallia, and also queen and princess of this and that, and kovneva and stromni of other fair places on Kregen. She was honest enough to admit to herself that, while all these fancy titles might mean more to her than perhaps they ought, they weighed evenly in the scales beside her sisterhood in the Order of the Rose.

She could remember her father the emperor continually complaining because his advisers and pallans and counselors would protect him and not allow him to go running headlong off into danger. She had had a fair share of danger. But she was Delia. Of course, she was well aware that she had been influenced by her husband. He, the great hairy clansman, had been powerfully influenced by her, to their mutual joy, and he was adjusting nicely to being emperor. In this situation neither of them would be likely to run off.

The blood in their veins might boil hotly at injustice and they would do what they could to set things right. But they were no plaster saints. If they scented adventure, they were after it like a leem after a ponsho.

So, now, Delia waited quietly in the shadows, her decision taken and her mind firmly made up.

She'd dance attendance on this woman and her brother,

these two Gillois, and not only would she find out what they were up to—the pair of scoundrels!—she'd see to it that their precious schemes came to nothing. And if the pair of them ended up dead, that would be their misfortune.

Nath the Muncible moved quickly to the steps of the coach. Watching, Delia saw how he moved in a fussy and yet hesitant way. He assisted a cloaked figure to alight. Delia watched avidly. Another member of the cutthroat gang, clearly, come to join in the plot. Well, he'd lose his head as easily as the others.

The face in the hood of the cloak lay in shadow. Torchlights struck twin gleams from the person's eyes. The Lord Gillois na Sagaie stamped and turned, his sword swinging.

"Everything will be prepared for you, Sana, immediately.

The woman in the cloak acknowledged the information. The hood twisted around. For a moment, a matter of a half dozen heartbeats, she looked directly at the spot where Delia hunkered down in the darkness. Delia held her breath. The world fined down to that hooded face and those twin gleams of light from hidden eyes.

The hood turned away.

"Very well, Cranchar. I am in need of a bath and clean clothes. I do not think I shall attend your sister's dance. Convey my regrets."

"Yes, Sana, of course."

Movement followed as the Sana was escorted away by two serving girls from the coach and by Nath the Muncible. If the Sana was a wise woman or a witch, Delia could not tell, the ancient title of sana being used indiscriminatingly for any woman whose powers were beyond those of normal folk.

Time to be moving.

Nyleen would be calling for Sissy and Alyss to go off and assist the new arrivals. Delia moved like a hunting cat of the jungle, smooth and feral, soundless in the shadows.

The flagstone made a faint chiming gong note as the last corner dropped. Motionless, clad once more in her silver tissue and beads, she glared around. A hard shadow moved against a distant torchlight.

"Who's there?"

Armor clanked. A broad form blotted out the light.

"A Chail Sheom? What are you—?"

Delia leaped.

She was not fussy. She was quick and professional.

The guard's armor and helmet and sword and shield did not save him. He had marched in with his lord, and now he lay on the ground with a broken neck for all the good his zeal in guarding had done him. Delia flexed the muscles in her arms and shoulders. The fellow had needed a shave. She ran fleetly away, skillfully taking the shortest and darkest route, fled up the backstairs.

She made it back to the refectory with a second to spare.

"Sissy! Alyss! There you are, you ungrateful girl. Attend the lord my brother. Mind you are punctilious."

"Yes, mistress."

"Well, then—grak!"

They grakked.

Luckily for Lord Cranchar Gillois na Sagaie, he wanted nothing more from the girls than attention to his well-being. Hot water, towels, wine—these they provided. Anything further would have distressed Delia, for she wanted to find out about the plot against her before she slew him.

She had to allow Sissy to deal with the mysterious cloaked figure addressed as a sana, and when the two girls could talk afterward, she asked the obvious question.

"Oh," said Sissy, tossing her head, for all her uncertainty determined not to allow this new girl Alyss to oust her from her position as the number one handmaid, "Oh, she's a witch. No doubt about it."

"Ugly?"

"She had nice hair."

"Beautiful?"

"Her body was too thin."

Delia did not really care what the witch looked like; what counted was her power.

This gave credence to what she had heard at Lancival about sorcery being employed by the Sisters of the Whip, for Delia believed she had stumbled on a hotbed of that order here.

"She complained there was only one handmaid to wait on her. She was horrible." Truth to tell, Sissy did look upset. "You were lucky with the Lord Cranchar. Now he is here we shall see a few things!"

When they returned to the refectory the dance was the Pandamon Jut Gallop, a dance brought over from the island of Pandahem. Delia did not dance. She wondered just what those few things might be that Lord Cranchar would show them in a household of women. The magic grated on her, despite her shutting her ears. Presently she stood up and went across to Sissy. Nyleen was prancing with her brother.

"Sissy. Don't you want to dance? I'll play the harp."

"You can?"

"A little."

"If you make a mess of it, my lady will have us—"

"Don't worry. Look, here is a chord—" Delia swept her hand over the strings, and then pressing the round of her palm against two strings finished up with that thrilling vibrato with all its mysterious over and undertones that only a harp can fetch forth from the soul of music.

"We-ell," said Sissy. "All right."

So Delia played the harp.

The Strom of Valka had once told her in genuine and abashed amazement that he'd no idea at all that she could play the harp. Well, by Vox, and hadn't she sweated blood for season after season learning the mystery? She played divinely.

Presently the other musicians stopped scraping and blowing and banging.

Presently the dancers stopped dancing and crowded around.

Delia played on. Her repertoire was vast, culled from many races and cultures of Kregen, and she played now with a release of her feelings, letting herself, for the moment, forget her problems in the spiritual uplift and the earthy chuckle of the music. She forgot she was slave, she forget she was empress; she was just Delia, playing the harp.

When she finished and the strings thrummed into an echoing silence, she sat back, at once filled and exhausted.

No one said anything until the Lord Cranchar, slapping his thigh, exclaimed: "Sister! You have a slave there worth a sack of gold!"

"Yes," said Nyleen comfortably approving of this new source of wealth dropped upon her. "When I decide to sell her."

In his decorated evening robes, flushed from the dance, high of color, Cranchar might consider that he looked splendid in the eyes of many a woman. The women here, except one or two including his sister, kept away from him. He always had ample body space. They did not look squarely upon him, and if by chance their glances happened to meet his, they would look away with a furtive sliding motion to which he could only respond with a bearlike roll of his shoulders.

In looks he superficially resembled his twin; but his hair was of the darker Vallian brown, and his face, far from being of an icy complexion was fiery, choleric, and with the veins sprouting blue. He stamped his feet a lot. Delia rose from the harp and, demurely, made her way to where she had been bidden to sit in attendance upon the kovneva.

From then on Delia was commanded to play the harp as a regular part of her duties. She still had to run with the fur-rimmed silver bowl and the towels. But more and more as the days passed the harp-playing overtook all her other work.

Fresh batches of slaves arrived, and a certain amount of readjustment took place in slaving duties. The fortress was being turned into a luxurious palace, and remaining a fortress despite all. She was unmolested, and as she played she listened to the conversations between brother and sister, between the kovneva and her cronies—and she learned no more of the plot against the empress.

The witch, who was called Fiacola the Gaze, remained closeted in the chambers reserved for her use. She was regularly attended by Sissy and some of the newer slave girls whom Sissy attempted to train. Delia was content to remain with Nyleen, play the harp, and listen.

But, she promised herself, she would not wait forever.

If nothing more transpired of this famous plot, she'd escape and bring the army down on this decadent place. If they were all swept away down to the Ice Floes of Sicce, there'd be no more plot. Yes, by Dee Sheon!

CHAPTER THIRTEEN

Nyleen Enjoys Herself

When Delia was thrashed she told herself that she had had enough and that as soon as her back stopped hurting she would escape.

The afternoon before had not appeared any different from any afternoon. The twin suns shone. Food was eaten and wine drunk. The harp was played. Toward evening the woman in the green gown, girded with keys, Paline Pontora, the chatelaine, told her mistress that a batch of male slaves had been brought in. Nyleen nodded. Her teeth caught up her lower lip. A slumbrous look about her eyes and a marked flush of her cheeks denoted a greater significance to this information than was at once apparent.

This time the refectory was cleared of tables and benches, not for dancing but for games of a more sinister nature. The Lord Cranchar did not attend. He bore the cognomen of Cranchu, and this, alone, was enough to mark him as a man of savage temperament and cruel ways. Yet he did not attend.

The bewildered men slaves, stark naked, were herded in by Jikai Vuvushis, armed and armored. Spear points prodded narrow buttocks, whips licked expertly around shanks and backs and ears. The men yelled in pain and shuffled on in their chains. They were an unremarkable collection of men, some tall, some short, some fat, some thin. They stood in a bemused huddle as first two and then another two of their number were selected. The ladies sprawled in fascinated attention on divans and chairs about the cleared central space. Guards stood at alert, waiting for any rebellion. No doubt some of them relished the chance to lick a whip around a fellow's bottom. The sports were varied and ingenious.

All of them meant pain, humiliation and indignity for the men, and death at the end. That death was not quick in coming. The screams bouncing from the ceiling of the refectory would have chilled a listener's heart. The men were not gagged. That, it transpired, would have blunted the women's pleasure.

Delia watched not so much in horror and pity, as in a dull and futile rage.

Whatever of inhumanity woman could show to man was performed there, in iron and lash and blood, in sporting events that led through agony to fresh agony, until death could be the only winning post.

The races of the iron spikes, the hurdles of the sawed blades, the fights between men who believed that the winner might be allowed to live—only to discover their mistake when they screeched their triumph—the whiplash contests between girls who prided themselves on the skill and cunning of their whip arms—all these passed in a miasma of distant horror to Delia. She had to believe what she was witnessing. After all, many a girl had said in a passion that this was what she'd like to do to a man, to any man, to all men. It was understandable.

Nyleen craned forward on her chair, anxious to catch the moment when a man with a shock of fiery hair decided he had had enough and would beg for his death.

She snapped her fingers at Delia.

Dutifully, Delia brought forward the silver bowl.

She did not care to look at suffering and death. Also, she did not much care to watch Nyleen. The kovneva moved. Just how it happened, Delia was not sure. Nyleen was sure.

"You stupid bitch! I'm wet! Look—" Nyleen lifted herself. She shouted: "Ilka! Drag her off. Stripe her! Thrash her!"

"Yes, mistress. How many?"

"How many? There cannot be too many. . . ."

Ilka lifted her silver rod. "The harp, my lady?"

"Oh, yes, of course. Sissy, bring a fresh towel. Give the bitch twenty, then. Mind they are good and strong—no, wait. In the morning. Yes. I will watch myself in the morning."

So, in the morning, they stretched Delia's naked body out and chained her down and so thrashed her with a thin and whippy rod. A Jikai Vuvushi hit her. Ilka counted on her slate. And the Kovneva Nyleen watched.

Because she was acting the part of a slave, Delia shouted.

Truth to tell, she was not sure that she possessed the fortitude and willpower not to scream her head off.

She felt terrible. She did not faint, but the world went away from her for some time. The fire traced scorching fingers down her back. Liquid agony poured into her. Each narrow stripe shocked through her, as though some devouring monster closed his fangs on her head and chewed her right down to the soles of her feet and then back again—each time.

They let her rest all that afternoon. In the evening she was expected to play the harp.

The harp badly needed tuning, which was a difficult task. She did not consider herself to be particularly adept at tuning, although, of course, this she could do. Nyleen came in and watched her for a space, and then said: "And are you sorry, slave?"

Delia was sorry, all right. But not for what Nyleen imagined caused her that sorrow.

"Yes, mistress."

"You will not be so clumsy in future."

"No, mistress."

The girl wearing the black and white skins hauled on her couple of werstings, and the hunting dogs snuffled and followed obediently after the kovneva. There were other hounds in the other ward, opposite the yard holding the kitchens, but just how many couples Nyleen owned Delia had no way of knowing.

The kovneva walked toward Delia. Her icy face showed no emotions of compassion as she said: "They have treated your back?"

"Yes, mistress."

"That is good. You are valuable."

Nyleen put her hand on Delia's shoulder where the pearl beads clustered. She ran her hand down, over Delia's bare and scorching back. Delia gasped. The kovneva turned her hand, moved it down around the ribs and onto Delia's stomach. She rubbed, reflectively.

"When your back is mended I will have other tasks for you. More enjoyable tasks. If you have learned your lesson."

"Yes, my lady."

Nyleen fondled for a moment more and then walked off trailed by her retinue. Seething with emotions that, in this situation were ludicrous, Delia returned to the harp. Sissy had said Nyleen was gentle. Given the opportune moment, Delia did not believe that the empress would be gentle.

To make an effective escape she would have to have a riding animal. Those werstings, tame and blunt-fanged though those she had seen might be, could still run down a poor half-naked girl escaping through the forest. Run her down and hold her for the hunters to ride up with their whips and chains and nets.

She could barely manage the harp. She had no great hopes of riding an animal until her back mended.

Because she had dipped in the Sacred Pool of Baptism her back would mend far faster than these slavehandlers could expect. There was need, therefore, to pretend she was worse than she truly was. Well, by Vox, that was not so difficult!

As though her punishment was the signal for jealousy to break out, Delia found that many hitherto smiling faces were now frowning. Fault was found with her. During this period as her back mended she hoped that she sustained her spirits not by mere thoughts of revenge. She was acutely aware that she could so easily succumb to this nightmare. She could go under without a trace. But she hoped she managed to last out on a little better spiritual fare than mere revenge.

The practical teachings of the SOR as well as their mysticism helped. Perhaps she was most fiercely sustained by her loving thoughts of those dear to her. The idea that she would never see them again tortured her far worse than the scouring pain of her back.

The kovneva's personal needlewoman, a pinched-faced soul who was seldom seen, had been refused permission to practice her arts and insert acupuncture needles to ease the pain.

"Through pain shall the shishi learn to cleanse herself," pronounced the kovneva.

As a principle of life, that was pretty shoddy, considered Delia. That it sometimes occurred made no difference. Pain could so often turn a person inside out and drive them savagely against any form of kindness or human warmth, embitter them, make of them soulless devils.

She took not a grain of comfort from the fact that she had brought this on herself. If she had escaped when she had the chance, she'd have been clear away, this place would be a smoking ruin, and her back wouldn't hurt. So much for going out and seeking adventure!

And then, being Delia, she knew damn well that she couldn't have done any differently. As for doing it all again if the chance should come—well, that she would have to take under advisement, with counsel for the defense her sense of the rightness of the universe, and counsel for the prosecution these damned pains scorching down her back.

Already, therefore, she was feeling better.

Her husband often said that Kregans had a funny old sense a humor. People said that the emperor seldom smiled or laughed, yet with her in the good times he was always laughing and joking. When the bad times came and he put on that expression people called his devil face, her heart ached for him. He had been forced to do many things he abhorred, as had she. Such was the price of being fetched to be emperor and empress. She was coldly aware that without him her career as empress, had she succeeded her father, would have been much harder, more bitter and infinitely unhappier.

She knew also, without pride but with much thanksgiving, that without her he would have been morose, even more savage, intemperate and utterly lonely.

The evening passed. Delia played the harp and was aware that she did not play particularly well. Nyleen remained unrelenting.

"Play, slave!" she commanded. "Do not stop until I give you leave."

A few of her cronies gathered in her retiring room, hard, ambitious, cold women. Most of them came from Evir. They followed Nyleen Gillois in the hope that her schemes would bring rank and riches. "When the empress is dead . . . !" were words heard more than once. Delia did not catch just what the plans were after that occurrence.

She marked these women, their faces and characters, their names. She had once had a very good friend who came from Evir, and she had been totally unlike this bunch. Thelda, who had married Seg Segutorio, had been pushy and over enthusiastic, yes, always attempting to do the right thing and more often than not ending up in total confusion. But Thelda had been good-hearted, and she'd considered herself Delia's best friend, as she never tired of telling everyone, including Delia. Well, she was believed dead, now, and the last Delia had heard about Seg was that he was just about over his grief for his wife. Now he was making attempts to build a new life—going off adventuring with the emperor, for a start.

One of these sycophants, a woman hard and grainy, with a face like the blunt end of a tent peg, said: "It is a pity, Nyleen, that the fool girl died. She, at least, knew what the empress looked like."

"Do you criticize me, Ethanee?"

"No, kovneva! Of course not."

Nyleen picked a paline from the silver dish. Sissy was most attentive. "That is well. The girl died before I could make proper inquiries. I think the pity is that none of our girls went through Lancival at the time the empress was there, when she was princess majestrix. We must recruit more."

"Assuredly, kovneva."

Nyleen sucked another paline, and her face resembled the outer crags of ice that wall off the Ice Floes of Sicce.

Favoring the scorch that was her back and playing minor melodies, Delia listened. She kept her attention on two items, and two items only. One—playing the harp. Two—listening to what these people said. She would not allow her thoughts to dwell on what had happened to a Sister of the Rose who was questioned about the empress. Not yet.

"There is no more news?"

"Only that the emperor is still absent from Vondium, the Lord Farris rules as Crebent Justicar, and Drak the Prince Majister prances around in the west country fighting the rebels. The army is split between Hamal and the frontiers in Vallia. If only that bitch of an empress would come!"

"And there is no news of her since she left Mellinsmot?"

"None." Nyleen threw a paline at Sissy. She did not laugh, as Sissy, attempting to catch it in her mouth—to pop a paline—missed and the yellow berry hit a wersting, who snarled and gaped blunted fangs. "None at all. I think she went to see her SOR friends. There are rumors that their misbegotten mistress is ill. I hope she is. But—where is the empress now?"

"Lancival?"

"I expect news from there shortly."

At these words Delia hit a false note. The string twanged angrily until she stopped it. She went on playing without looking up. This one false note, apparently, was allowed to pass as a result of her beating.

If these Whip Women suborned a sister who knew Delia and she turned up here, the minions of Hodan Set would be let loose in the cant saying. Both fur and feathers would fly, not to mention silver tissue and pearl beads.

The likenesses stamped on coins, no matter how beautiful the original engraving, would never betray her. Her portraits hung mostly in the homes of friends. During the great festivals of the calendar season she would be seen by thousands of cheering people; but to them she would appear as a distant golden figure, haloed in light. The clusters of nearer nobles and guards would know her face. If she met one of them, they would treat her as the empress. It had been her misfortune to be taken up by a pack of rascally slavemongers who actively plotted against her.

Nyleen was never left alone with Delia.

Always the folk of her retinue accompanied her. Nadia and her guards; the wersting handler, a creature of northern Evir called Rinka the Stripe; Ilka the Silver Rod; Paline Pontora the chatelaine; various slaves to run and fetch and wave fans. Her cronies came and went. Her brother made punctilious appearances. If Delia could get Nyleen alone. . . .

Yes, that was one way she'd extract the information she required. She'd ask outright, fair and square. And Nyleen would answer. Yes, Delia considered, equably, Nyleen would answer.

Her back mended. She gathered other scraps of information. More people were in the plot than she'd at first suspected. The witch stayed close. And then Nyleen announced she was leaving for a visit, she did not say where, and she would be taking her retinue, including Sissy, but excluding Alyss. Recognizing that if she had not completely failed there was no more she could do, Delia made up her mind to escape this very night.

CHAPTER FOURTEEN

Cranchar the Cranchu Carouses

When she was in a hurry Delia used needle and thread in a fine free way. Her stitches were uneven, rambling, usually overlarge, generous in the amount of material she expected them to deal with. When she had the time—which was pretty damn-well never, by Vox!—she could make herself be a fine seamstress. Then her stitches were marvels of neatness and exactitude, cunning in their beauty.

Now, with the silver tissue on her knees, her head on one side, and her face puckered up into a scowl, she made herself put in neat, precise stitching. An open window in the small room she and Sissy shared let a gentle zephyr play on her half-naked body. Sissy was washing her hair in the corner, making a tremendous fuss with spilled water and splashed suds, chattering all the time.

"You should not, then, have let her tear the tissue," said Delia, and bit a thread, her teeth even and white and sharp enough to bite clean through Nyleen Gillois's jugular.

"How could I stop her —ow!" and Sissy groped in agony for the towel. "My eye!"

Rising and laying the stitching aside, Delia passed across the yellow towel. Sissy came from Evir, from a family who owned land in a small way. She was wrapped up in the fortunes of Nyleen, but she was a scatterbrain, really, and hardly responsible.

"I am sorry you are not to come with us. The kovneva likes your playing. But we could not take the harp with us, and you are in disgrace, anyway."

"You sound pleased."

Sissy stopped toweling herself and one bright eye peered out. "Oh, no, Alyss! I did not mean that!"

"I believe you."

Oddly enough, Delia did. Sissy was too open to nourish jealousy. She was far removed from the hard brittle women who clustered about Nyleen Gillois.

Now, toweling herself vigorously, she spoke in what Delia could only believe was an unthinking way.

"Still. I did laugh when you wet the kovneva."

Threading a fresh needle, Delia felt it politic not to reply. Almost immediately Sissy stopped toweling herself. With her hair standing in spikes she stared sickly at Delia. The handmaid's face shook, her mouth trembled. "Oh," she said and the saying was a gasp, "I did not mean that!"

Delia replied equably. "No one heard you."

"You did!"

"But I am your friend—am I not?"

Sissy nodded with great eagerness.

"Oh, yes!"

"So that's all right, then." The needle was sharp and Delia was careful. The silver tissue was drawing together nicely, but it was fastidious work, demanding great attention. Why these great folk liked to clothe their slave girls in this diaphanous stuff, drape them in exotic costumes, almost escaped Delia. She could see why, of course; but the act reflected scant credit on any warmth of humanity. At least, and for this she was devoutly thankful, Nyleen did not chain them up. They were not true Chail Sheom, chained obedient slaves for erotic pastimes. The chaining of women was just one of the reasons for the reactions of women like Nyleen and her cronies.

"You won't tell?"

"No. I thought you liked the kovneva."

"I do! But—she frightens me. I wish. . . ."

"Yes?"

"I wish I was strong, like a Jikai Vuvushi, and could use a sword! Then. . . ."

"Yes?"

"Nothing. The lady Nyleen is gracious and a true jena, a true lady. I joy to serve her."

"Yes," said Delia, and dragged a stitch through the silver tissue, and so spoke her mind on that, whereat Sissy gasped.

"Alyss!"

Then Ilka stormed in, brandishing her silver rod and uttering threats, so Delia had to cobble the last few stitches together, Sissy brushed out her hair at lightning speed, took the silver tissue and popped it about her shoulders and ran out. Slaves would take down her small traveling bag. Ilka looked at Delia, and switched her rod, and smiled—a smile of no friendship—and went off. Delia threw the sewing things back into their basket, closed the lid, then sat back. A puff of disgust parted her lips.

Tonight, as ever was, by the gracious Dee Sheon!

As for the name Alyss. She had used the name before in some of her nefarious schemes for the SOR. Her husband had chanced upon it, and had laughed immoderately. When Delia asked him what caused this merriment, he replied that, yes, by Zair, Alyss did live in Wonderland.

So she was left as Nyleen Gillois na Sagaie, Kovneva of Vindelka, rode out with her entourage.

The kovneva's brother, the Lord Cranchar Gillois, known as the Cranchu, remained in the castle. Almost at once a change came over the place. Instead of the light sound of women's voices, the heavier beat of men's voices echoed along the passages and halls. Serving wenches stayed close to their slave mistresses, and a wary look entered all their eyes.

Chica the battle maiden brought in a new bunch of slaves, garnered from some hell hole. The men were sent about learning what the whip could do to their backs. The women and girls were reserved for a different fate. As Delia discovered, what Cranchar and his henchmen planned would not happen if the kovneva remained in the castle.

Within a slave structure differences of status must exist. Delia, because she had been born into a slave-owning society, understood the hierarchy. She had renounced and denounced slavery. But she knew that these women dragged into the castle stood on the lowest rung. Slaves like Sissy were very near the top, and she would not have been slave at all if her parents had not run into debt and sold her. Better for Sissy had they found her a decent husband; but then, some folk could not trust gold at second hand.

Four hulking great fellows blundered into the kovneva's retiring room and took the harp down to the refectory. Delia waited for the summons. She donned a clean yellow breechclout and a tunic, old but serviceable, of a dull brown color she'd found wrapped around a silver bowl in a wooden chest. Her biological rhythms seldom gave her trouble, sometimes there was a little discomfort but almost never any pain, she was far too active a girl. She did not think that would make much difference to the slave girls below. There was much to ponder and think on as, summoned by a girl with a black eye and half her grey tunic torn off, she went down to the refectory.

The stink of spilled wine and sweat and cheap perfume stung her nostrils as she entered. Many torches blazed from sconces along the walls. The tables had been pushed to either side to form a cleared area in the center, and along the walls sat Cranchar's retainers, supping and drinking and shouting and banging their goblets on the tables, roaring.

Four girls stood at the center wearing layers of variously colored veils, and shivering. So it was to be the Dance of the Nine Veils. Each girl, of course, would be wearing only eight.

Nath the Muncible looked up from where he sat at Cranchar's right hand. His face flushed. "Here she is!"

Cranchar did not turn around.

"Play, girl. . . . You know the tune."

Without a word, Delia went to the harp, sat down, tilted it into her knees, rested her hands on the strings.

Well, now. . . .

The refectory had at a stroke been turned into a male province of hell. Half-naked wenches ran with brimming pitchers. The heat poured from the fires in the alcove where Nan the Bosom laid about her with her ladle. The food heaped high on silver platters. Many amphorae had been overturned in some tussle, and their contents ran and spilled between the cracks of the floor. No one took any notice. The stink of wine and greasy food, the yells and bangings on the table, the fights that broke out here and there and which ended in a thwack and a curse, all this pandemonium formed the background to the playing of Delia of Delphond.

She touched the strings, and brought forth that mysterious, heart-searching note from the soul of the harp.

Everyone turned toward her.

Cranchar wiped his lips and bellowed.

"Dance!"

The girls had probably been picked up from some low tavern, even a dopa den. They knew the dance, and performed it with a trembling languor that changed with the tempo into a most vigorous demonstration. Their limbs flashed. They smiled. They twirled their arms, pirouetting, posturing, and the veils flew off and floated free. When it was finished and the men set up a crowing racket of approval, the girls ran out, more drink was poured and drunk, and the next item began. This consisted of girls contorting themselves in weird and wonderful ways. Again, observing not so much with distaste as a deliberate blanking of her feelings—for now—Delia saw that these girls were professionals. They'd quite clearly been trained from very early ages to contort and twist themselves so. They were clever and agile, no doubt of that.

There was a difference in the performances of the contortionists and the dancers that did not escape Delia.

The men applauded wildly, shouting and drinking and roaring, enjoying themselves. They could not see anything odd in a girl shedding veils in a dance for their delight. The more beautiful she was, the more artful in her dance, the more they appreciated her. They did not see that to a woman who danced in this way an act of indignity was being forced on her. There were pros and cons, of course. But Delia was well aware that the Kovneva Nyleen would see in this spectacle only a familiar story of men persecuting women. She would fill her mind with thoughts of revenge, and fail to look deeper at the fundamental relationships between men and women.

The revenge taken by Nyleen here in this very room was her way of striking back. That it would solve nothing did not matter. There were ways to redress the balance; Nyleen's way was not one to be recommended. Delia sat back from the harp as the contortionists finished, wondering if her grandiose thoughts were all to be proved wrong when the next item wheeled in.

Chica must have stumbled on a traveling fair, a troupe of perambulating actors, for now a play was presented. That it was bawdy in the extreme and thus caused enormous merriment probably accounted for the gang of ruffians watching. They were scarcely followers of the playwrights acknowledged as masters and mistresses of the boards. It was all pretty crude stuff, with a deal of bladders and feathers, false noses and tails—the impersonation of a Kataki was particularly splendidly done—and a deal of falling about and head thwacking.

Delia glanced across to the alcove where the kitchen staff gawped away, fascinated. Nan the Bosom, no doubt, was busy picking up techniques of head thwacking.

During the short interludes between acts and scenes, Delia

was called on to provide incidental music, which she did. While the players postured through their buffoonery, she studied this Chica and this Nath the Muncible. She very soon came to the conclusion that what Sissy had said was right. They did not get on. Chica, so Sissy had said, awed, would slit a man's throat as soon as kiss him.

"And has Nath kissed you, Sissy?"

Whereupon Sissy had giggled in her own not-silly way, and left Delia with the assumption that Nath the Muncible and Sissy were farther along the road of romance than anyone suspected.

The atmosphere thickened. Smoke from the fires began to twine tendrils into the refectory, and a subsequent tremendous racket sorted out the damned stupid incompetent whip-fodder slaves to attend to their fires. Some of the men enjoyed that. They flexed their arms afterward. The fires were attended to; but Lart the Boil had a broken arm and Nath the Turnips had not one but two black eyes, and others of the slaves nursed their bruises.

Catching Nath the Muncible's eye as he looked at her, Delia half-smiled, and made an unmistakable gesture that she wished to leave. Nath bent to the lord. Cranchar Gillois did not turn around. Nath straightened up and shook his head.

Delia would stay and play until she was given leave to go. That was the word of the lord.

In the nature of the fight that broke out at the far end, no one knew exactly what the cause was and cared less. Two men leaped into the center, swords whickering as the players might have said, and started to knock seven kinds of brick dust out of each other. Their comrades applauded and bellowed, and bet on one or t'other. When the first lay senseless upon the floor and the second staggered with a broken left arm, the bout was considered ended.

More wine flowed, the slave wenches were chased, more wine flowed, and still no one had struck up a song. And more wine flowed. Half a dozen more fights erupted, more wine flowed—and still no singing.

"Shishivakka!" someone yelled and fell over backwards off his stool. His wine pot fell on his head.

Most of the cutthroat crew in Cranchar's band were apims, but there were a few diffs, a Khibil, a Rapa, and a Fristle whose catlike face blazed up as he yelled, "Fifivakka!"

Nath the Muncible spoke again to Cranchar. In the Muncible's posture was eloquence and urgency. Cranchar hoisted his goblet—of gold and encrusted with jewels, a pretty piece of ostentatious bad taste—and laughed and shook his head.

"Let them race," he shouted. "And a bag of gold on it!"

"Hai!" the men roared. "Hai for Lord Cranchar!"

"Clear that harp out of the way," directed Nath.

Despite his romance with Sissy, the Muncible was, Delia had little need to remind herself, a traitorous slave-mongering acolyte of Cranchar Gillois. She could expect no favors from him.

The Vuvushi Race, where girls ran and used sharpened steel to hinder their opponents, was one thing. Down at the end of the hall girls were herded in for quite another.

Slaves lifted the harp. For the first time Delia became aware of the stain in the wooden floor as a rug was skidded away. She knew how that stain had come there.

The man who had been impaled, early on in Nyleen's own games, to have bets wagered on just what he would do, the quantity and caliber of his screams, the amount of blood, and of course how long he would last before he died, had died in the end and the floor under him had been stained. Slaves had scrubbed; the stain remained. Delia moved away.

The harp was set up again to one side, nearer to Cranchar. Delia walked slowly across, carrying her stool. She did not hurl the stool at Cranchar the Cranchu. She did not wish to throw her life away uselessly.

He wore a rapier and main gauche, the Jiktar and the Hikdar. They were overly ornate. Now he took the left-hand dagger out and rapped it on the table before him.

He obtained a degree of quiet.

"Strip them. You start *there* and you finish *here!*" and he flung the dagger into the floor before the table, where it stuck and quivered. "That is your winning post."

Rapacious fingers ripped the tattered clothes from six girls, who tried to cover themselves in the uproar. The men were all jovial now, more laughter and jokes flying. If they gave a thought to what the girls were feeling the Ice Floes of Sicce might go up in steam.

Disputes arose among the men over who would be the first six. A tall fellow staggered out, ripping off his own clothes, shrieking he would ride, damn you all, and fell flat on his face, out to the world, drunkenly snorting. He was kicked aside and the six men who elbowed their way to their mounts prepared. The race was simple. The girls would gallop, run, crawl on hands and knees to the winning post, and the men would sit astride their backs and whip them on.

That was the race known as the Shishivakka.

A bag of gold pieces jingled for the winner.

Cranchar need turn his head the merest fraction to see Delia. That florid face, brilliant and flushed, swung toward her. The mouth, crimson and full, parted.

"Play for the race, girl."

"No," said Delia.

CHAPTER FIFTEEN

Shishivakka

In the general uproar, Cranchar barely heard her. He most certainly did not believe what she had said could be what it sounded like.

"We'll have 'The Agate-Winged Jutmen'—that's a good rousing tune. Play, girl."

"No," said Delia.

He heard her.

He still could not believe what his ears told him this slave girl said.

"Play!"

"No."

The noise at the far end of the refectory bounced off the ceiling. The caterwauling mingled with the jingle of bottles, the crash of overturned benches as men crowded to get a better view. Cranchar put a hand to his ear and sticking a finger in rubbed vigorously. He shook his head.

"You say you will not play for the race, slave?"

The blood rushed and collided in that already fully blown face. He gave her no chance to reply, spilling out words in a froth of passion.

"You refuse to obey? You are slave and you will obey!" At Delia's small shake of the head he roared on: "Then you will be flogged jikaider until your back is a pudding! Hai! Chica!"

But Chica was no longer in the refectory. At the first shouts of shishivakka she had gone.

A bright thrumming thrilled through Delia's head. She felt like one of the strings of her harp just touched by a cunning finger, vibrating and resonating through her out to the whole world. She deplored, at the same time laughed at, the pretensions of women like Nyleen Gillois; but she felt as a woman that she could not bring herself to play for this race. That unpleasantness would ensue was without doubt. She acted as a slave; this showed her that, despite all, she did not possess a slave mentality.

Cranchar the Cranchu bellowed his outrage. He surged to his feet, roaring. His men stopped their own roaring to stare stupidly at him.

"The slave harpist refuses to play!" The words rattled around. The men stared. And, suddenly, Delia saw this as a direct confrontation with the will of the master. The lord had ordered; a slave had disobeyed. In so petty a matter, surely, the men would say, the lord will brook no opposition.

"The whips!" screeched Cranchar.

Nath the Muncible stood up. He spoke swiftly into his master's ear. Cranchar gestured irritably, as though brushing away a pestiferous fly; but then he listened.

With graphic gestures, Nath indicated Delia's back, the harp, and then—so Delia guessed—mentioned the amount of gold the slave was worth to the kovneva. "If," no doubt Nath was saying, "if you have her whipped, how will you explain this to your sister the kovneva?"

"Very well!" Abruptly, Cranchar erupted into jovial good humor. He laughed widely, swinging his arms. "Very well! The slave will not play for the race. That is of small consequence. She shall race herself!"

Before his men had time to digest any suggestion that their lord had climbed down before the fear of his sister, Cranchar was roaring again.

"Fetch her down!"

"Make room!" shouted the Muncible. He was leaping for Delia before anyone else moved. His face blazed with anger and passion. He looked a remarkably ugly customer. He took Delia by the upper arm. He bent close.

"Listen, my girl!" He looked ferocious; he spoke softly. "You're in for a thrashing if you make another mistake. I cannot save you. You are alone. Do as you are bid and no worse will befall you."

Quietly, Delia said: "I will race; I will not play. And I do not stand in debt to you."

"Women!" said Nath the Muncible, and dragged her off.

He treated her gently. They reached the waiting group of female steeds and male riders and the old brown tunic vanished in a twinkling, torn off by greedy hands. When calloused fingers reached for the yellow breechclout, Nath struck them away. He bellowed a raucous comment on the beauty of this steed. Then he roared: "I'll do the honors. We don't want to damage the merchandise."

The yellow breechclout whisked away. Delia stood forth.

A broad hand thrust against the small of her back. She was aware of the room and the ranked tables and the inflamed faces of the men, of brandished wine goblets and heat and uproar. Then the hand knocked her over and she was on all fours on the floor.

Nath appeared in front as she twisted her head up to see. He held a rapier aloft. This would be the signal.

A hard yet soft bulk squashed down on Delia. She let out an involuntary gasp. Whoever was straddling her was broad and heavy and hot. Hands grasped her hair. A thick and hairy leg stuck forward past her left ear, and its fellow jutted forward past her right ear. She almost squashed flat into the floor. But that she would not allow.

She bunched her muscles and fought back against the weight.

The bedlam in the room continued unabated. The heat puffed into her face. The man sitting on her back felt as though he weighed as much as the Heart Heights of Valka, mountain upon mountain. She drew two ragged gasps, and Nath slashed the rapier down.

Instantly a thin, hot, scorching pain laced across her buttocks.

The bastard up there had a switch and was whipping her on.

She started to crawl forward. The floor razored off a layer of skin at every movement, or so it seemed. She felt as though she was pressed down as flat as a sheet of paper. She struggled on, her mind a blank, hearing a shrill continuous uproar, seeing only the floor ahead and the next painful place on which to put down her hands and her knees.

Seven naked girls ridden by seven men, they scrabbled their way along.

Her knees were pits of fire.

Through the blankness of her mind the idea that this just would not do rose up in letters of flame. She stood up.

The man on her back yelped and wrapped his legs around her body. He held on, one hand in her hair, the other over her shoulder. If he'd fallen off that would have been his hard luck. Delia stood up, swaying, feeling the weight. She bowed a little forward, got her breath, and then started to run.

The run was more in the nature of a stagger, a lurching struggle from side to side, one foot after the other. She knew how to put one foot in front of the other when every instinct screamed at her to lie down, roll over and die. She kept on.

The noise grew prodigious in the refectory.

The man on her back shifted his grips, deliberately, dragging on her. So that confirmed his chances.

She stumbled on.

No other girl and rider preceded her. As for winning this disgusting race, that was nothing. She just wanted to get to the winning post and free herself of this incubus.

What she looked like she had no idea. She was aware of the table at the far end, slowly, as she neared it. Cranchar was roaring with the rest, waving a wine goblet, inflamed.

She began to think she could never complete the course. Her body felt as though it were being crushed down into the floor with each step she took. The man on her back held her in such a way that it was difficult to breathe. If he pulled her hair out by the roots she would not be surprised. On and on she struggled, and her doubts grew. She could never make it to the far end! Never! But she would. Pride—damned stupid pride. What had pride ever done for her? Now—all it did was make her struggle on with this man on her back instead of falling face down, to be kicked and whipped on like anyone else.

Something like ten strides remaining. Strides! Ha! More like ten feebly tottering steps. Lurching, rolling like a dismasted vessel in a gale, she staggered on.

Eight steps, seven and six. A splinter in the floor jagged her heel wickedly, and she barely noticed.

Five and four.

Now Cranchar, drinking his wine at a gulp, tossed the goblet over his shoulder and reached for a fresh. Three steps, two . . .

The left hand dagger stuck up from the floor.

That was the winning post.

One last step. . . .

Beneath her feet the floor seemed to her to be swooping up and sinking down, nauseatingly. The man on her back clawed at her, yelling in her ear, thrashing her with the stick. She ignored him. The whole world fined down to two objects, circled in roseate fire, limned, coruscating, beckoning.

One—Cranchar Gollois the Cranchu.

Two—the left-hand dagger.

The first waved his new goblet so that the wine flew like golden rain, his face a scarlet bloom, his mouth open and bellowing. Sweat clustered on his face.

The second jutted up from the floor, its point stuck, its hilt ornately chased, and its blade a silver length of death.

The limpet on her back with his legs wrapped about her had to be dealt with. The matter scarcely warranted comment. She had not dislodged him before, and she knew why. Now she gave a rolling twist to her shoulders, smoothly shining, and shed him as she might shed a sack of laundry. He went over, spilling untidily onto his back. She gave him not a glance. The throw was merely a throw taught any girl who went through Lancival.

She lunged for the left-hand dagger.

Astonishment gripped her.

She was slow.

Agonizingly slow.

A fierce and condemnatory anger suffused her at her own lethargy. Her muscles shrieked protest. Her body felt as though she were forcing it through molten metal.

Her right hand scrabbled for the dagger.

The main gauche would not fit comfortably, the quillons and the pierced and scrolled shield baffling her desperate attempts to take up the dagger as a fighter would. She had to turn her hand over and take up the blade with her thumb to the pommel and her little finger to the blade. Upside down for a rapier and dagger fighter. . . .

Cranchar gaped for only an instant. Then he was leaping backwards, dropping the wine goblet, groping for his rapier.

Delia leaped for him.

The main gauche glittered as she struck.

A long thin rapier blade slashed in from the side. That licking splinter of steel struck the dagger down. Delia lurched on and the dagger struck ferociously into the wood of the tabletop.

Cranchar shrieked insanely.

"Spit her, Nath, you fool!"

Nath the Muncible held his rapier down over Delia's outstretched arm. She panted, heaving with the effort of drawing air into her lungs. Her legs and arms trembled. Her hair swung forward over her face, half-obscuring the fury and desire to kill blazing there.

"Lord! Your sister—"

"Then if you will not, I will!"

Cranchar's rapier was in his fist. It snouted up.

Delia drew in a painful lungful of air, twisted herself around. Nath's rapier withdrew. For a horrid instant, as she lay sideways against the table, panting and naked, she thought he would thrust her through.

The next instant as Crancher drove forward savagely, she slipped away, fell along the floor, and the dagger remained fast wedged in the table. Cranchar's rapier hissed past her head.

As she rolled over she saw a pair of thick and hairy legs above her. A bloated belly jutted above. A red face lowered toward her.

"Stay there, slave!"

The man who had ridden her in the race shouted. He shouted hard and high.

"The gold! Lord! I won—the gold you promised!"

Cranchar looked bewildered. His rapier flicked back, ready for another thrust when he could see his target. The slave girl had vanished beyond the table. Now he shook his head.

"The gold? Magero? What gold?"

A bedlam of shouts broke out at this from the men.

Magero hollered louder than all the rest, bloated, red-faced, triumphant, and not to be cheated of the gold he had fairly won.

"The bag of gold for the winner. Lord! I claim my right!"

If she'd had the dagger now she'd have stuck it straight up and Magero would have been less of a man than he was.

But he had told her to stay there, to lie still. Now he was yelling angrily that, by Vox! he'd won the gold promised. He reached for the bag upon the table, near where the dagger jutted.

"My gold!"

Something soft crashed into Delia and she sprawled half-under the table. A naked girl with limbs flailing fell with her and the man riding the girl's back toppled over them. The rest of the field followed. Most of the girls dragged forward in complete exhaustion. Blood stained the floor in their tracks. One girl, with blonde hair and a heavy body, screamed and screamed as the man riding her whipped her on.

Magero was yelling for his gold. Cranchar was shrieking for the slave wench to be dragged up for him to spit. The girls were crying and sobbing, two or three simply flopping over and sprawling still, and their riders were fiercely arguing that Magero's mount had cheated. Nath the Muncible appeared.

The whole scene sickened Delia. She felt nauseated.

"You said you do not owe me anything, Alyss. This may be so. I do not stand to suffer for you." The Muncible's face was pale, his nostrils pinched. He reached for her and took her shoulder in a firm grip. "Up! And speak small before the lord."

She was standing, swaying with Nath's hand on her shoulder. She realized she would probably fall if he had not supported her. That made her think. She had thought very little since she'd first said "No!" to Cranchar the Cranchu.

"The girl won fair and square," said Nath. "Magero has won the gold, lord. Your sister the kovneva—"

The rapier in Cranchar's fist glittered in the torchlights. He moved uncertainly, scowling.

"I know, Muncible—and you run in peril—"

Nath let go of Delia's shoulder.

Instantly, she fell down.

Truth to tell, that collapse was not entirely fake. She felt as though she could not have stood up a moment more. She fell and sprawled on the floor, covering herself, and so lay motionless.

Let the bastards sort this one out!

A considerable commotion persisted, with catcalls and yells boiling up as men argued intemperately among themselves. Delia lay still. Some said she had won fairly, others that she had cheated by standing up.

The man who had come in second struck his girl.

"You stupid shif! Why did not you run?"

The girl held her knees and crooned in pain.

"I could not, master—"

"My gold!" Magero would not be put off.

"Cheat!" Shrieked the man he had beaten.

"Say that again—"

"Cheat!"

Magero roared into action. He and the man who had come in second, Naghondo the Squint, tore into each other.

In a wild and unscientific flurry of heavy-handed blows they started to bash each other about the head. Magero landed a pile-driver and Naghondo staggered back, only to yell and spit out a tooth and come windmilling in again. They wrapped their arms about each other, massive hairy bodies fast locked, and fell down, struggling and writhing and trying to throttle each other. Delia lay still.

Nath hoisted her up.

Over the din he shouted: "The slave has fainted. You!" to a scared slave girl, whose pitcher of wine slopped in her terror. "And you!" to another, who dropped her platter of palines. "Take this stupid slave girl to her quarters! *Grak!*"

Helped by Nath, the two girls somehow heaved Delia up and started to carry her off. The fight between Magero and Naghondo rip-roared on. Men ran out from the tables to form a ring and cheer. The girls, trailing blood from their knees, staggered away. The bag of gold lay on the table by Cranchar, the left-hand dagger sticking up at the side. Cranchar stared hotly at Nath and the two slave girls, at Delia's form as she was carted off, a limp and lovely burden.

"I haven't forgotten!" he said. He slapped the rapier down. "She will recover from her faint. Then we will see."

Nath, bent over, hurried on. The two slave girls, whimpering, grasped various portions of Delia's anatomy and helped.

Swinging back to the fight, Cranchar, his blood up, bellowed his bull roar over the noise. He was caught up at once in the new combat.

"Fight for your gold, Magero! If you win, you win the gold. If you lose, then your mount cheated!" He looked enormous, bloated, scarlet-faced, once more in command. "Let the gods decide!"

CHAPTER SIXTEEN

Magero's Gold Piece for his Little Paline

Most of the next day Cranchar spent with his women closeted in the chambers of the tower reserved for his use. His men rampaged within this tower, and the noise broke over the walls and roofs of the fortress like surf driven before a gale. Slaves cleared up the refectory and put the place to rights before the kovneva returned.

Of the other three towers built of stone, one contained Nyleen's quarters and the small rooms of her handmaids and slaves. The next contained her fighting women bodyguards. The last tower's contents were unknown to Delia.

She felt humiliated, dirtied, her pride grossly affronted.

She tried to tell herself these were irrational reactions. They left her alone that next day to recover. This was, she surmised vaguely, because Cranchar was either roistering on or sleeping it off, and there was no one left prepared to take action. As for her own feelings, these were murky and passionate.

Some of the girls, apart from the pain in their knees, had accepted the Shishivakka race as a mere part of entertainment, what men expected, and therefore tolerated because there was nothing else they could do. Certainly, and to Delia incongruously, Magero sent up to her by a little slave girl a single gold piece.

"Magero the Obstreperous bids me give you this, Alyss," said this girl, wiping her nose. She was scrawny, unkempt and as appealing as a cold haddock. The gold piece shone on her dirty palm.

"Put it on the table, Limi," said Delia. "And go."

"Do you not send thanks?"

"Get out!"

The door cracked shut. Poor Limi . . . And, this gold piece

in thanks from Magero meant he had won the fight with Naghondo the Squint. He was big enough, the hairy monster.

So then, of course, to add to her woes she had to feel guilty about shouting at poor Limi, who was just a skinny little slave girl. As soon as she was up and about she'd make it up to her; probably an extra helping of whatever was the tastiest dish of the day would soothe Limi's hurt feelings. Delia was only too well aware that slaves had feelings.

Jumbled up with her own feelings about the race were the problems surrounding this Nath the Muncible. Certainly, when she brought her armies down on this place, this sink of iniquity, why should he not die along with the rest?

He had gone out of his way to afford her what protection he could. He had run perilously close to disaster. If this puffed-up bladder, this Cranchar, had been half the lord he fancied himself, then Nath would be walking around headless. Had Cranchar been of that breed of lord of Kregen who did not lightly tolerate interference with their desires, Nath would be done for.

Only the thought of Nyleen, the kovneva, kept her brother in check. Nath had played on that. Delia found, and with alarmed surprise, that she was actively looking forward to the return to Nyleen.

Almost unimaginable!

During the late afternoon she found strength enough to rise. She bathed and washed her hair and brushed it out. The thought of that flagstone with its loot hidden beneath tempted her. Well, and why not? Surely there would be fresh unpleasantness when Nyleen got back. Cranchar would fabricate some story to have the impertinent slave girl up to her neck in trouble. Gold was gold, and pride was pride. The two Gillois hungered for the one and allowed the other, perhaps, to overpower their actions. Once Nyleen was persuaded, Cranchar would have a free hand. Delia did not relish that prospect. Tonight, then, and may the luck of Eos-Bakchi the Five-handed be with her!

She prepared herself, physically and mentally, for the tasks ahead. Stealing a kerchief of food was not overdifficult, the most dangerous part being to dodge the swipes of Nan the Bosom's third largest ladle.

Silly Nath was all agog about the race; but Delia shooed him away—very gently—and skulked back to the room she shared with Sissy. The odd thing was, without the girl there the room appeared bare and lonely. She locked the door with Sissy's bed jammed against it, put a pot to hand in case anyone tried to break in, and then composed herself on her own ramshackle bed.

Obnoxious.

Yes, that was the word she would use about this place. The slaves were cowed in their fashion, and full of energy when a master or mistress appeared. They carried on their own way of life, as it were below stairs, and contained their own febrile strengths. But this place was obnoxious. She did not know its name, although she'd heard Nyleen and her cronies speak of Veliganda as though they might be referring to this fortress. Anyway, whatever its damned name, it was obnoxious.

She lay on the bed, then she got up and prowled about the room. She picked up the earthenware pot, and hefted it, and swung it through the air a few times.

Here she was, cowering in her room until dark, frightened of every footstep in the corridor outside, wondering if some drunken lout would break in. It just wasn't fair. Girls could learn tricks, stratagems, cunning twists and grips to deal with men, but a man's brute strength remained a man's brute strength. By Vox! If any drunken bastard broke in here he'd have a smashed head and caved in ribs and go reeling out clutching himself and with a face as green as Green Genodras!

It was all very well taking a lofty world view when you sat on your throne in your palace wearing a crown and with regiments and fleets and aerial forces at your beck and call. But when you sat in a little room with only an earthenware pot to defend yourself with—world views reduced in importance and took a back seat.

Cunning, intelligence, skill and courage. They were just about the only weapons she had. She might have taken a pride in her use of the old standby of women through the ages down in the refectory. Women who were blinded by anger, like Nyleen, would condemn and have only contempt for that particular stratagem. But the faint had been splendid. She'd fainted clean away, swooning beautifully, and that had got her out of it.

Footsteps passed in the corridor, and she tensed up, and then only half-relaxed as the heavy tread passed on.

If she could have taken on in a fight all Cranchar's men,

and bested them, she would have. But that behavior did not belong in the logical world, that was of the stuff of the shadow plays and mimes hawked along the souks of the great cities of Kregen. Actors might fight whole armies and win, tiny girls might put to rout regiments; she was a mortal girl.

The slot of light falling from the window in mingled streaming jade and ruby slanted further along the floor, began to creep up the wall. The Suns of Kregen were declining. When the shadows fell, she would move. And woe betide anyone who got in her way!

With these brave thoughts to make an attempt to sustain her, she waited.

Once, and once only she allowed herself to think of her husband. If he was beside her now, had he been there, last night, in the refectory—well, and perhaps the shadow plays would have been proven true.

Even though he had changed greatly, she knew with utter conviction that before anyone bestrode her in the Shishivakka race, her husband would be dead. And, equally, the refectory would have been awash in the blood of Cranchar's men. As for the Cranchu himself, a Krozair longsword would make his head leap from his shoulders. . . . Idle dreams, girl! she told herself. It's all up to you, and you alone. . . .

The gold coin sent up to her by Magero lay on the table. It gleamed erratically as the slanting light of the suns glanced across the surface. It showed a worn portrait of Delia's grandfather on the obverse, and a trophy of arms on the reverse with the exhortation to Support Vallia.

She did not touch the coin. The exhortation to support Vallia reminded her that these people here causing all this woe were Vallians. She had demonstrated her reactions to Magero the Obnoxious and his gift by shouting at a poor little slave girl. Limi had jumped with fright. That reaction, it seemed to her, was perfectly natural. But, wait a moment . . . Magero had bothered. He had shouted at Cranchar. There seemed the distinct possibility that he held some petty rank, that he was not as cowed as the other henchmen. This gave her to ponder.

When he'd changed his grip on her, she had promised to chop him. But he might merely have been making sure of his hold, not wishing to fall off. That reading of what had happened was admissable, grotesque though it might seem. The way nature had constructed men and women with only two arms meant that certain holds could not but fail to fall in certain places, willy-nilly.

She glared at the kerchief of food. That would be required after the escape. But she was hungry. Slaves were entitled to eat, for they had to maintain their strength in order to serve their masters and mistresses.

Going down the backstairs to the kitchens this time called forth a greater degree of resolution. She felt as a small animal must feel, penned at the end of its burrow, knowing the savage predators approached nearer and nearer with every passing heartbeat.

A new chief cook was on duty. The old one, Naghan the Meats, had been ill and unable to work, and Nan the Bosom had stepped in. Now she showed her feelings about being relegated back to her soups by thwacking about with her various-sized ladles, each increase in size a measure of her mounting displeasure. The new man, a slave with uppity airs, was Ornol the Rasher, for his specialty was vosk rashers served in a hundred and one different ways. He looked at Delia as she came in, and Silly Nath darted across with an urgent query about the well.

"You should be out there, Silly Nath, not lollygagging about here!"

"Yes, master. But the handle is split. . . ."

Ornol the Rasher threw his hands up in despair. He looked porcine, flabby, with a sheen to his skin. His grey slave tunic bore a yellow and ochre favor. "All right. I will look."

Nan the Bosom, when they had gone, said: "He'll never last." Delia ducked the swing of the third largest ladle.

She found a hunk of bread and a bowl of soup, and Nan looked the other way. As any slave would say, a slave has to eat.

Had she cared to consider the matter, it was a measure of her own personality that these kitchen slaves had not turned hostile and jealous when she'd been promoted out of the kitchens, rising in the slave hierarchy, to be harpist.

The soup was good, a thick ordel, and she wiped the bowl with the crust of bread and wolfed the lot down. She decided not to return to her room but to wait out the last of the Suns here and then steal out into the yard.

Then she made a mistake.

Thinking to take herself out of harm's way, she went off to one of the small storerooms. This one held flour sacks. She spread a few empty sacks and lay down, continuing to build her strength for the night's operations. There Magero found her.

He was not drunk. He had been drinking, and he carried a flagon of good red, and he was flushed and jovial and sweaty, but he was not drunk. He smiled. His teeth were gapped. He wore a lounging robe of a lurid pink and blue, and he carried a basket of food of better fare than slaves were provided. Quiveringly alert, Delia was aware of his bulk, and of his belt of plain leather—with cheap bronze fittings—and of the rapier and main gauche. The belt also swung lockets for a clanxer, the straight cut and thrust common sword of Vallia.

He called her his Little Paline. This was a compliment.

"You ran well, girl. I won the gold. That buffoon Cranchar could not deny me, not after I knocked Naghondo's squint straight for him. Ha!"

She said nothing. She drew herself into herself, warily.

"I like you, my Little Paline. For a slave you are beyond beauty—I have never seen anyone to match you." He put the red wine down and spilled some food in placing the basket. "I feel we are soul mates. We have much in common. We serve a master who does not appreciate us."

Delia wet her lips. "The kovneva—"

"She will whistle, and Cranchar will come groveling like a beaten cur. I have seen it." He smiled gappily. "But I have not come here to talk about onkers like that. You had the gold piece? Or did that slave shif steal it away?"

"No, no," said Delia. She did not want to bring more trouble on Limi's head. "I had the gold piece."

"You see! You see how generous I am. And I can be much more generous. Much more, if you are nice to me."

Delia decided on a course of action that would have aroused contempt in women like Nyleen Gillois.

"You are so big and strong, and you fight well. Yet you speak ill of the lord. Perhaps it is not safe to know you."

"Safe? Of course it's not safe! Cranchar fears me, for I can see through him. Come here, girl, and take off your tunic."

"Should I not dance for you, first?"

"You have no veils, and I am sharp set."

He reached for her, and she slithered away on her bottom. Standing up, and making herself smile, she undulated around him, keeping out of the reach of his hairy arms. This was ludicrous; she had to have him dead to rights before she hit him, he was such a great lummox.

"You entrance me enough! You need not dance for me!"

"Oh, Magero, you great zhantil of a man! Do I not dance well?"

She was gyrating and swaying, and weaving her arms about and smiling, her head on one side. Magero gaped. Sweat stood on his brow.

"By vox! You overpower me, my Little Paline!"

She reached up to the latch on her tunic, and undid it, and flapped the grey cloth down and then up. The tunic was one of Sissy's, and was a tightish fit. She danced lightly around, avoiding him, and he lumbered after her, sweating with passion. Now if she'd choosen the firewood shed, there'd be a handy length of lumber to hit him over the head with. . . .

"Come here, sweet! I am ready for you!"

Despite the desperate appearance of this situation, Delia felt close to hilarious laughter. It was comic, this tantalising of this great man mountain. She'd have to take him with bare hands, get him in a grip, and hope to finish him quickly. But he was so big, and—unfairly, unfairly!—so mannish brutish strong.

Her plan was this—she undulated around flapping the grey cloth down and up tantalisingly so that his eyes boggled out on stalks—she'd come in close, let him slobber all over her, and she'd have the rapier and main gauche out quicker than he could think. Then the weapon used would be up to her . . .

She circled to face the door and advanced. He broke into a great slobbering smile and opened his arms wide to enfold her. She moved in quickly, and felt his paunch slog into her stomach with a grunt. Her hands dropped to the hilts of the weapons. He was kissing her neck—and over his shoulder she saw the door open and Naghondo the Squint appear. The man's face bore an expression of vicious hatred. He lifted the bludgeon and brought it down with savage and unerring accuracy on Magero's head.

Magero dropped soundlessly, sliding away from her.

Naghondo leaped in.

"That'll teach the bastard! And I'll carry on where he left off! C'mere, girl! You're mine now!"

CHAPTER SEVENTEEN

A Zorca for Two

To speak thus to Delia when she was unarmed was one thing. Even had she been wielding her earthenware pot, perhaps. But to speak thus to Delia with a rapier and left hand dagger in her fists was to commit a grievous error.

The point on which she chose to check this Naghondo and show him his error amused her. It created a pleasant frisson.

"You claimed I cheated in the Shishivakka race, you great blowhard oaf! Draw your rapier and we'll see if I cheated."

"Do what?" He looked completely flabbergasted. The billy lowered. He looked stupidly at the rapier and dagger whose points hovered before him. Then he let rip a great bellow.

The roar was compounded of amusement, not even of contempt.

"C'mere, girl! I'll show you what fun is!"

Had she been of the truly murderous kind she sometimes thought she was, Naghondo would have been dead by now. When she thrust, he had time to skip back to the doorway. He looked puzzled. Then his face cleared. "You wish me to show you? Right!

He whipped out rapier and main gauche and bore in.

"I'll show you a few things, my girl, and then I'll show you a few more. Hai!"

She realized he intended not to spit her but to hit her with the flat, punish her for her effrontery. That was his misfortune. She did not stop to curse herself for not having the courage to stick him through on the instant. She set herself, met his first attack with ease, set up her own attack, and missed the final thrust as he stumbled away and only took a sliver from his ribs.

"You bitch!"

Now he came in with more deadly intent.

Circling him, feeling the strength of his wrists, the speed

of his reflexes, sounding him out, she was aware of faces looking in at the door. Well, this was a free show. Come one, come all. She'd have to remember to put out a hat or a bowl to collect the copper obs after the show.

Then she banished thought and allowed the transparency of the sworder to enter her soul.

Naghondo was a fair hand with the rapier, but he was not in her class, nowhere near. She circled his bald attacks, checked his twinned onslaughts, the left-hand dagger held and deflected out of the true line. She stuck him through the arm and he yelped. Then she stuck him through the other arm, and he yelped again. He staggered over Magero's prostrate mountain of a body and twisted and fell.—She stepped in, smoothly, rapier ready to dart down and finish him.

Hands grabbed her shoulders and waist. She was dragged back. A rapier pointed at her midriff, and Chica said: "Enough, girl. You think you are a sworder—well, desist, or you will meet someone who knows the Jiktar and the Hikdar."

"Treat her gently," said Kovneva Nyleen, over Chica's shoulder. "She is worth gold. Bring her to me when I summon. The rest of you carrion crows—back to work! *Grak!*"

The rush and scurry to obey cleared the area outside the door of the flour storage. Nadia with her bodyguard crowded up, carrying their weapons. Nadia's full-fleshed face looked savage.

"Let me at her! I'll show her what rapier work is!"

"Yes, yes, Nadia, you are very good," said Nyleen. "But the girl is deranged. She is a harpist. Not a Jikai Vuvushi."

"All the same, my lady," said Chica, taking the rapier and dagger from Delia. "She seems to know one end of a sword from the other."

Nyleen looked scornful. "Naghondo cannot make a fist of rapierwork. He should stay with his clanxer. That is more his mark. And I shall want to see my brother over this."

"Quidang!"

Nadia looked disappointed she was not to have a bout, and Chica led Delia off. Nyleen did not even bother to speak to her slave harpist.

As for that same slave harpist, she was so savagely condemning herself as would have made all the saints in The Golden Grottoed Halls blush. *Why* had she been so stupid?

Why hadn't she just got on with escaping? *Why* hadn't she killed these men instead of trying to be so clever? The excuse that Nyleen had returned and so scotched any escape plans was merely an excuse. Damn the woman! *Why* had she skulked in the flour storage? It was all so—so *infuriating!*

Also, it was deadly. . . .

Nyleen was saying in her hectoring voice: "What's that there, Magero? Give him a kick and rouse him. Is he dead? That would not worry me. He is getting too big for his boots. My brother, will have to watch him . . ."

The sound as of some leviathan of the deep breaking the surface and uttering a distress signal would be Magero the Obstreperous regaining consciousness.

Naghondo the Squint, carried off, complained loudly and bitterly that the fool girl had only stuck him because he'd fallen over that oaf Magero. Since when did a slave shishi know anything about swording?

The reason for the puzzlement and clash of sympathies in these women was perfectly plain. They were women. A man, a common brutish man, had attempted another woman, who had defended herself—and with naked steel. But the woman was a slave, a nothing, one of the grey ones. Where should sympathy lie?

The last Delia heard before she was assisted up the stairs was a fruity bellow from Magero, frothing.

"The girl was my steed, Naghondo the Squint! Not yours! And she has a fire you don't understand." The spluttering voice pounded out words that must have caused Magero's aching head to throb even worse. "If you touch her I'll have your tripes!"

Stupid to warm to man-mountain Magero the Obstreperous. . . . Still, the idea of having Naghondo's tripes spilled out wasn't altogether a bad idea, at that. . . .

When they'd dumped her back in her room, Nadia looked back, scowling, and said, "One of my girls will stand outside your door until my lady sends for you. Keep you out of mischief. Mind you behave yourself, slave."

She stretched out on the bed, feeling her bruises, and contemplated with thoughts that were exceedingly hot the fiasco of the evening. What a leem's nest she'd made of it all!

Not being in the habit of feeling sorry for herself, she

didn't lament over that end of the mess. And to start longing for what might have been was worse. She'd just have to start over.

But it was cruel, damned cruel, by the disgusting diseased left eyeball of Makki-Grodno!

So that little memory of him made her feel even more determined and, truth to tell, even a little better.

Then Sissy waltzed in, prattling on, all agog, and with a few words upended all Delia's plans. Delia experienced a piercing shock. She trembled and went pale. Sissy, chattering on, did not notice.

"Yes, Alyss, I know you have had an exciting time. But my lady is fond of you, as she is of me, of course. And dear Nath will do all he can." Sissy's rounded shoulders drew back as she thought of Nath the Muncible. Then: "And with the poor kov so near to death in the Lud Tower, who knows what is to become of us?"

"Kov?" Delia's words croaked.

Sissy, busily unpacking, rattled on. "Poor Kov Vomanus. He is like to die, and the needlewoman can do nothing. It is very sad."

Delia stood up. She swallowed down and some of the bile went away. Vomanus was a reckless scamp; but he *was* her half-brother.

"In the Lud Tower?"

"So dear Nath said. Alyss! You cannot go out. There is a Jikai Vuvushi, and she was very strict with me when I came in. Alyss!"

Delia opened the door.

The Battle Maiden was hefty, big-breasted, thick of thigh, with a high color. Delia put an arm around her neck, above the gilt-rimmed corselet, and twisted. She did not kill the girl. She dragged the unconscious body into the room and, unheeding Sissy's squeals of terror, stripped the armor. She put it on. It fitted here and there, for, and she would not say it herself, there were few, very few, women in all of Kregen with so perfect a figure as Delia of Delphond. She strapped on the weaponry.

Sissy, hand to mouth, face green as Genodras, watched. The girl's eyes rounded into enormous terror.

Delia tied up the Battle Maiden herself.

"Now, Sissy, you know nothing of all this. You will not

tell anyone, not Nath, not anyone. If you do, I shall come back and cut off your head."

Sissy started to cry.

Delia resisted the impulse to put her arm around the girl's shoulder and chide her for a silly goose. She looked very fierce, said, "Remember, Sissy, your head!" and marched out.

The helmet was of that curved pattern that both allowed freedom of movement of the neck and shielded the cheeks. Delia's face was, therefore, partly shadowed. She tilted the helmet forward. She marched with a swing, just like any of your battle-hardened Jikai Vuvushis. She stared with utter contempt and loathing upon Limi who was creeping along carrying a linen-covered bowl. Limi shrank away. Delia strode on.

Sissy ran out after her, distraught, and then raced off in the other direction. If the girl had any sense she'd have stuffed the Battle Maiden under the bed first. And, if Sissy babbled out her news—why, then, that would mean that Delia would have to start fighting in real earnest. Somehow her blood was up. Somehow she was invigorated. And, she told herself sternly, that could not be just because she was concerned about someone other than herself, could it? That was to admit to a silly kind of perverse self-love.

Making her way to the Lud Tower at this time of evening when some of the torches were lit and others were not was not overly difficult. No wonder she'd not discovered what existed inside the fourth tower. The ward rang hollow under her Battle Maiden's sandals with the iron studs. Her equipment clanked. That wouldn't do for any regiment Delia commanded. A guard stood at the lower doorway. The torch was lit and helped by contributing its quota of shadows to conceal her face.

"What do you want, dom?" inquired the guard in an unfriendly voice.

"Why, dom—nothing that concerns you—" The blow was swift, unexpected, and hard. The girl collapsed. Delia dragged her into the shadows inside the doorway and then started up the stairs. The place stank of damp and dust and disuse. Nyleen hadn't as yet gotten around to redecorating in here, then.

The kovneva was very sure of the kov. There remained only two more guards and a couple of werstings on the second landing.

The guards, being human, could be knocked out without trouble. The werstings presented a more formidable obstacle. . . .

The black and white striped hunting dogs snarled at her, exposing yellow fangs. Their tongues lolled. They were chained through slots in the wall so that she could not pass without putting herself within their range. Their fangs had not been blunted. She took out the Jikai Vuvushi's terchick, hefted the little throwing knife, hurled. Even as the first wersting yowled at the steel sliver in his neck, trying to bite and scrape it off, so the long slender steel of the rapier slid into his mate. Feeling disgusted, Delia stepped back.

With the blood-stained brand in her fist she ascended the last flight of stairs and pushed open the door at the top.

In the dimness she could see little apart from a vague rectangle of radiance from a door in the room's far wall. Something moved, and a trembling voice said: "Majestrix!"

"Quiet," said Delia.

A chain clanked. The voice said: "I would give you the full incline, majestrix, but these cramphs have chained me up."

He spoke in a low voice, heeding her injunction to be quiet. Evidently, he knew her. She said: "Kov Vomanus?"

"In the inner room, majestrix. I fear he is near death."

She went in, kicked over a stool, peered about. Her eyes could make out objects better now. The man was, indeed, chained. His straw pallet was filthy. A few scraps of bread in a wooden platter looked stale. His hair stood up in spikes.

The far door beckoned her. But she paused to say: "You are?"

"Larghos Ventil, majestrix. I serve the kov—"

"Yes. I will see what I can do for you."

She went through into the far room. She put a hand to her nose instantly, gagging.

The light from the arrow-slit fell across the haggard face. Vomanus did, dreadfully, look close to death. She held herself within herself. Sickness . . . Suffering . . . Disease! How she loathed all this ghastly business!

"Delia?" The fluttery voice barely stirred the stifling air. "Delia?"

"Yes, Vom. It's me. I'm taking you out of all this."

"Yes, but—Nyleen—?"

"Do not fret."

Vomanus looked as though he might be in the process of being starved to death. That would be like the dark revengeful soul of Nyleen. He tried to rise, and she shushed him, and turned back to the outer room.

"Larghos—the keys?"

"The guard, majestrix—with the werstings."

"Yes. And do not call me majestrix, as you love your life. If you must, call me Sishu."

"Yes, my lady, yes, Sishu."

She went out and down the stairs, the rapier held just so and ready to rip into the throat of anyone attacking her up the stone stairs. The guards still slumbered. The werstings looked pathetic, slumped in their own blood. She tapped the two guards again, just to make sure, wondering when the guard Deldar would come by to change the sentries, snatched the keys off the uglier girl's keyring and darted back up.

She had been gone a bare score of heartbeats, but already Vomanus was querulously demanding where Delia was.

"Hush, Vom. I'm here." She threw the keys at Larghos Ventil and went through to bend over her half-brother.

"Nyleen," he said. "She tricked me. I thought she was—"

"Yes. Where are your clothes?" Then, berating herself, she looked. The clothes, splendid wedding gowns, lay bundled in a chest. She dragged them out and then Larghos was with her and they began to dress Vomanus. He was wasted to skin and bone.

"Nyleen is a wicked woman," he babbled. "She is mad, quite makib. She plans to be empress of Vallia."

"Yes, yes, Vomanus, my dear. Put your arm through here. Larghos! Do up those laces! Hurry!"

"Yes, Sishu."

"She plans to kill you, Delia. Kill you!"

"I know."

"She sent the wedding invitations, all smiling, and she waited to kill you and you didn't come. I was glad."

"How did she manage to bring you to this?"

He shivered.

"Fiacola the Gaze. . . . Sorcery!" He glared up, and reached out a withered arm to grasp at her dangling pteruges. "Witchery!"

"If you don't let go I can't dress—there, that's better. Larghos, a blanket! And how was she to be empress?"

"Why, she plans to marry the emperor. Then, she will kill him, too. She and her brother—"

"Kill the emperor!"

And then Delia saw the comic side of that. "*Marry* the emperor!"

"When you are dead."

"Well," said Delia, Empress of Vallia, lifting the shriveled form of her half-brother off the bed. "Well, we will see about that!"

"Oh, she will marry him. Her witch is strong. I—I—"

"Yes. Now keep quiet. If there is any fighting to do I shall have to drop you."

"Sishu? Should not I carry the kov?"

She laughed. A small gurgle in the dimness. "So that I can do the fighting myself? Unimpeded? Why, Larghos Ventil, I was hoping you would help with the fighting."

"Yes, majes—yes, Sishu."

Down the stairs they went. "Give those two another tap, Larghos. Do not kill them."

He picked up the girls' abandoned weaponry, and tapped them, and then crept on. The guard at the bottom still slumbered, for Delia had dealt with her more severely, but Larghos tapped her, just to make sure. A big fuzzy pink moon floated above, the Maiden with the Many Smiles, and this did not please Delia. The overpowering scent of moon blooms reached her, strong on the night air. Sounds of the usual fortress business floated up; there were no shouts of alarm.

She started off for the tricky busines of penetrating back to the yard and Larghos said: "The stables are this way."

She stopped. Of course there would be other stables. She said nothing, but followed Larghos as he led off in the opposite direction, skirting the tower, heading for the far corner where the stone walls ended jaggedly and the new wooden ramparts joined. In the angle stood a small door. At the side leaned sheds. A zorca stamped his hooves and blew.

There was one zorca.

Delia let fall an unladylike remark.

A girl slave passed carrying a bucket. The moon shone. The moon blooms drowned the night in perfume. And there was one zorca.

The girl slave vanished around the corner. Delia lifted Vomanus into the zorca's saddle which Larghos, with practiced skill, had already cinched up. The saddle animal was a splendid example, belonging to the guard on perimeter patrol, and, like all zorcas was so close-coupled as to make riding two up difficult. With a little give and take and a squash it could be done. She had felt the strength flowing in her arms and back and thighs when she'd lifted her half-brother. He would have to go, of course. But she could scarcely ride off and leave Larghos Ventil. She could do so, of course, and he would understand and accept the proprieties of her decision. For she was the empress. And that was the kind of thing empresses did.

Delia was not and never could be your ordinary mundane kind of empress. If she wanted to do something and it didn't hurt anybody else, she'd damn well do it. If it didn't discommode them too much, she'd do it. . . . But in this . . . ?

Torchlights blazed up from the darkness. Through the gateway separating this ward from the next lurid light flickered. Orange highlights bounced on the stonework of the tower. Shouts raised, heavy angry bellowings. The heavy beat of warsandals cracked out, iron studs ringing against flagstones.

"Up with you, Larghos. Hold the kov firmly."

"But, majestrix! Sishu!"

"Up, man! Hurry."

"But I cannot leave the empress—"

"Do as you are commanded. Escape and fetch help. Now, Larghos, when I open the gate, ride as though your hide depended on it. For by Vox, believe me, it does!"

"Quidang!"

The wooden gate opened easily enough and the faint squeal vanished in the increasing uproar beyond the other gate. Larghos bent his head, Delia gave the zorca the subtlest of taps, and the superb animal, responding, leaped through. Delia swung the wood closed. No time to lean against it for a gulp of air and a moment's respite. Truth to tell, she doubted if she could have brought Vomanus safely through to the other stables in his condition. Larghos would care for Vomanus, stop him from falling off, and, the sooner the better, return with help.

By that time Delia planned to be long gone. Her confidence nerved her; she trusted in herself for a very long way, but what others might never see or suspect in her she was very well aware of herself. Her confidence and self-assurance were frighteningly thin. Her nerves had been scraped raw.

By Krun!—all she had to do now was get across to the stables and select a mount and ride off. That was all.

She suspected she had just about enough courage left for that.

Through the open gateway ruddy light flared, like the single enormous eye of some diabolical pagan idol drowned in the jungles of Chem. Two guards catapulted through, to land with twin crashes on the flags. Furious bellowings reached her. The coruscating lights of the torches reflected in whirling radiance from the weathered stones of the tower. Iron studs gonged against the flagstones, and guards appeared. The two who had been thrown through staggered up. The group hesitated, and then with naked steel turned.

Clutching her bloody rapier, Delia peered about into the shadows, desperately seeking a place to hide.

CHAPTER EIGHTEEN

The Artistry of a Sword Mistress

Hunkering in the shadows next to a shed that contained something unmentionable—something best left undisturbed judging by the smell—Delia glared out into the ward. Torchlights cast ominous flashes and gleams of fire. Silhouetted and animate, the guards gathered themselves. Evidently a new coffle of slaves had just come in and someone retained spirit enough to resist. More than one slave was being loaded with extra chains and bashed over the head in the next ward. Delia had to cross that space and then get past the kitchens to the stables. Setting themselves, the slave handlers rushed back through the archway and the noise increased.

Delia glared. She glared in a veritable passion of frustration and sheer bad temper.

By Vox! By Krun! By Dee Sheon! By all the gods and goddesses and spirits of Kregen! Just when she'd got Vomanus away and at last—at long damned last—things were going reasonably well and she could envisage herself astride a zorca and speeding away, this maniacal crew of idiots had to come shouting and scattering torchlight and whipping on packs of yowling werstings.

As a man she knew might have said, it was enough to make her throw her hat on the ground and jump on it, by Zair!

The rumpus and the lights drew back from the archway. She waited, seething, feeling her temper boiling up and scalding away her doubts and uncertainties.

She could remember her mother in her strict yet loving way saying: "Now, Dilly, you will say you are sorry to Opaz every time you lose your temper, and no sweets for a week."

This pack of rasts here in Veliganda led by Nyleen and Cranchar were like to have her off sweets for the rest of her life.

Her mother used to call her Dilly. That was a long time ago. At least, Vomanus had called her Delia, even if, so distressed she had been, she'd called him Vom. They were the affectionate names of their youth.

If her mother had married her father first, instead of Vomanus's father, then young Vom would have grown up to be emperor. That would have saved a very very great deal of grief for her and for the hairy clansman she had wed.

The snarling racket of leashed werstings made her react. By Krun! She felt invigorated, the action driving the blood through her. She felt capable of anything. At first she had guessed the alarm to be raised because a sentry on the battlements had spotted Vomanus and Larghos riding off astride their zorca. Then she had fancied it must be because missing sentries had been found. But the torchlight, spilling in through the gateway and bouncing in lurid reflections from the stone of the tower, remained stationary. It did not advance menacingly. And the snarling growls of the werstings spat no nearer.

She took a breath, and spat. That shed reeked. Standing up, she hitched up the weapons belt. Gripping the rapier, she advanced out from the shadows.

The surge of confidence brought her to the gate. The flagstones glistened with the running fire of torchlight, orange and golden in the night. The diffuse pink lighting from the Maiden with the Many Smiles washed away, haltingly, before the harsh glow of the torches.

One of the male Fristle guards hovered by the stone arch. He was ill-at-ease. Like most Fristles who are not armed and armored by their masters, he wore a leather jack, brass-studded. The racial weapon of the Fristle, a curved scimitar, kept slipping up and down in its scabbard as the catman pulled and pushed. He looked ready to run, given half the chance.

Silently, Delia approached.

The uproar beyond the gateway markedly reduced. One or two words spurted up. They might have been key words, they might mean nothing. "Decadent. . . . Take them away. . . . screws. . . . error. . . . ways. . . ."

Delia marched on. She angled her head so the torches

threw deep shadows across her face. The rapier, unwiped, went back into the scabbard. She made herself take the long and exaggerated steps some Jikai Vuvushis affected. Her accoutrements jangled.

The Fristle jumped.

"Out of the way, man!" snarled Delia, and strutted on.

The pecking order of this fortress was made transparently plain, as Nyleen made it plain dealing with her brother, when the Fristle said nothing but shuffled away. He waited until the Battle Maiden had stalked past, and then he resumed his place. He, it was clear, would prefer to be very far away.

Apart from the noise going on around the group of people who were moving—spasmodically—away beyond the wall, another and altogether different species of noise emanated from the kitchens. This noise seemed to be, first; Nan the Bosom thwacking, second: Ornol the Rashers screaming ineffectually for obedience, and, third: Silly Nath bellowing that someone had stolen the bucket from the well.

The stables were so filled that some totrixes and freymuls were tethered outside. The animals did not care for the noise, and blew and stamped. Delia had her heart set on a zorca, for obvious reasons, although if she had to steal a freymul, the so-called Poor Man's Zorca, she would do so. Saddle animals were scarce since the Time of Troubles. The general busy scene around her afforded some protection. The mob of people kicking up the most noise vanished into the fortress. The kitchen hullabaloo sounded louder. Then Silly Nath ran out, all awkwardly scrambling, and Nan the Bosom chasing him, with her largest ladle going like a slave-powered trip-hammer used to break stones.

"Give me back my bucket, Nath!"

"Shan't! Need it for the well!"

"I'll stuff you down your well, head first!"

With a smart side-step, Delia darted out of the torchlights. She moved fast around the edge of the yard in the shadows.

In the stables she drew in a breath redolent of straw and droppings, pungent with liniments and sweat. She put her hand on a zorca, gentling him. His single spiral horn jutted up to a fine length, well-proportioned. Not all first-class zorcas possessed large horns; some zorca-copers claimed it as an infallible sign of breeding. She put her hands on the animal, not bothering to saddle him, and a thin and scorching fire slashed around her legs.

She fell down, and was dragged to the door.

Struggling over, she tried to rise, and another whip joined the first about her, and tripped her. She lay there on her back, glaring up helplessly at Chica, who stared down in mocking triumph. Chica's atra swung on its golden chain from her neck, and the little good luck charm glittered in distant torchlight. The amulet was of a particular kind, the golden ornament a miniature of a man in agony being transfixed most unpleasantly by a stake. Chica smiled.

"Alyss. So this is where you are! We did wonder."

She snapped her orders and the two whips withdrew. Jikai Vuvushis seized Delia, stripped away her weaponry, dragged her up with her arms twisted behind her back.

"The kovneva sent for you, Alyss, and you were not there. Only poor Thafti with a bruised neck, all tied up. Why did you do that?"

Delia just stood there and said nothing.

"You were going to escape! Of course. That's it. Poor girl. You were going to run away from the kovneva. How ungrateful." The mockery was crude, heavy, and cut with the effect of a blunt wooden lath upon steel.

The grips the two Battle Maidens fastened on her were efficient; she could have broken them with a trick taught by the SOR. Then she could have started to run off into the darkness. Waiting at the side stood three Jikai Vuvushis. Each one held a bow. The bows were of the compound reflex type, short and sharply curved. Three arrows were nocked, three strings were partly drawn. Three steps, three arrows, no more Alyss the slave girl.

Chica flicked her whip. The black length of the lash, shining, thick at the butt and tapering to a thin and evil slenderness, writhed up. The tip struck Delia upon the thigh.

The Battle Maiden's pteruges absorbed most of the sting; the shock remained.

"Bring her along. The kovneva is indulging us in a small entertainment tonight. This will add to her pleasure."

Coiling her whip up along her arm, Chica swung about, a tall, agile and commanding figure.

Forced along by the guards, Delia considered this Chica. She was called Chica the Fangs. Her legs were long and sturdy, and she walked with a step lithe and free, almost bouncing. She favored dark clothes, with the silvered corselet shining bravely, and she looked very much like a desert reptile, quick and sudden and deadly.

With sword points at her back, Delia was woman-handled into the refectory. The tables were pushed away to the sides. Stakes were set up. The saw-edged barriers were in place. Nyleen was preparing another entertainment for her cronies.

Swathed in a profusion of gems and feathers, her silver hair glimmering in a net of emeralds, Nyleen sat in the high-backed chair where her brother Cranchar had sat for his entertainment. Her pallid face twisted with grotesque pleasure when Delia was brought in. Nadia, full-fleshed, lumpy with passion, half-drew her rapier.

"Ah, my dear," said Nyleen. "So they have found you. I do not think you will play the harp for me this evening."

Delia made no reply.

"No. No, I thought not. But we will find other amusements. Do not fret over that."

Nadia pushed forward. She looked ugly. "This shif thinks she can handle a rapier, my lady. Let me teach her—"

"Tsleethi-tsleetha," said Nyleen. "Softly, softly. Let us first enjoy a small spectacle."

That small spectacle disgusted Delia. She closed her eyes. Presently the screams of the men faded, and their tortured bodies were dragged away.

"Ah!" said Nyleen, and she helped herself, daintily, to a handful of palines. "That has quite refreshed me. But then, of course, it is no more than men deserve."

The keys jangling from her chatelaine, Paline Pontora walked swiftly in. Her green gown rustled. She bent and spoke urgently in Nyleen's ear. The kovneva sat up straighter in her chair. She looked murderous.

"So the kov my stupid husband has run off! Well, the worse for him. He will soon be brought back and punished."

She bent her gaze on Delia, who stood to one side of the table. "And you, Alyss the Harp. Did you know of this? Why else would you wear the armor of a Jikai Vuvushi?"

Delia just didn't bother to answer the unpleasant woman.

"You—!" shrieked Nyleen.

Nadia drew her rapier. "Let me teach her, my lady!"

Nyleen slumped back. Her eyelids half closed, and she smiled. Her teeth closed over her lower lip. Then, slowly, she opened her mouth and half-turned to her Battle Maiden

Hikdar. This Nadia quivered. She served in the office of cadade, captain of the bodyguard, and she was raging.

"Yes, Nadia, my fighting leem. Let us see what she can do."

"Rather, my lady," said Chica, and she spoke with some regret. "What Nadia can do. I would welcome a chance to claw her."

"That chance will never come, Chica the Fangs!" Nadia drew her left-hand dagger. "I will cut her up artistically. . . ."

They removed the armor Delia had donned. They thrust a rapier and main gauche into her hands. Wearing only a slave-grey breechclout, she was thrown into the center between the tables.

The feel of the hilts in her hands did, with the natural magic of any mistress of the sword, feel good. If she was to die, why, then, she would do so and seek to find the sunny uplands beyond the Ice Floes of Sicce. But, before that, this rapier and this dagger would no longer glitter pure silver.

She turned, almost casually, with a lazy movement, and lifted the weapons.

"I am ready," she said in her small voice. "Bring on your vermin, Nyleen the Vile."

A gasp ran around the watching women. For an instant Delia thought she had overstepped the mark, had overdone it. But Nyleen laughed her pearly laugh and waved her hand. This spectacle, it was clear, would excite her, would be wonderfully enjoyable!

Nadia did not waste time. She leaped forward with a parade, her steel flashing. She was determined to show to all that she was the greatest swordswoman there, and to cut up this stupid and impertinent slave girl with great artistry. She would make the silly shif suffer. She was supremely confident.

Whoever had trained Nadia had been efficient and thorough. Of necessity, for her to have risen through the ranks of the Jikai Vuvushis to become a Hikdar meant she knew her business. To be chosen to be the cadade of a kovneva's bodyguard meant she also understood the management of women—and men, too. She fought with great competence and skill. But, very soon, Delia felt her out. She was wooden. She did not possess that spark, that indefinable transparency of the great sworder. Soon, dreadfully soon to the bewildered Nadia, her attacks failed, her cunning feints vanished, and blood stained along her arm, her thigh, over the rim of her corselet.

The sighing sound of the watching women susurrated, and faded. Entranced, unbelieving, they watched.

Delia was not cruel. Once she had the measure of Nadia she did not cut her up out of spite. And, too, she found that she had no interest in merely killing the overblown woman.

There was little need to exert herself unduly. The steel scraped and slithered, chiming with the unholy carillons of combat. Blood flowed. Nadia's blood flowed. . . .

Presently, with a sweet little passage she remembered with some fondness, she stuck Nadia through the thigh, and, withdrawing, instantly stuck her through the other. The armored pteruges could not deflect thrusts of that degree of skill.

Bleeding, in pain, unbelieving, Nadia sank down to the floor. Her weapons slipped from her hands. Delia put the point of the rapier at her throat.

"Yes, Nyleen?" she said, still in her small voice. "And?"

Silence for a moment, for two moments, and then amid a babble of expostulations, Chica leaped forward.

"Let me!" screeched Chica. She snapped her whip.

The lash snaked toward Delia. With a single contemptuous flick of her dagger, Delia checked the strike, lopped the tip of the whip. The women gasped.

Nyleen called above the hubbub. Everyone stopped to listen to the kovneva.

"Vile men have their jikordur and their hyr jikordur, in which the ritual of personal combat is sanctified. Well, and are we any the less? What is there a man may do that we cannot?"

The howls broke out then, women screaming for blood. Delia stood, the rapier and dagger held ready, watching. The kovneva motioned to two Battle Maidens, who stepped forward and leveled their bows at Delia's breast. In this the kovneva showed her cruel streak. She joyed in her power, and what she could command. "Chica, you have been challenged, I think."

"Aye, my lady! Let it be done!"

CHAPTER NINETEEN

The Whip and the Claw

Nyleen Gillois na Sagaie, Kovneva of Vindelka, torture mistress of untold numbers of men, would-be murderer of her husband, would-be wife and murderer of the emperor, had studied long and assiduously in the histories of Loh. With her lip caught up between her teeth, as a young girl in cold Evir, she had read of that mysterious continent of Loh and of the Queens of Pain.

To be a Queen of Pain of Loh!

She had never considered herself to be a cruel woman. She was merely the instrument chosen to redress the imbalance between the sexes. The witch Fiacola the Gaze had perhaps contributed more to success than Nyleen cared to admit. But, in this coming confrontation, she saw more than mere revenge.

The satisfaction on her icy features reflected her inner joy that she had the power thus to test Chica the Fangs. Nyleen was always conscious of the necessity to preserve and display her power. This slave girl had skill with the rapier. Well, then, let Chica the Fangs discipline her, cut her, and let Nyleen take the frisson from Chica's lash, from her Claw, and the risk the Fangs ran!

Nadia the cadade was carried out, groaning, wondering what cyclone had hit her. Delia was stripped of weapons. She regarded Chica the Fangs warily. She could feel a pulse in her temple. She well understood what was in store. Her chin lifted.

"Very well, then, Chica the Fangs. You stand challenged."

"Give her a whip, and fetch my own old Fang. And bring the balass boxes." She turned, a hard, bright, agile woman, to face Delia. She sneered. "You challenge me, you fool! It is not only whips."

So, Delia knew.

Well, perhaps if she'd practiced more she wouldn't have this fluttery feeling in her chest.

They brought her a whip, a long snaky length of vileness. They gave Chica her favourite whip, old Fang, and she flicked it out. It was long and hard and supple, and it could strike in the pain ways and in the death ways. And Chica was its mistress.

The balass boxes were brought. Bronze bound, triply-locked, they were placed on the table before Nyleen. At once, Chica threw back the lid of one and took out her Claw. She held the thing aloft, a marvel of cunning linkages and bright steel and lacings and razor-sharp talons.

It glittered, held aloft in the torchlights. "Hai!" she cried, exulting. "Now you face death!"

From the second box Delia took out the Claw. It was a good, serviceable model, and when she tested it with a tentative thumb, reasonably sharp. There was no doubt that, if she had to use a Claw she would prefer to partner it with a rapier. But a Whip would serve. Would have to serve, seeing that was the forte of this Chica. She held the Claw for a moment, and Chica laughed contemptuously.

"Help her strap it on. I will give her every chance. But it is clear she has no idea of a Jikvar, no idea at all."

Leading her cronies, Nyleen gloated. The Claw was strapped on Delia's left arm and hand. She flexed her muscles, rotating her arm, pulling back and jerking forward. The Claw fitted her surprisingly well. She looked at Chica the Fangs. That need not be her real name. She had gone through Lancival. Once, she had been a Sister of the Rose. That was the sadness in this, for Delia; that and the thought that sorcery had been used to debase this girl and deflect her from her vows.

Nyleen leaned forward. She was breathing more rapidly.

"Alyss. You do understand? You are to die. The manner of your death will be more unpleasant if you do not stand up to it. We here are all Sisters of the Whip. We know. The Claw has its uses, as you will discover." At this the women laughed, sensing the mood of their mistress. Nyleen went on: "But it is the Whip that must be used to chastise all men, everyone who stands against us. Why you set free the kov my husband, if you did, is of small consequence. What matters is your death here. Try to use the Claw. Use the Whip. Die like a woman!"

Then she sat back and with her cronies settled down to

enjoy the spectacle of a half-naked girl being cut to pieces by an expert.

And, of course, Chica the Fangs was an expert.

In the desperateness of this situation, Delia had time to reflect on the comicality of her instinctive reaction. To herself, fervently, she said: "When I get out of this I promise Dee Sheon most devoutly to practice more regularly!"

Then Chica's Whip flicked and the fight was on.

As any bully-fighter might do, Chica sought at first to torment Delia. The Whip snapped and hissed. Twice she struck Delia in the painways, and Delia gasped with the shock. Once, in Lancival, seasons ago, she had heard a girl describe Delia as the Flower of the Sisters of the Rose. And, like any silly empty-headed girl she had hugged the description to herself, mightily proud. Later she had seen the folly of that, and had been displeased. Now, had her sisters been able to see her, they would have seen the Flower with petals drastically wilting.

When Chica's whip flicked like a surging ripple of black destruction in the next passage, she got the Claw in the way, twisted, and yanked. But Chica was not to be caught like that. She disengaged and struck back, and Delia only just had time to skip sideways.

"The shishi learns!" crowed Chica. "This is becoming more enjoyable!"

Delia circled. The Whips abruptly leaped, and struck, and twined, and parted. Both girls leaped back.

The thing to do, Delia reasoned as she circled warily, was to get rid of the Whips. They fouled the issue. If these women followed the strict procedures, if the Whips wrenched away and were discarded, rapiers would be thrown into the ring. Chica would be as good as if not better than Nadia. That was probably the cause of the cadade's open desire to excel with the rapier and dagger. Probably.

On the next sudden onslaught Delia swirled away from the tip, snapped her own Whip and slogged the lash into Chica's side. It was not as clean a blow as she had hoped for; it slapped against the corselet and made Chica jump.

"You bitch!"

Delia said nothing but reeled the Whip in, coiling, ready for the next attack.

When Chica, incensed, struck again, Delia jumped forward. She let the thicker section of her antagonist's Whip coil about her body. Its major force spent, it merely stung. She cracked her own lash up, high, sliced it down in a rippling line of destruction. The tip blazed across Chica's face.

The girl screamed and spun away. Her own Whip began to uncoil from Delia's body. She clamped it with her left hand, dragged it savagely back. She rippled her own Whip, and struck again. Again Chica screamed.

That damned helmet! It blocked the major force. But those two blows had opened up two vivid weals across the girl's face. Chica's lash snagged in Delia's left-hand Claw. She dragged again and the razor-sharp steel sliced through the Whip. A length as long as a girl's leg fell away.

Instantly, Delia leaped. She slashed with fury with her Claw. The blow hissed past Chica who stumbled back, shaken, off-balance. She staggered. And then she had recovered and come screaming back, her Claw gouging for Delia's naked side.

With a routine block and twist, Delia checked the onslaught and instinctively slashed back. The return missed only just, only just—and both girls stood back, panting.

"What, Chica?" called Nyleen. "Do you toy with her still?"

Chica bit down on her lip. She looked frighteningly savage.

"She will rue these blows, my lady!"

"Then, Chica, my dear, pray let us see. We are waiting."

The next passage was not quite the same as that preceding. The Whips became entangled. Chica, relying so much on her lash, took a moment too long to attempt to untangle the lines, and Delia stepped in. The Claw razored down.

Only a woman in the Jikvar of Chica's skill could have twisted herself away from a stroke of that expertise.

The Fangs slid the blow. Just. One steel talon ripped across the shoulder, slashing through the metal-studded leather of the latchings. Around the watching women ran the gasp of excitement—of pleasure. Who among them was dismayed that Chica was meeting her match?

A man had once said to Delia that the sight of women fighting did not so much disgust or offend him as sadden him. To which she had replied, tartly, that if a woman has to do a certain thing in life, then a woman will do it.

Delia did not proceed to demolish Chica. For one thing, the Fangs was too good for the slightest chance to be taken.

But Delia did, having seen that first latching go, cunningly contrive to slash the other shoulder. At that, the return blow whispered past her face and only a last minute wrench away and recovered lunge saved her from losing half her features.

The Fangs took three steps back. The black length of the Whip rippled to stillness along the floor. Her silvered corselet sagged away, held by the waist belt and rib-straps.

"Very well," said Delia, flicking her Whip and making Chica jump. "I will give you a few moments to make yourself comfortable."

Sucking in the sight, Nyleen felt her insides deliquesce. This was better sport than she had ever imagined!

Furious, still not accepting that she had met a superior in the Jikvar and the Grakvar, Chica ripped away her breastplate. She wore under the padding a thin supple-leather vest. She was not a big-built girl, being of the wiry and agile variety. But she was a woman. For that, alone, Delia was cautious. . . .

Waiting quietly for Chica to get set, Delia reflected that just about the only truly authenticated example of a man using a Claw came from the Life of Velda the Tempestuous, whose old room Delia now lodged in at Lancival. The man—apparently his name had been Nath or Naghan the Flute—had hungered after an initiate of the SOR. He had broken into one of the provincial colleges to an assignment with her. Everything had gone wrong, and in the ensuing fracas he had slain a sister. He had snatched up and donned a Claw. Then he ran into Velda.

If Delia did to Chica what Velda the Tempestuous had done to this Naghan or Nath the Flute, they'd have to carry the Fangs out in baskets. Or, rather, to make less mess, in buckets.

Chica slished her Claw through the air. She snapped her Whip.

"I am ready, dom."

Delia, using the Disciplines to relax herself in this pause in the fight, deliberately slowing down some rhythms so that others might be speeded up, smiled.

"You call me dom, Chica the Fangs. Strange address, surely, from a Jikai Vuvushi to a mere slave girl?"

The Fangs rippled her Whip. "Yes, you are a slave girl—now. But you have, I think, been through Lancival."

"As have you."

"I am done with them! They betrayed me. Now, I am a Sister of the Whip!"

"That is your misfortune."

Nyleen shrilled from her chair: "What are you two standing lollygagging about for! Get on with it! Chica—cut her up. Bratch!"

Delia made a small elegant gesture with the Claw. "That, Chica the Lost, is your mistress."

"She is what she is. Like me, she hates men. So—"

"So you hate everyone? Indeed, you are Lost."

"Fight, you bitch, and have done!"

In the moment before the Whips rose and leaped Delia said: "I think, my girl, it is you who are done."

"Bratch!" The shriek from Nyleen made her cronies start.

Chica the Fangs put out everything of which she was capable. Perhaps, Delia had just time to consider before surrendering herself to the demands of the Whip and the Claw, just perhaps Chica had grown soft in whipping poor defenseless slaves instead of facing opposition. Leaping streaks of darkness, the hiss and crack of cunningly applied lashes, the quick intake of breath, the sliding scrape of feet upon the floor. . . . The glitter of the Claws blinded. The Whips coiled and struck, withdrew, rippled, slashed again. . . .

Chica put the lopped tip into Delia's ribs, and she gasped with the dizzying pain. On the next passage she sliced the supple-leather vest from Chica, spilling it away in two clean halves. Without waiting, she roared in, the whip slicing and the Claw slashing. Chica just saved herself. And, in stumbling away and avoiding that savage attack, she entangled her lash with Delia's. The two Whips writhed together.

Both girls reacted instinctively. Both hauled back with all their strength. Chica was brought staggeringly forward, off balance, gasping, as Delia reeled her in. At the last moment the Fangs released her grip on her Whip and flopped away.

Delia threw the entangled mass onto the floor.

She stared at Nyleen.

"Well, Nyleen?"

Nyleen chewed her lip.

Now it should be rapiers. . . .

Chica screamed at the kovneva.

"Kovneva! My lady! *Daggers!*"

Nyleen nodded. She felt sweet and moist and satisfaction

coursed through her. She would like Sissy to be here to minister to her. But the fool girl was missing. . . . She'd be in for a flogging, of course. But, now, Nyleen gloated and would not miss a single moment of this fascinating passage at arms.

Two Jikai Vuvushis threw two daggers into the center.

They stuck, quiveringly, light splintering from hilt and blade.

Chica leaped, ripped the nearest dagger free, brandished it. "Now, sister, you will understand!"

Delia took the other dagger. It was a Vallian dagger. It was long and slender and sharp. Its quillons were marvels of curious ornamentation. It was not, most certainly was not, a left-hand dagger. The major problem with Vallian daggers was to find steel of the quality required. So long, so thin, the blade, inferior metal would snap. These looked to be weapons of quality. Delia felt the hilt in her hand, and she held the dagger in her own way.

Delia was accounted a mistress of the bow, having been taught by Seg Segutorio. She was a mistress of the rapier, having learned much from her husband. She was a mistress of the churgur's art, the use of the battle sword and shield, having been taught by Balass the Hawk. She was a mistress of the Whip and the Claw, having been through Lancival. But of the Vallian dagger—ah! Of that superbly cunning instrument of death there was no one in the whole wide world of Kregen, it was said, who could teach Delia a single tiny thing.

The Fangs used her own Claw to rip away the two parts of her supple-leather vest. She ripped them and tossed them down. She fronted Delia.

Catlike, she half-crouched, and began to circle. Delia circled with her. Like two primordial felines out of the mists of time, the women circled each other, seeking an opening, panting only lightly, their legs long and supple moving them with infinite grace.

Now there would be no long-range work. Now they would meet, body to body, arms and legs thrusting, seeking to rip and claw. Their skin glowed in the torchlights, sleek and rounded, the hollowed shadows tinged in violet and carmine. Chica tossed her head back, and weaved left and surged right, and Delia let her go past and used her Claw to rip a bloody chunk out of that glowing skin.

Chica screamed.

She threw herself at Delia, dagger and Claw lifted.

With expertise that spurted from her inmost depths, Delia feinted, blocked, caught the Claw and let her dagger slide on. The stroke was cunning, perfectly delivered, superb. It would penetrate between Chica's ribs, slice on unerringly, burst into her heart.

Infallibly. . . .

Why? Why did Delia turn the dagger slightly, turn the direction of the thrust? Why did she let the blade score along Chica's ribs instead of rupturing her heart? Why?

Again, Chica screamed, and fell back, and Delia was on her like a leem.

The Claw flamed before Chica's eyes. The talons, each razor-sharp, each capable of dragging flesh from bone, of gouging out an eye, hovered over the Fangs' face.

Among the watchful women were many who understood the techniques of fighting. They might not practice; they could judge. They saw. They saw the diversion of the blade. Now they saw Chica's horrible disfigurement, her death in agony.

Chica glared up, froth on her lips, her eyes wide and yet blank, drugged with the awful knowledge of impending destruction.

"A fight, dom," she said. "A fight."

"And you have lost, Chica the Lost, as I said. I will not kill you. I have other plans for you."

With that, Delia turned the Claw and used a blunt and heavy edge and knocked Chica the Fangs backwards. The girl sprawled limply across the floor. The Claw flopped with a clank of steel. And the dagger flew from her hand, skidded across the floor to smash into the kovneva's feet.

Standing up, Delia let Claw and dagger dangle. She stared at Nyleen, and her face expressed contempt. Splendid, she looked, Delia, Empress of Vallia who was just Delia. Only a light sweat glinted on her body. She breathed deeply. Superb, superb, and consummately deadly. . . .

Nyleen was staring past her, at the door, and the kovneva's eyes opened wide. An expression of great joy filled her icy face. She smiled. Then she giggled, as at a supreme joke.

"Slave! You fight well. You have skill. Chica was good, in my service, very good with Whip and Claw. But now, I think, now you will face a greater! Now you will be tested to the utmost!"

Delia did not turn. Hell and damnation! She'd fought and fought well and won. If they shafted her, well, she'd try to deflect the arrows in the way her husband had shown her. But that was difficult, by Vox! When the door bashed open and this newcomer entered, she had felt the flicker of a hope she had resolutely refused to acknowledge. An obvious hope, a pent-up desire that would burst out like flame. He had done it before. She'd been naked, chained up, staked out as a sacrifice, menaced by steel and talons and fangs. And he'd come storming in like the maniac he was, and rescued her.

But not this time.

She'd won, and she could feel the tiredness creeping up on her, a fatigue she pushed aside and ignored which yet insisted on trembling her legs and jerking her muscles. And now the bastards were bringing on another champion.

From what Nyleen said, from the expression on her face and the satisfied oohs and aahs from her cronies, this newcomer was going to be very good indeed.

If she was better than Chica—and she would be, she would be!—she'd be the very devil to handle.

Oh—why hadn't she practiced more!

"Drag Chica away!" commanded Nyleen. "Give the slave her Whip. Now we shall see some *real* Whip and Claw."

She called along the length of the refectory, a glowing, commanding woman, joying in her power and enjoying her own joy. "Come in, my dear. Lahad and Lahal. You are more than welcome. Now you can show us how it should be done. As you can see, the onker Chica could not manage it."

From the swiveling movement of the watching women's heads, Delia realized they were watching the newcomer walking from the door toward her unturning back. She did not hear her. That, alone, boded ill. If only she'd put in more practice sessions. . . . Chica had not been easy. And the dismal truth of the coming encounter was made crystal clear as Nyleen crowed her own pleasurable anticipations.

"Here is a slave shishi for you to—well, my dear, I hardly dare call it fight—for you to cut up. Step forth, my dear. For you are supreme, far far better than Chica with Whip and Claw."

"Cut her! Cut her!" screamed the waiting women.

When a Claw struck and cut it could rip your face off. . . .

Delia turned around.

She saw the woman walking down between the tables. She saw. The newcomer, this redoubtable champion, lifted her head and spoke.

"You wish me to fight this silly little slave girl and cut her up for you?" said Jilian Sweet-Tooth.

CHAPTER TWENTY

All for Vallia. . . .?

Jilian swirled off her enveloping black riding cloak. Dust stained the hem. She wore black fighting leathers, trim, taut, still shining although scuffed. At her waist the belted rapier and dagger swung to hand. Terchicks snugged across her shoulders. Her Whip coiled up her right arm. Somewhere in her baggage would be her bronze-bound balass box. She did not look at Delia.

"I do not think, kovneva, I shall fight this girl."

"Not fight her, my dear? Oh, of course. You are tired from your journey. I see! Well, this shif must be tired, too, since she has defeated Nadia Woodraven who used to be my cadade, and Chica Trevalmin ti Alvondsmot, whom we used to call the Fangs."

Jilian let her dark intense gaze pass broodingly across Delia. She drew off her left-hand glove, supple and black. She did not remove the right, for the Whip coiled its sinuous lashes about the leather gauntlet.

"If Nadia and Chica are both defeated, have you not found yourself a—Jikvushi who would serve you and fight for you—if you treated her well?"

Giving the kovneva no time to reply, Jilian gestured with her right hand. "Slave—bring me wine, a light yellow, for my mouth is as parched as the Ochre Limits."

The slave girl thus addressed scuttled to obey. Delia stood motionless. Jilian looked almost just the same. Her pale face bore its normal look of brooding intensity, her dark hair cut low over her broad white forehead setting an added luster in her dark eyes. Her whole face looked almost the same; pleasing, broad and well-proportioned and with a warm and mobile mouth. But there hung about Jilian Sweet-Tooth an air of dejection, of more than usual brooding hurt. She took the wine and quaffed it and threw the goblet at the slave girl as Nyleen arched her back, like a cat, her face rigid in its icy smile.

"You have been unsuccessful, Jilian?"

"Yes and no. I have almost certain news of the rast. Almost certain. But I must follow up even this slender lead. I came to advise you that I leave for Pandahem tomorrow."

"Do not forget to bring back his head—or some other part of Kov Colun's anatomy—for our inspection and delectation as you tell your story."

"If there is anything of him left."

"Ah! And, now, Jilian, mayhap you will cut this slave shishi up for our inspection and delectation—*here and now?*"

Still Delia stood motionless. Truth to tell, in all their practice bouts together, she and Jilian had never settled the issue—who was the better. It had not mattered. They had joined in combat, joying in the tussle, in the skill and expertise. In the nature of practice bouts they had used rebated weapons and heavily padded Claws. Whips, one against another in practice, were uncommonly difficult to manage. Delia just did not know who would win, if she and Jilian fought in the Jikvar and the Grakvar with razor-edged Claws and Whips that could flay.

Again, truth to tell, she was aware of the odd trifling deficiency in Jilian's technique. She had told her friend. And Jilian had told her, in her turn, of Delia's mistakes. Perhaps, if it came to a fight to the death, just perhaps, Delia felt she might win. But that victory would leave her a ruin. Then she thrust those thoughts aside. So Jilian had renounced the Sisters of the Rose and had joined the Sisters of the Whip. Very well. That did not mean she had renounced her friendship. Being Jilian, she would do what she wanted to do, and Delia found herself confident that Jilian would unravel a way to settle this without fighting.

She hoped so, she devoutly hoped so. . . .

Moving with her lithe easy swing, Jilian crossed the open space and hitched herself up onto the edge of a table. Her body sat erect, and one long leg swung backward and forward, backward and forward. If anyone here could think it of anyone else, then that swinging leg in the tall black boot was a most insolent gesture, most insolent indeed.

Jilian took up a goblet of wine. She said: "Let me compose myself, kovneva. As I said, I have ridden hard and long."

She drank the wine down. Then, with her bare left hand, she wiped across her mouth. Deliberately, she said: "By Mother Zinzu the Blessed! I needed that!"

Delia showed no startlement. She just hadn't given a thought to the idea that Jilian would tell the kovneva and her cronies who this slave girl was. Delia showed no startlement; but she was profoundly moved. Jilian, a member now of the Sisters of the Whip, could so easily have told, so easily done what would amount to a betrayal of her friend. But, by saying what she had after she drank, Jilian was reassuring Delia. Jilian had never, to Delia's knowledge, visited the inner sea of Turismond, the Eye of the World. But she had heard the emperor, many times, say those words when he was dry and downed a draught.

"By Mother Zinzu the Blessed, I needed that!"

Yes, those words had been used many times, and Jilian was reaching out to Delia. Now, she went on in a conversational tone: "People call me Sweet-Tooth. Many people—and, I think, all men—believe that because I was born in a Banje shop and like sweet things, I was given that name. That the Tooth does not refer to any tooth I have in my head is so; men do not know."

Nyleen's frustration grew visibly upon her. Now she took what Jilian said in an entirely different context from that intended. Jilian was speaking to Delia, reassuring her that her secret was safe; Nyleen imagined she was making excuses for not fighting this slave girl.

"Do you tell me, Jilian, that because she is a girl you will not fight her?"

"Give me the moment I ask, kovneva. Then, as surely as a leem takes a ponsho, you will see . . ." She pointed negligently at the length of whip sliced from Chica's favorite Fang. "Chica relied too much on her Whip. You did well, kovneva, when you brought her away from the Sisters of the Rose, for she spied for them in Delka Ob. Now, they know nothing of our plans."

The horror hit Delia then.

Could Jilian be a party to the plot to kill the emperor?

That did not seem credible to the empress.

The emperor had rescued Jilian and brought her out of humiliating bondage to a position of respect. Jilian was a loved and valued member of the household, who had raised her own regiment of Jikai Vuvushis to fight for Vallia. At first she had known the emperor only as Jak the Drang, a now famous cognomen. Delia understood well enough the ties Jilian might form.

Between the emperor and the empress existed ties that had not been broken by the sundering of four hundred light-years, by the interference of superhuman beings, immortals, godlike beings of supernal power. Those bonds had not been broken by the petty slanders of evil tongues. Other attachments, for these two, were matters of supreme indifference. Yes, considered Delia, poor Jilian might well have formed a romantic attachment in her mind. Perhaps that had gone sour.

Perhaps she *was* in the plot to kill the emperor.

If so, then she was going about it in a remarkably peculiar way. . . .

Also, this explained what had happened to the spy sent by Thalmi Crockhaden, pro-marshal and spy mistress of the SOR. A girl of Chica's caliber would be needed for that work. Yet she had turned sour, gone rotten, been suborned, turned herself over to the Sisters of the Whip.

The cause of that rapid overturning of the beliefs of a lifetime and the embracing of inferior beliefs, now entered the refectory.

The witch, Fiacola the Gaze, walked in on the arm of the flunkey woman, Ilka the Silver Rod. Following, spitting and snarling, prowled two couples of werstings straining the leashes held by Rinka the Stripe. The intrusion of the witch brought everything else to a halt.

Even so, in the respectful hush, Nyleen called crossly to Ilka: "Where is that tiresome girl Sissy? I shall surely stripe her when she comes crawling and sobbing to me."

Ilka made a small gesture with her free hand. "I have not seen her, my lady."

Fiacola the Gaze kept her face hidden by the deep folds of a dark blue hood. She moved heavily to a chair quickly vacated at the side of Nyleen's chair. She sat, and Ilka fussily arranged her robes. The hood was not thrown back.

Only those two eyes caught the torchlights and gleamed a deep crimson in the shadows of the hood.

Not for nothing was the sorceress Fiacola called The Gaze. . . .

Standing quite still, Delia took note of what went forward. She was able to feel amusement that amid this respectful hush, Nyleen still could react in her cross way, and Jilian could still swing that long booted leg back and forth in her insolent fashion.

When Fiacola spoke her voice surprised Delia. That voice sounded deep and clear, like a note from a woodwind, like a sonorous chime.

"Does Jilian Sweet-Tooth forget what she now is?"

Jilian's booted foot stopped swinging.

"She says she is tired, Sana—"

"I am aware, kovneva, of what goes forward here."

Delia clamped her mind shut. Witches did have powers; of course, this Fiacola could merely have been listening at the door. But, all the same, it was a mightily powerful performance.

The witch's hood turned and inclined and Delia was aware of that sliding crimson gleam upon her. In the silence the hoarse breathing of many of the women sounded like the scraping of sword upon shield, the grating of a badly balanced spinning wheel. Even the werstings slobbered into silence.

The witch spoke again. "You promised me a diversion tonight, Nyleen. I do not object to seeing women cutting up other women if they deserve it. But that does not compare."

"You are right, Fiacola," responded Nyleen instantly. She lifted her right hand and gestured. She made of the gesture an imperial demand. "Begin!"

"Leave the slave girl to me." The ominous ring in the words was not lost on Delia.

The two Jikai Vuvushis with half-bent bows shepherded her away to stand near the side table. Jilian sat on the edge of her table across the central space. And, into the space from the flung open doors, on the kovneva's command, advanced a familiar, a sorry, a horrible procession.

The women who used their whips upon the naked bodies of the men were careful. All the shuffling men wore chains loading them down. There were various sizes and weights of chain in common usage among slavemasters. Sometimes they would refer to a slave as a one-chain man, or a three-chain man. This gave an indication not only of his troublesomeness but also of his strength and the care they took over restraining him until he was brought to heel and trained into the ways of slavery.

Most of the men wore one set of chains.

One man wore two. One man was a three-chain man. One was a four-chain slave. And one was loaded down with no less than six sets of chains. He could walk upright, which he did, defiant, arrogant, his four arms cruelly chained up his back.

"Oh!" said Delia to herself. "My poor Djangs!"

The two-chain man was Jordio the Hawk. The three-chain man was Lathdo the Eager. The four-chain man was Dalki, and the six-chain man was Tandu, his father.

So Jordio and Lathdo had fallen safely from the storm-wrecked airboat and had been taken up, at last, and so, eventually, brought here to be tortured to death. And her two ferocious Djangs? Surely, she reasoned, surely they must have ridden up to take service with the kov, bearing the letter from the Lord Farris, and had been sent on, and so been entrapped. They would not have been taken easily. . . .

Dragging their chains, herded in a mass of suffering, the four men did not see their empress and queen beside the table at the far end. They saw the prepared stakes, the saw-edged barriers, the instruments, and they understood what was to be their fate.

Now the excitement rippled around the watching women. Everyone brightened up. Nyleen and her cronies prepared themselves for a pleasant divertissement. Only the witch kept her gaze bent on first Delia and then Jilian. She looked from one to the other, and back, like a reptile measuring its prey.

The occult powers of sorcerers and sorceresses could be very real, or could be shams to rook the gullible. Delia believed this Fiacola must be mistress of some of the arts, for to suborn away a Sister of the Rose from her vows must take thaumaturgy of a high order. Perhaps not. Delia could not answer for the integrity of every Sister. . . .

But—Jilian! No, that was certain sure. Witchery had ensorcelled Jilian, quite apart from glib promises of help in tracking down Kov Colun Mogper of Mursham to his just desserts. If Delia could not believe in and trust Jilian, then her whole concept of integrity was proved valueless and ridiculous.

The first men were prepared for blood, agony and death.

Delia put one hand on the edge of the table. Sticky wine fouled her fingers, but she did not grimace with distaste. Spilled wine, sticky and unpleasant though it be, was as nothing beside the spilling of blood now being enacted out there on the floor. The Claw still strapped up on her arm fit her hand like a glove. The dagger, blood-befouled like the Claw, hung limply in her fist. The two Battle Maidens kept on taking their surveillance away, kept on darting looks at what was going on out there among the shrieks and the vomit and the blood. But they did not relax their vigilance. One movement, and one or other of the Battle Maidens would shaft her. . . .

Aware of the grisly scrutiny of the witch, Delia deliberately kept her own gaze averted. She did not look at the suffering human beings out there; she looked at her Djangs, and at Lathdo and Jordio. They stood sullenly, chafing their chains, so overloaded they could barely move. Their clothes were in a mess, ripped and stained, and their faces were bruised and bloodied. But they did not look cowed. In this, at least, they were prepared to face a ghastly end with fortitude.

She noticed an odd circumstance about Dalki. He was the four-chain man. But, somehow, he seemed only to have three chains lapping his body. As she watched a loop of chain tumbled free of his tunic. Weirdly, like the trunk of a mammoth beast withdrawing, it slithered up and vanished from view. Delia blinked. Dalki seemed to be in movement although he remained still. Most odd. Another chain dropped, and was checked, and so drawn back. She felt the pulse in her throat. In some unaccountable way, Dalki was freeing himself of his chains. He must have been working on them from the moment they were first loaded upon him, and, no doubt now, he was cursing away that it had taken so long, and that he was in sight of freedom when he was also in sight of death.

A victim shrieked and died. He was glad to die, and the women were sorry that entertainment was over. But they looked eagerly for the next. Nyleen stood up. She walked with her smooth gait out onto the floor to inspect personally the gruesome wreckage. Other women crowded up. The guards moved forward.

Nyleen liked, now and then, to take a hand herself. She could flick and slash her Whip, and although she would have been cut to shreds in short order by any mistress in the Grakvar, she still liked to posture.

"Chain some to the posts," she commanded. "We will have a competition."

"Oh, yes, kovneva," chorused her cronies. And, still, Delia found it hard to hate the silly woman. Her craving for power and glory, her mimicry of the ways of the Queens of Pain of Loh, as Delia shrewdly surmised, her genuine belief that she had a mission to chastise all men, all these things added up to a woman bereft of essentials and adrift on tides of unchecked emotion. That was unfortunate, reprehensible, and in its effects evil; but Nyleen, Delia guessed, was also the victim of sorcery.

"Chain up some fine specimens, strong ones." Nyleen pointed. "Those! They are sullen enough, by the Breath of Evirani! We will make them wish they had not been born men."

Lathdo, Jordio, Dalki and Tandu were chained up. In an odd way, Dalki managed to conceal his handiwork and was chained up with the others. Delia marveled. Three other hard and hairy men were chained up alongside to the stakes. Nyleen preened herself and took the whip a girl slave ran out and proffered.

The first blow missed. No one laughed. Jilian's booted foot quivered; but it did not swing. The second blow chunked into one of the hairy men, and he yelled. The third blow almost took Nyleen's eye out. She glared around pettishly. She threw the Whip down and drew a long Vallian dagger.

"I have a keener way with men, my dears!"

"Yes, kovneva!"

She advanced with the dagger held aloft.

"Wait!" The deep bell-like voice of Fiacola the Gaze caught everyone. Nyleen stopped and looked around. The dagger slowly descended.

"Yes, Sana?"

"The Jikai Vuvushi, Jilian, will now fight the slave girl."

"But, Fiacola—"

"Fight! *Now!*"

Jilian put her feet on the floor and stood up slowly.

She turned to face the witch. On Jilian's pallid face that brooding look compressed into a deep and intense absorption.

"And Sana, if I do not choose to fight?"

The witch cackled. The mellow voice broke into a harsh cackling croak, as of great enjoyment.

"I did not think you would. Would you fight some other girl? Say, that Jikai Vuvushi there?"

Delia felt her heart contract.

"Oh, Jilian!" she said to herself. "Careful!"

But Jilian tossed that dark hair back. "If I was commanded," she said, carelessly.

The Witch nodded within her hood, and the sliding crimson gleam came and went. "Take the dagger from that slave girl. Take the Claw away from her. Why, Kovneva Nyleen, do you think Jilian Sweet-Tooth will not fight this one particular little slave shishi?"

Nyleen looked bewildered. "Why, she says she is tired. But she will fight. We will see to that."

The hood swept back. Fiacola's face was revealed. Delia saw the smooth round plump features, like those of a young girl who in all innocence and purity follows the sacred procession, clad all in a long white gown, trembling with the spiritual fires of devotion. A clawed hand lifted, and a black fingernail pointed.

That hooked talon pointed directly at Delia.

"Jilian would fight another, if you commanded, Nyleen. But you will not make her fight this one! I know! I have the power. I have the Gaze!" Her voice rose, booming around the refectory, echoing, demanding. "For that silly slave girl is Delia, Empress of Vallia!"

Into the stunned silence Delia's scornful laugh rang like a sword striking stone. "The witch is deranged. I am just a poor girl caught up into slavery—"

"It is useless, Delia of Delphond! You are the Empress of Vallia."

A massive bull bellow smashed above the sudden chatter. Over the exclamations of wonder and surprise, and then of understanding and satisfaction, that gargantuan roar broke like a hurricane.

"My queen!"

Tandu turned into a writhing onslaught of flesh and bone and sinew, striving against the chains.

The witch laughed. "This woman is, also, as you will doubtless know, the Queen of Djanduin."

Her pure childlike face turned toward Jilian. Brightly she looked upon the Sweet-Tooth.

"Jilian. You are a Sister of the Whip. I have said the kovneva will not make you fight your friend, the empress. But, for me you will fight her. For me you will cut her and cut her again, and slay her into little pieces. For me, for Fiacola the Gaze, for I have the power over you, Jilian Sweet-Tooth."

Watching her friend, Delia felt the agony for her, the sorrow. Jilian trembled. She swayed. Her pallor now turned her face more icy than Nyleen's. Sweat dropped.

"You have the power, Fiacola. And I believed you."

"Continue to do so. What is there that can stand against what I may make you do? Fight the empress, Jilian! Fight and cut and kill!"

As though a mere inconsequential irritation in the clash of wills, Nyleen chattered out quickly: "If this is true! It must be true! Then we have won! But, Jilian—fight her as Fiacola commands. But I do suggest you do not kill her. Let us chain her up and let her die—differently—yes?"

"Chain her up?" said Jilian. She swayed. "Fight Delia to the death and then not kill but turn her over to you for . . ."

"Only if Fiacola approves, of course."

Watching her friend, Delia said nothing.

Jilian's bare left hand brushed the dark hair back from her forehead where it immediately fell back into that curved line above her eyebrows. "Lace up her Claw," she said to the Battle Maiden plucking at the lacings. "Fetch my balass box."

Delia sucked a breath.

The box was rushed in and placed upon the table, and all the time Tandu struggled and writhed and roared. No one paid him any attention. Jilian unlocked the box and threw the lid back. She withdrew her Claw. That glittering fang of death was a supreme example of the Jikvar armorer's art. She glanced across at Nyleen.

"You would do what you say, kovneva?"

"Of course. What else? Now, Jilian, my dear, do as Fiacola commands and let us get on with this evening. It is going to be absolutely splendid now. Now that the empress will be dead we can all go forward with much greater heart. It is so exciting."

The Sweet-Tooth moved as a bamboo and paper puppet moves behind the screen in a shadow play. Always a girl of a brooding and intense nature, she now seemed to draw in upon herself. She spoke in a slurred way. "You command me, Fiacola the Gaze?"

"I command, Jilian, and I have the power over you."

The Claw turned in Jilian's right hand, turned and lifted and positioned ready to be fitted snugly up over her left hand and arm. Each steel segment, cunningly curved, articulated, oiled, catching sparkles of fire from the torchlights, would be honed to razor sharpness. Once that hand of death fastened on Delia's face. . . .

Delia said: "Fiacola claims she has the power, Jilian. And you have been led into a belief she speaks the truth."

Fiacola's head swiveled from her wrapt attention upon Jilian to stare in a liquid crimson gleaming upon Delia.

"Silence! Shastum!"

"Fiacola the Gaze," said Delia, and she felt a stroking pressure upon her, like spider silk drawing and tightening. She lifted her head. "You claim to be a witch. But there are powers of which you know nothing." The contempt in Delia's voice flayed as the lash flays in a flogging jikaider. "You do not feel. There are powers beyond your puny comprehension."

"I command this girl, and she will surely cut you and slay you into little pieces—"

"You, Fiacola the Malignant, command nothing. You may deceive this pitiful creature Nyleen and her abhorrent cronies. I do not think you can command against those powers of which you know nothing."

The childish features contorted. "I am Fiacola the Gaze! I have powers! Jilian—cut her, kill her, slay her into little pieces! I command you!"

The crimson gleam remained fast set upon Delia. She faced that Gaze, unflinching. She could feel the spider strands drawing upon her mind, and she resisted. There was no other chance of life beyond this. . . .

"Jilian," said Delia, and her voice rang and soared. "Jilian!"

Instantly, Tandu's roarings subsided. The witch, her gaze fixed on Delia, flinched. The Sweet-Tooth moved her head in a peculiar sideways motion.

"There is no hope for you, Delia of Delphond, Empress of Vallia." The witch chattered and her childish features twisted in concentration. The spider strands tightened.

Jilian said: "You command me to destroy my friend, witch. Your power is great. But Delia and I have a power, too. It is a power you fear and abhor because you cannot feel it."

And Jilian Sweet-Tooth reached her left hand up to her neck and drew one of the three terchicks that snugged in their sheaths over her shoulder, and threw. The throwing knife glinted just once as it streaked. The point penetrated Fiacola's right eye, and the blade went in up to the hilt.

Had the witch turned into a puff of blue smoke, Delia, for one, would not have been surprised.

The spider strands slithered unpleasantly, like cobwebs brushed aside in the dark, and vanished.

Nyleen shrieked, purple-faced. Her shock at the revelation that Alyss the slave who played the harp so divinely was the empress had been followed by joy that the woman was under her hand at last. And now—now the witch was dead. All her icy pallor fled. Engorged, she screamed orders. In a trice Delia and Jilian were overborne and chained. Nyleen cast a single glance at the crumpled body in its hooded gown. Fiacola the Gaze was dead. There were other witches. The scheme must go on. She must have the empress killed—kill her herself!—and then marry the emperor and destroy him. Then she, Nyleen, would be Empress of Vallia. The scheme *would* work. . . .

The dagger held aloft, she advanced upon Delia.

Tandu roared at her. His magnificent Djang head lifted and he told her something that brought the breath short between her teeth.

"Your tongue will be cut out, rast, I promise you!"

Dalki shouted across, adding to what his father had said, amplifying, going into graphic details. His description of Nyleen drove the color from her face. Her body shook in its panoply of gems and gold and silks. She looked like an Ice Queen of Myth, a Queen of Pain of Loh. The dagger trembled violently.

Delia heard Jilian say: "Once we get out of these chains we will make a bonny fight of it. Delia—I knew nothing—"

"Yes, Jilian. I know."

"How can you know? How can you trust me—?"

"I thought I knew my Jilian Sweet-Tooth. And I was right. I did. Fiacola the Gaze did not, for all her sorcery."

". . . pasty-faced, impotent, sag-chested, knock-kneed, moustached, bladder of a woman," quoth Dalki, merrily, going on into further disparaging descriptions of Nyleen.

She rushed at him, foaming, the dagger lifted. She struck wildly at his head. He moved his head sideways and the dagger gouged into the wood of the stake and stuck, lodged fast.

Nyleen pushed in against the chained man whose two arms

were viciously chained around the back of the stake and whose legs were chained all the way from thigh to foot. She reached up past his head for the dagger. The next time she would not miss.

She reached up, her body straining in the silks and tissues, looped with gems. She remained there. She lifted a little onto her toes. Dalki's arms, chained around the back of the stake, quivered with some intense exertion. Nyleen did not reach farther for the dagger, did not move, just stood there on tiptoe, pressed against Dalki.

Delia saw the Djang's face. He was not a real Djang, for he had but the two normal arms; but he thought and acted like a Djang. That face was compressed with effort, the eyeballs starting, the veins throbbing in the forehead, the mouth clamped and white with strain. Sweat rolled down Dalki's Djang face.

And the kovneva remained on tiptoe, pressed against him.

The women began to fidget, to call out. Ilka left the body of the witch and walked down the line of tables. The werstings snuffled and yowled. Jikai Vuvushis began to chatter among themselves. Some looked around in a bewildered way, as though wondering where they were.

And, still, Nyleen, Kovneva of Vindelka, remained unmoving on tiptoe, straining against Dalki.

Delia saw an odd movement at the kovneva's neck.

Something lifted there, like a collar, lifted and withdrew.

Nyleen fell.

She collapsed and sprawled to the floor.

Ilka reached her, bent, looked, turned and screamed: *"The kovneva is dead!"*

Jilian said, "And about time too. I am ready to throw off my chains, Delia."

"And I."

Delia, about to discard the chains that the inattentive guards had allowed to loosen, steadied herself. Just before she broke loose she looked not at Nyleen, dead upon the floor; but at Dalki. She saw.

His father was a Djang, no matter that his mother had been apim. Dwadjangs have four arms. Dalki, too, had four arms. But the second pair of arms were truncated, tiny, as long only as half a forearm each. But the hands were broad and powerful. Those hands withdrew into the rents in his tunic. They might have looked pathetic, muscular hands that could only just touch each other across his chest. They might have done. But those hands had taken Nyleen's throat between them and choked her out of this world.

Dalki had worked on his chains with those hidden hands, and now he stepped free and raced for his father as Delia and Jilian cast down their chains and raged out. Jilian's Claw went on in a twinkling. Her rapier licked out. Delia found the first rapier to hand, for the guard would no longer require the blade, and the two girls ranged shoulder to shoulder.

Not a single woman in the refectory would care to challenge one of them. Now there were two. . . .

"This will be a bonny fight," said Jilian. "If we are lucky it might be dubbed a jikai."

"It is nice," said Delia in her decisive way, "to have friends."

There was little need to spell out to Jilian what Nyleen had intended. She made no further attempt to explain away her conduct. There was no explanation this side of the black arts.

Delia said, "Now the witch and Nyleen are gone I think these poor fools will come to their senses. I hope so. I would like to avoid more fighting."

"So would I," said Jilian, making her Claw catch the lights of the torches and splinter back silver stars from each razored talon. "So I dearly would. But someone has warned that cramph Cranchar. Here he comes."

The doors burst open, and Cranchar and his henchmen rushed in, brandishing weapons, roaring for the devils who had slain Fiacola the Gaze.

Over the uproar, Delia called: "Cranchar! See to your sister."

He saw the limp gaudy form, cradled in Ilka's arms. His face bludgeoned. He stood stock still. He put the gauntleted hand gripping his sword to his forehead. In a low mad voice, he said: "Then are you all dead. Dead!"

"No!" shouted Nath the Muncible, striding forward with Sissy defiant and yet palpitating at his side. "There has been death enough to warm the Ice Floes of Sicce with spilled blood."

Tandu ripped the last of the chains free as Dalki helped him. Tandu stared up, engorged.

"My queen! Is this the chief rast?" Without waiting for an answer he leaped for Cranchar.

Cranchar was a dead man then. But Tandu caught his foot in a loop of chain and tumbled head over heels, all four arms going like a windmill, rolled into the tables and brought two or three down with pots of wine cascading onto his head. He roared.

Nath the Muncible was pushed out of the way as Cranchar hared for the door. He screamed at his men. They stood undecided, or followed him, or started to attack. Those that chose the latter course no longer figured in the annals of Kregen. Jordio the Hawk and Lathdo the Eager, freed, snatched up weapons.

Delia called above the hubbub, commandingly, as befitted an empress.

"I desire no further bloodshed. But I think Cranchar the Cranchu should not be allowed to escape. He did plan to kill the emperor, and that cannot be allowed to pass."

Men—and Jikai Vuvushis—ran out after the Cranchu.

He was a poor figure, Delia considered, broken now that his sister was dead. But anyone at all who attempted ill against the emperor her husband must know he ran in peril of his life. Some of the Jikai Vuvushis came forward, and some made the greetings of the SOR, and some of other Orders, and they bent the knee to Delia, Empress of Vallia.

She had to put up with this. For one thing, it meant the girls were getting back to sanity and order could be restored. For another, it was a visible proof that the thralldom imposed by the witch was passing. Some of Nyleen's cronies might not be happy, might plot revenge; they would have to be handled with tact and firmness.

Nath the Muncible walked forward. He held Sissy around the waist.

"Majestrix," he said. "I crave your forgiveness—"

Sissy goggled up. "Alyss! Are you really the empress?"

"Hush, dear heart," said Nath, discomposed. Jilian laughed and Tandu and Dalki bristled up. Lathdo the Eager bustled forward, ready to perform his duties.

Delia quashed it all.

"Yes, Sissy, dear, I am the empress. And if you and Nath are as happy as the emperor and me—" Then she stopped. That was a poor promise for a couple. Of course, these two would not face the near-inconceivable horrors faced by the